SANGUIS AMANTIUM - 1

# A MEMORY NOT MINE

## REBECCA BYRON

# CONTENTS

# CHAPTER ONE
# PROLOGUE

"Have you seen her again—the girl?" Robbie asked as they made their way up the rocky path behind the cottage, heading into the hills near Caisteal Abhail to check on Baird's herd of cattle grazing there.

"She's not a *girl*, Robbie—she's a woman. Near to thirty, I'd say." Baird flexed his hands and rolled his neck, trying to shake off the tension that had settled in his muscles. His loyal deerhound trotted alongside, oblivious to his master's mounting frustration.

"But ye keep seein' her?" Robbie pressed.

"Aye, Robbie—isn't that what I've been tellin' ye?" Baird said sharply, his irritation slipping through despite himself. This wasn't Robbie's fault, and he knew it. In truth, he was grateful to have someone he could confide in. Ol' Robbie was the only real friend he had left.

"Sorry...it's just...I thought all of this was behind me." Baird ran a hand through his hair, his voice tight. "When the visions stopped years ago, it felt like being released from a prison. I was finally free." He exhaled heavily, his broad shoulders sagging with the weight of it. "But now...they're back. I see her—sometimes two, three times a day. Her face just appears in my mind, uninvited. I've tried to shut it out, to block the visions, but...I haven't had much luck."

"And ye don't know who she is?" Robbie asked.

Baird shook his head. "Not yet, but I've a feelin' that's about to change." As much as he didn't want to admit it, Baird was certain the simple, solitary life he'd built on the island was about to get significantly more complicated.

# Chapter Two

## Mira

The house was dark when I came in through the back door. I flipped on lights as I moved from room to room, trying to chase off the weight that had followed me home from the bank in Boston's Back Bay. The drive to Marblehead had me gripping the wheel so hard my fingers ached. I kept my eyes on the road. I couldn't—*wouldn't*—look at the tote bag in the passenger seat.

Buried among the expected contents of my parents' safe deposit box—titles to the boat and my mother's car, a few pieces of her jewelry I hadn't found in the safe in the house—was a small, dust-covered box. The name *Garvie* was scrawled across the lid in unfamiliar block lettering. I hadn't opened it yet. I didn't need to. Whatever was inside, I could feel it—humming with energy, pulsing like a heartbeat just beneath the surface. It was going to trigger one of my visions the moment I touched it. I knew that much.

When I reached the dining room, I unceremoniously dumped the contents of my tote onto the table. I'd never felt a reaction like this—not without even opening the box. Whatever was inside, it was already working on me, a thunderstorm on the horizon, buzzing just beneath the surface. I took a deep breath, bracing myself for whatever was coming, and sank into one of the chairs.

I dragged the cardboard box across the tabletop to where I was sitting, and the same sense of dread I'd had at the bank hit me again. I was right—this was the source. Dust rose from the surface as I lifted off the lid, and ancient scents of stone, petrichor, and peat moss assaulted my nose, mingled with other scents I couldn't pinpoint. Inside, a smaller box waited. It was made of red leather, worn dark with age, its corners trimmed with gold leaf, the brass latch on the short edge corroded by time. The size struck me as just right for a necklace—about four by six inches. But when I flipped open the box, I found something unexpected: a finely painted portrait miniature of a young woman, delicately perched on a bed of red silk.

The hammering thud of my heart against my ribcage made it hard for me to concentrate on the painting, but as I tried to study the face more closely, a jolt of savage clarity hit me. The face in the portrait was so strikingly familiar, it felt as though I was looking into a mirror. Her ivory complexion was kissed with a soft flush on her cheeks and nose, a light dusting of freckles scattered across high cheekbones. Dark brown eyes, heavy-lidded and framed by thick black lashes, seemed to hold some unspoken thought. Her ripe-berry lips were slightly parted, as if she were about to speak. Then my gaze fell to the dimpled chin, exactly like my own—the one my dad always called the 'Garvie cleft.' It's the feature I'm never quite sure whether to love or hate, yet it's undeniably a part of me, the one that always comes up when someone describes my face.

I knew it was unwise to touch the fragile painted surface with bare hands, but I was compelled by a force I couldn't control, my peripheral vision dimming at the edges with each second. I poised the tip of my finger near the subject's exposed collarbone, the skin there so flushed with passion it almost seemed to glow, reminding me of the same way my own skin reacted when I was aroused.

As I pressed my finger to the surface, my heart was beating so erratically, I knew the blackout was inevitable. I made one final attempt to fill my lungs with air, but it was as if a wide leather belt was wrapped around my chest and pulled to its tightest notch. The crushing sense of panic was followed by a jolt of electricity through my body, and then the room went black.

*I feel him and recognize his scent before I see him. Cocooned in his arms, my head rests perfectly against the middle of a wide chest, wind blowing my hair, my eyes closed. My feet are firmly planted on a wooden surface, but the earth is gently rolling, and when I hear waves lapping against the sides of a boat, I know why. I inhale his scent deeply, unusual and somehow familiar all at once—sea salt, cedar, and leather touched by the sun. Encircled by these strongly muscled arms, I feel safe.*

*This feeling is one of "belonging," and it is entirely foreign to me. After a lifetime of feeling I don't belong, anywhere or to anyone...I feel like I belong right here. God, this feels so perfect. I don't want this to end. This man makes me feel "whole," like he is some long-lost part of me. But I also feel longing, and there is an ache inside me, in the deepest part of my belly that I know only he can fill. I don't even know how to deal with these sensations. I've never been more than an observer in all my previous visions, but here I am part of it, and these emotions are my own, not someone else's.*

*His strong hand reaches up from my back to the nape of my neck, and then drifts between us to my tucked chin, fingers curling under my face to lift it gently to the light and toward his lips, the pad of his thumb resting in the dimple on my chin as if it were made to be there. I open my eyes, and a halo of warm sunlight blocks me from seeing his entire face, but I catch it in fractured glimpses; thick dark chestnut hair falling over his forehead, streaks lightened by time in the sun, soft lips on a wide mouth, lowering to meet my own, his breath warm against my skin, and then he whispers a name, like an incantation, desperate with longing...*

*"Agnes."*

# CHAPTER THREE

# MIRA

I opened my eyes to a blur of light and shadow, my head pounding. The back of my skull ached sharply, and for a moment, nothing made sense. Then the shapes around me clicked into place—I was in my own house. On the floor. I must have fallen out of the dining room chair. That would explain the throbbing lump forming at the base of my head. I had no idea how long I'd been out, but long enough for the swelling to start.

As I sat up, the room slowly came back into focus. A faint whiff of cedar hit my nose, and for a bizarre second, I found myself wondering what kind of wood the dining table I'd been lying next to was made of—cedar? Oak, maybe? No, this was definitely walnut.

This vision was a wicked doozy.

Nestled against the silk lining inside the box, just beneath the portrait, was a small slip of yellowed parchment. *Agnes Garvie Campbell, 1785*, it read in delicate script. I hadn't noticed it when I first touched the portrait. So that was it. That's why she looked so much like me.

Some distant relative—long dead, but unmistakably mine.

The visions—some form of clairvoyance I didn't understand and couldn't control—came without warning, always triggered by touch. I'd pick something up, and suddenly I was somewhere else, seeing people, moments, emotions bound to the object. Most of the time, it was manageable. But every now and then, if the emotional weight was heavy enough, I'd black out.

Working in the estate jewelry business, I'd had more than my share of encounters with pieces that carried history like a pulse. Over the years, I'd learned to adapt—learned to spot the warning signs early, to brace myself when something felt off. Only once did I lose consciousness in public, and thankfully, my parents were with me that time.

The first time it happened, I was thirteen, working in my parents' shop over summer break. I was cleaning one of the display cabinets when I picked up a pearl necklace with a diamond clasp and fainted on the spot.

While I was out, I had my first vision. An older man sat alone at a desk, the necklace resting in its original box—*the same one I'd just touched*. He stared at it in silence, tears slipping down his cheeks. One by one, he ran his fingers over each pearl, and I could feel the sorrow in his chest like it was my own. A grief so raw it clung to me even after I came to.

When I opened my eyes, both my parents were kneeling beside me. They exchanged a look—quiet, knowing—something I wasn't meant to understand. My dad gently asked me what happened.

"When I touched the necklace, I got very dizzy, and it was hard to breathe, and then everything went black! I saw an old man who was so sad, and he had the necklace." I shook my head, still trying to make sense of what happened.

"What did the man look like, Mira?" Dad asked gently as he helped me up off the floor to sit next to him.

"I don't know, Dad—just some old guy, white hair—I think he had glasses on, maybe." I shrugged, a little exasperated by the question—shouldn't they be more worried about me passing out than about what I saw?

"I felt him more clearly than I saw him. He was just so sad. I still feel sad for him now." I said, trying to shake off the black cloud of sorrow that threatened to swallow me up again.

"I bought that necklace from a gentleman out on the Cape last fall—Mr. English," Dad said, his voice softening. "His wife had passed not long before, and none of his children wanted the piece. He'd given it to her as an anniversary gift, years ago. Sixty-two years they were married." He paused, his brow furrowing as he searched his memory. "Parting with it wasn't easy. I think he was heartbroken it wouldn't stay in the family. White hair, glasses...kind eyes, if I remember right." He reached over and gently patted my hand, then glanced at Mom with a look that conveyed some shared secret.

"Well," he said, turning back to me, his expression both serious and proud, "I've told you before—our family back in Scotland has a long history of clairvoyance, in one form or another. Mira...it seems you've inherited what we Garvies call *the Sight*."

# Chapter Four
# Mira

I was still in a fog from the vision I'd had the day before, emotions
carved so deeply into me, it was hard to believe they weren't my
own. Harder still to admit I'd never felt anything like that for a man
in real life. That daze lingered as I walked into the restaurant to meet
Anne and Dillon for our monthly *endless mimosas* brunch—a ritual we'd
kept faithfully since graduating from UMass in 2016. I spotted them
out on the patio, already settled in with a pitcher of grapefruit mimosas
glistening in the sun.

My circle of friends was small—by design. I liked to joke that I hate
people, and while that wasn't entirely true, it was close enough. Most
people drained me. But Anne and Dillon? They were the exception. I
loved them, even when I couldn't quite explain what was happening
inside me.

Group hug complete, I dropped into a chair beside the low patio
table, the fireplace already roaring against the late fall chill, eager to tell
them what had happened. When my parents were killed in a car accident
this past summer, Anne and Dillon had wrapped themselves around me
like insulation, trying to shield me from a grief that sometimes felt too

heavy for an only child to carry. But as the months passed, I'd started to find a way forward. The pain was still sharp some days—grief came in waves—but I was beginning to feel like myself again. Not exactly the same, and maybe I never would be, but close enough to recognize the outline of who I'd been before I lost them.

"Well...what's the latest? Tell us about the thing you found in the safe deposit box," Anne asked as she poured a glass from the pitcher.

I shrugged, trying to downplay the chokehold yesterday's vision still had on me.

"I thought I was done playing executor," I said. "But a bank statement showed up last week—turns out Dad had a safe deposit box I didn't know about. I found the key buried in his desk."

I hesitated, then pushed on. "Inside was a small portrait of a woman. Some distant Scottish relative I'd never heard of. And when I touched it..." I shook my head. "It was the most intense vision I've ever had. If Dad were still alive, I'd ask him about her. But that's not an option anymore."

I'd wanted today to be fun—something *normal* after months of anything but—and here I was again, teetering on the edge.

"Are you sure it was a good idea to move back into the house?" Dillon asked, concern marking his brow. "Honestly, I thought you'd put it up for sale immediately."

I suspected the last part of that comment was more wishful thinking since I was now almost an hour away from where these two lived near downtown. "Nah...you know I have a soft spot for old things. The creaky wood floors and wavy glass windows that don't want to go up—they make me weirdly happy."

I'd broken my lease, hired movers, and returned to the yellow Colonial on Washington Street in Marblehead, the house I grew up in. The main structure dated back over two hundred years, expanded over time with two wings and a detached garage before my parents bought it. It needed a coat of paint, but the roof was new, the furnace solid. It stood the test of time.

Like many of the homes on the street, it sat just ten feet from the sidewalk, most of that narrow setback swallowed by a tangle of overgrown hydrangeas. By late October, their woody stems were exposed, green leaves mostly faded or fallen. In winter, the house looked tired, worn by years and seasons. But in spring, when those same bushes exploded with rich blue mopheads, it became one of the most beautiful homes on the block. This was the house that made me. And in some strange way, I saw myself in it—sometimes bright and full of promise, sometimes broken-down, sad, and in need of improvement.

"How's the love life?" Anne asked, pivoting the conversation like a seasoned pro, clearly hoping I'd moved on from the on-again, off-again architect I'd been seeing for two years before my parents died.

"Nonexistent, but thanks for the reminder," I said, with just enough sarcasm to smother the sting. Right on cue, the voice of my therapist, Dr. Elizabeth Patrick, echoed in my head like a judgmental fairy godmother. She was always reminding me that I wasn't listening to my intuition when it came to dating. Apparently, my pattern was: ignore the red flags, jump into bed with the nearest handsome disaster, then act shocked when it all imploded.

According to her, I didn't have commitment issues—I had a radar for emotionally unavailable men and a black belt in self-sabotage. She said I should be looking for someone who *gave* me energy—not someone who drained it out of me like an emotional vampire.

Great in theory.

In practice? A lot harder when the sucker in question has six-pack abs.

"Maybe the wide path of destruction—*also known as my dating history*—just means I'm not cut out for a long-term relationship," I said with a theatrical shrug, the kind that practically begged for a sitcom laugh track to drown out the quiet desperation behind it.

"I don't believe that," Anne said, tossing back her long blond hair like a rom-com heroine delivering a plot twist. "He's out there—you just haven't crossed paths yet."

That was the thing about Anne. She never let cynicism win. I could be knee-deep in the rubble of another romantic implosion, and she'd still be out here planting hope like wildflowers—reckless, bright, and utterly convinced something beautiful would grow.

Then, just as I was preparing a monologue about my lifelong attraction to men with red flags and gym memberships, she switched gears.

"Did you ever tell Dillon about that woman who called you?"

I blinked, caught off guard. With everything that happened after my parents died, that bizarre call had completely slipped my mind.

Michael, the architect, was my big gamble. Eighteen months of trying to make something last. He was tall, dark, and charming, a divorced dad who knew exactly what to say and when to say it. Looking back, I was almost certain it was love-bombing.

And I fell for it—hard.

Pretty quickly, though, he seemed to lose interest in sex, which completely baffled me. I enjoy sex, and most men do too, so this was unfamiliar territory. Then came the excuses—he was too busy to drive the twenty miles to my apartment, had sudden business trips, followed by long stretches where he was unreachable by phone or text.

Looking back, it was all painfully obvious. But at the time, with barely any real relationship experience, I assumed this kind of friction was just part of the deal. So the relationship dragged on for nearly two years, me voicing frustration about the lack of intimacy, him apologizing and promising to try harder, the emotional seesaw slowly beating me into submission.

One day, only half-joking, I said, "If I could just fuck someone on the side, maybe this relationship would actually work."

He turned on me instantly, called me a slut, a nymphomaniac. And in that moment, I saw it for what it was, a form of abuse. I stayed calm and asked him to leave.

I hadn't thought much about it since, until that call, out of the blue, about eight weeks ago.

"I told you, he was either gay or fucking someone else!" Dillon proclaimed, eyes gleaming with *I told you so* energy when I explained how this woman called to say she'd been dating Michael for the last three years and had found text messages between us on his phone.

"At first, I thought this woman was calling to blame me, so I quickly told her I had no idea what was going on," I said, filling Dillon in to bring him up to speed. "She told me she'd confronted Michael with the texts, and he confessed. Not only had he been dating both of us, but those so-called business trips? They were just excuses to meet up with other women from dating apps. And to top it all off, he'd never even finalized his divorce—he was still legally married."

I paused, then added with a dry smile, "You're the only gay boyfriend I've ever had...or at least, the only one I *know* about."

Dillon and I had dated briefly, and one night—after pizza and a couple bottles of wine—he had confessed something he'd never told anyone else:

14

he was attracted to men. I had held him tightly, moved that he trusted me with such a vulnerable truth.

We broke up soon after, but our friendship endured. Still did, to this day.

"You know," I said, half-laughing, "her call was almost like a public service announcement...woman to woman."

I laughed, but underneath, I felt a wave of disgust with myself for not walking away when the cracks first appeared. My therapist was right, I poured so much energy into trying to get Michael to spend time with me, only to find myself watching the clock, waiting for him to leave the moment he arrived. Cheater or not, I was never meant to be with that man.

What I really needed was someone I *couldn't stand* to be away from. But honestly? I was starting to wonder if that kind of guy even existed.

"Okay, you two—enough with the emotional spiral," I said, slicing through the heaviness like a knife through stale birthday cake. "I have an announcement to make... I'm going to Scotland."

They both blinked at me, mouths open, like I'd just announced I was joining a cult or getting married in space.

"I think it's time I track down some of these famously clairvoyant Garvies and figure out, once and for all, why I have this 'curse.'" I added air quotes for dramatic effect, because if I didn't laugh about it, I might actually scream.

# Chapter Five

# Mira

Dillon and Anne were the only people—aside from my parents—who had ever known about my clairvoyance. Not even my therapist knew the real reason behind the panic attacks that had landed me on her couch in the first place. In hindsight, withholding crucial information from the one person trained to help me probably wasn't the most effective strategy—but hey, radical transparency has never really been my brand.

Officially, I was going to Scotland to meet my father's last living relatives. Unofficially? I'd become mildly—okay, maybe *wildly*—obsessed with learning more about Agnes Garvie and figuring out how the hell we were connected.

I had recently connected with some distant relatives on my dad's side, north of Dundee, through Ancestry.com, and I couldn't shake the feeling that they might be my last real chance to understand where these visions were coming from and what they meant.

I'd always wanted to understand why I had this ability, this so-called gift that felt more like an unreliable party trick. It had never given me anything useful, like winning lottery numbers or a hot stock tip. Just vague, unsettling glimpses that left more questions than answers.

My dad had it too. He said the only truly valuable thing the Sight ever gave him was my mom.

When he was in college, he said he'd dreamed about her for weeks, a petite woman with big brown eyes, rosy cheeks, and braids wrapped around her head. Then one afternoon, while driving down a country road, he spotted a woman struggling to change a flat tire on a beat-up baby-blue Volkswagen. He pulled over to help. When he asked if she needed a hand, she looked up at him with the same eyes from his dreams, her thick hair braided and pinned up like a crown.

She stood, brushed her hands on her skirt, introduced herself as Faith, and shook his hand. She pointed to her dirndl skirt and apron, as if to explain what she was wearing, and said she was late for a shift at the beer garden in Northampton. But Billy Garvie didn't need an explanation, he already knew.

That night, he dropped in for a beer and a plate of schnitzel. By the end of the evening, he'd asked if she wanted to see a movie sometime. From that moment on, they were inseparable—thirty-five years together, side by side—until fate took them both on a rain-slicked interstate, not far from the quiet country road where they'd first met.

# Chapter Six

# Mira

After coffee the next morning, I sat down to check my email. After clearing out a handful of marketing junk, my eyes caught on the one I'd been hoping for—a reply from a Scottish art historian in Edinburgh who specialized in portraiture.

*To: mira.f.garvie@gmail.com*
*Date: October 21, 2024*
*From: jblackwell@nationalgalleries.gov.scot*
*Subject: Re: Portrait Miniature of Agnes Garvie*
*Mira – I think I can attribute this to a specific painter who lived in Edinburgh around this time, as I've seen a handful of similar pieces from this timeframe, but I hesitate to say for certain without putting eyes on it myself. I've only seen one other in the original leather box with the subject's name, so yours is quite a find to be so complete. But there is a bit of a mystery I'd like to tell you about, if my hunch is correct.*

*As to the subject, I found some information for a couple of women who lived in Scotland at that time, one the daughter of a family with a woolen mill here in Edinburgh, and an Agnes Garvie Campbell, buried in a small cemetery on the northwest side of the Isle of Arran, in our gravesite database. She died in 1785. I don't know if they are the same woman, or if either of them could be the subject of the portrait, but the dates line up. Not sure you'd be able to learn much more to definitively rule her in or out, but the island is a lovely place to explore. My wife and I honeymooned there almost 40 years ago. It's a bit of a trek from Edinburgh, and then a ride on the Ardrossan ferry to the island. But it's doable if you fancy a trip here.*

*John Blackwell*
*International Society of Appraisers*
*National Galleries of Scotland*

I'd been referred to Mr. Blackwell by a jewelry appraiser I knew who freelanced for the Isabella Stewart Gardner Museum. I had sent him several photos—the front and back of the portrait, the handwritten name and date on the slip, and the detailing of the leather box—hoping he might be able to tell me something about the woman in the painting or identify the unknown artist behind it. I quickly sent off a reply, asking him if he was available to meet next week.

"Yes, I am worried about you," Anne said, concern evident in her face as she watched me pack for my trip, her long legs crossed in half-lotus as she sat on my bed. "How long do you plan to be there?"

"Maybe two weeks? Longer, possibly, if I find any good treasures at the flea markets or auction houses. I've waitlisted for a jewelry fabrication workshop at the Goldsmiths' Guild in Edinburgh. Say a prayer for me that someone drops out. If I get in, I can write off most of this trip as a business expense. I have an appointment with that appraiser I told you about too, Mr. Blackwell, next Tuesday afternoon."

"Are you sure this isn't just a distraction, something to avoid dealing with what's really going on in your life right now?" Anne asked, voicing the same nagging thought that the curmudgeon on my shoulder had been whispering in my ear ever since I decided to go to Scotland.

"So what if it is?" I snapped, throwing my hands up in frustration. "My therapist keeps telling me to trust my gut...and my gut says I need to do this. I know it's not logical or rational, but my life has been ruled by logic and reason for twenty-nine years. And where has that gotten me? I'm sad and lonely—but I was lonely before my parents died. I'll probably still be sad and lonely when I come back. Maybe it's time to try something different."

I think Anne was surprised at how strongly I felt about this decision.

"Tell me about your dad's relatives there—you're meeting up with them?" Anne questioned, trying to steer this conversation back to positive territory.

"Yes, Dad's people live north of Dundee, in Kirriemuir. They raise sheep," I said, as if that explained everything. "Maybe they can shed some light on why I'm the kind of weirdo who feels other people's emotions when I touch things." I shrugged, though the question had haunted me for years. "Dad was never much help when I brought it up. He didn't feel things in the same way I do. His clairvoyance was...different."

I took a deep breath before continuing. "I'm also planning to drive down to the Isle of Arran while I'm there. Mr. Blackwell found a grave for an Agnes Garvie Campbell on the island. She died the year the portrait was completed. Not sure if it's the same Agnes Garvie, but I figure I should check it out."

The skeptical look on Anne's face told me she was still not quite on board with my plan.

As I laid out panties and bras to pack, Anne perked up.

"Oh...*sexy!* La Perla and Eres? Planning to bang some hot Scottish hunk while you're there?" She punctuated it with loud, exaggerated smooching noises—just to get under my skin.

It worked. Her teasing cut through the tension like sunlight through fog.

"You *know* I'm a snob about lingerie," I said, mock serious. "But it's been a while, so if the opportunity arises..." I gave a shrug and a grin. "I'll be ready."

I held up a lacy bra for emphasis. "Besides, I've probably got ten, maybe fifteen good years before gravity drags these tits into early retirement. Might as well let them see some daylight while I can."

I set aside T-shirts, sweaters, jeans, sensible low-heeled boots and tennis shoes, and a pair of black crepe pants with pumps, just in case I needed to dress up. I'd throw in a raincoat, and that should cover it. As I packed, I felt a flicker of excitement, an odd but welcome change from the grief and numbness that had consumed me since Mom and Dad died. Anne sensed it too.

With this shared acknowledgment between us, Anne said at last, "I may have been wrong—maybe this trip is exactly what you need."

# Chapter Seven
## BAIRD

He'd seen Bunny dart toward the tree line after a red squirrel just moments before they returned to the SUV. The heifer he'd been checking on in the upper valley was due to calve in the coming weeks—the last of his herd for the season—and since it was her first time, Baird was worried a cold snap might hit before the calf arrived. She wasn't showing the usual signs of imminent labor yet—no obvious softening of the pelvic ligaments or swelling of the udder—but he wanted to keep a close watch. First-time mothers had a way of not playing by the rules.

When Bunny didn't immediately return, he puckered his lips and let out a sharp, rising whistle that sliced through the quiet like a knife. A pause, then another, shorter and more urgent. His eyes scanned the tree line, hand cupped around his mouth instinctively, as if to carry the sound farther. Again, he whistled. No response. That wasn't like her—she always came when called. A flicker of unease passed through him. Some local farmers still laid traps for badgers and foxes; he prayed she hadn't stumbled into one while chasing the squirrel. The thought of her caught or injured sent a tight bloom of worry through his chest. He'd had a string of dogs over the years, each with their quirks and charms, but

Bunny might be his favorite. She had an uncanny sense for his moods, always curling up beside him when he was low, offering a silent, steady comfort. As if she were saying, *I'm here. I've got you.*

He was about to go after her when it hit him—sudden and unbidden. Yanked from his worry about Bunny, the woman surged into his thoughts again, a cascade of images vivid enough to steal his breath. A woman he didn't know, yet one whose face was achingly familiar. So beautiful that the world around him fell away. Whisky-colored eyes fringed in dark lashes, lips full and soft—he could almost feel the memory of a kiss that had never happened.

What unnerved him wasn't just seeing her—it was how completely the vision consumed him. This wasn't some idle memory slipping in while he worked. No, when it came, he wasn't present at all. Nothing else could occupy his mind while she was there for those fleeting moments.

Baird leaned against the Range Rover, bracing himself, waiting for the images to ebb.

From far off, he heard a rustle coming through the underbrush, and as his mind came back to him, he looked down and saw Bunny now at his feet, sitting quietly, gazing up at him with wordless concern.

"That's a good lass," Baird crooned. "I was worried about ye. Looks like ye are worried about me too."

# Chapter Eight

# Mira

I boarded my flight to Edinburgh and settled into my business class seat, my tote bag tucked at my feet and packed with all my favorite in-flight comforts: popcorn, books loaded on my iPad, and the goose-down travel pillow my mom made for me. She'd found a bolt of cabbage rose chintz fabric at an estate sale in Maine years ago and sewed me half a dozen pillowcases to fit the oddly shaped cushion—just the right size to wedge between my head and the airplane window.

As I thumbed the edge of the pillowcase, memories surfaced of Mom sitting at her sewing table, cutting and stitching the fabric with quiet focus. That familiar ache returned, the one I felt every time I came across something she made for me and realized I probably never thanked her enough. All those quiet acts of service, hours spent doing small things to show her love. The ache was sharper than usual tonight.

With dinner, I had a couple glasses of red wine—one during the meal, one after. I took an Ambien with the last few sips, hoping to squeeze in a few hours of sleep before landing. I read a couple chapters of *Wuthering Heights*, the words swimming as my eyelids grew heavy, and I finally drifted into a restless sleep.

*I'm sitting on a settee in a room filled with dappled sunlight and tropical plants, orchids, and palms, the scent of orange blossoms filling the thick air. An artist stands at an easel, face partially obscured to me, gracefully placing thick strokes in charcoal on the canvas to capture a rough study of my image. His slim body moves like a dancer from one side of the easel to the other. My upper body is angled toward him, and he speaks in French-accented English, directing me to turn my head this way or that so he can capture the light. Nothing in his voice registers malice, yet my heart begins to pound, and I feel the hair on my arms rise. My palms go clammy, and I feel the sudden urge to run, but my body is held tight against the settee by an invisible force. The artist seems not to notice my growing distress, and when I try to speak, the voice is not my own.*

*"What do you want from me?" the strange woman's voice asks. I hear none of the distress I expect, only a soft, tremulous question from my own lips, more sensual than afraid, and terror floods my body. Somehow, I am trapped inside her, this woman who looks so much like me, and surrounded by danger. The artist takes a small step to his left, and I can see more of his body. Sunlight shining through the greenhouse windows makes it hard to get a full picture of this man, but I see delicate facial features, almost feminine, curly black hair that falls to his collar, perfect white teeth in a mouth twisted in a smile that seems to turn cruel, and then I see his eyes; silver-lit from within, like moonlight on a clear night. Pulled to him by an invisible force, I get up from the settee and walk toward the man, everything in my brain screaming to stop, but my feet continue forward against my will.*

25

*My perspective changes suddenly, as if I am now floating above the scene, twisting without gravity, spinning over and over again in a starless black sky, and when I look down, finally I see a woman—or is it me? I'm not sure... She's motionless on a stone floor, blood pooled under her upper body, and a man's harrowing screams come from the corner of the room, his pain stabbing my own heart like a dagger.*

# Chapter Nine
## Mira

I was still shaking from the nightmare I'd had on the plane just a few hours before landing in Edinburgh. I remembered jolting awake to the flight attendant calling my name, her hand on my shoulder, trying to shake me out of it. Embarrassed, I blamed the episode on a trifecta of Big Pharma, red wine, and Emily Brontë, but deep down, I knew better. This wasn't just a bad dream. It was connected to the vision I'd had when I touched the portrait. I could feel it in my bones.

My first stop after dropping off my bags at the hotel was Jonathan Blackwell's office. It was just six blocks away, and I walked over, trying to shake off the last of the jet lag.

The office looked exactly how I imagined it might from our email exchanges—organized chaos. Behind a desk stacked with dog-eared auction catalogs, printed emails, and an assortment of stained teacups sat a cheerful, balding man with a pot belly, unruly white eyebrows, and a neatly trimmed beard.

As I took a seat, I pulled the red leather case from my tote and handed it to him. Without a word, he slipped on a pair of white cotton gloves—an unexpectedly formal gesture considering the cluttered, borderline hoarder vibe of his office—and carefully opened the latch on the box.

He looked at me and then back down at the portrait, and then to me again, and said in a booming voice, "Jings, lass—no doubt about ye being a Garvie now, is there? She could be your twin, even down to the dimple in yer chin. If ye had longer hair, I'd swear it was you." He turned the portrait over, raising the magnifying glass from the desk to get a closer look at the surface.

"Rag paper," he said with a quick nod, examining the slip beneath the portrait with the name and date. "Made from linen fabric scraps, common in the 1600s and 1700s, before they started using wood pulp."

He turned his attention to the leather case next, falling mostly silent as he inspected it. Every so often, he murmured to himself, nodding slightly, humming a few bars of a tune I didn't recognize. The quiet stretched out, broken only by the soft rustle of gloves against the worn box.

Finally, he closed the portrait back inside, latched the case, and looked up at me.

"Well, I was right," he said, settling back in his chair. "I believe it's the same artist I mentioned before—the one I've attributed to three other portraits, all painted sometime between 1755 and 1800. Each example is watercolor on ivory, though that in itself isn't unusual for the period."

He tapped the edge of the box thoughtfully.

"What *is* interesting," he continued, "is that all the known works by this artist are of women—dark-haired, dark-eyed women. That's not typical. Most painters at the time took commissions of men, women, children—when there was coin on the table. It was a 'hired gun' situation, if you will. But this one...this artist only painted women. And there's a pattern."

He leaned forward, lowering his voice slightly. "All the subjects look slightly flushed, their hair a bit unkempt—there's something subtly sensual about them. Not overtly erotic, but intimate. Most portraiture from that era was rigid, posed, formal. But these...they feel different. When I first saw one, I assumed it was painted for a husband—something to remember his wife by while he was away. A private moment captured for the bedchamber, maybe."

He paused, eyes narrowing slightly in thought.

"But all the examples I've seen have that same quality. And because the women also look so much alike, I started to wonder...what if the painter wasn't just the artist? What if he was the lover?"

Then Jonathan raised both hands, palms out, signaling that he was about to make an important point and I needed to pay attention.

"Even more curious," he said, leaning in slightly, "I've seen an example that I *swear* was painted by this same artist—but it was dated almost one hundred and fifty years earlier. That one turned up in France. And then, two more from the mid-1800s showed up in England. We're talking about a time span of over two hundred years. So it couldn't possibly be the same painter."

"Could it have been a student—or an admirer of the original artist—someone trying to copy the same style?" I asked.

"Perhaps..." He shrugged casually. "But in those cases, the original artist is usually well-known—famous, even. Not lost to history like this one. And honestly, it's rarely difficult to spot when someone's imitating another painter. There are always tells—inconsistencies, subtle differences in technique, the way they pose their subjects, or changes in materials based on what was popular or available at the time."

He brushed a strand of hair off his forehead, cotton gloves still on.

"But not here. The ones I've seen? They're all watercolor on ivory. Just like yours."

He paused, then added, "And the reason I didn't include any of this in my email to you? Reputation. The moment I put something like that in writing—speculating that one artist may have created work spanning nearly three lifetimes—they'd call me a daft eejit, and I wouldn't work another day. So if you please, let's keep my wild ideas between us, aye?"

# Chapter Ten

# Mira

When we were done, Mr. Blackwell walked me over to the Portrait Gallery on Queen Street to see one of the unattributed portrait miniatures he mentioned back in his office, this one painted almost twenty years after the portrait of Agnes. Sitting in a small glass case on a pedestal, the plaque next to the portrait said it was donated by a family from the Scottish Highlands, the subject believed to be an unnamed distant relation. The style was so similar; another raven-haired beauty with deep amber eyes and flushed cheeks, her dress a muted blue in a diaphanous Renaissance style with an empire waist and a wide neckline with one shoulder slipping off.

Watercolor on ivory again, just like mine.

I said goodbye to Mr. Blackwell and headed over to the National Museum to catch the Scottish Renaissance jewelry exhibit. The level of craftsmanship from that period floored me—especially considering the rudimentary tools and technology available at the time, not to mention the limited daylight hours they had to work with.

I snapped a few photos of standout pieces for inspiration back in the studio: the Fettercairn Jewel, an intricately enameled gold pendant housing a large garnet, believed to have been made between 1570 and 1600; and the Penicuik Jewels, a delicate pomander bead necklace crafted in gold.

I'd started designing my own line of jewelry a few years ago, always drawing from historical antiquity for inspiration. That's what led me to sign up for the workshop at the Goldsmiths' Guild. This was the kind of content my Instagram followers loved—showing how vintage and antique pieces could be mixed with modern designs. The contrast between old and new made both feel fresher, more alive—less formal or stuffy.

I was completely exhausted by the time I stumbled back to my hotel and decided that tonight called for some serious self-care. And by self-care, I meant cabernet sauvignon from the mini-fridge and a slice of room service chocolate cake.

I climbed into bed early, snuggled under the covers, and picked up where I'd left off on my flight, reading a few more chapters of *Wuthering Heights*. But even Emily Brontë couldn't keep my eyes open for long. With a yawn, I set my iPad aside and let sleep pull me under—knowing I needed the rest before the drive to Kirriemuir in the morning.

I was finally going to meet some Garvies.

*I see myself on a terrace overlooking a formal garden, the night warm. I'm dressed in a heavy silk gown, enveloped in yards of fabric, and under my skirt is a fine wool petticoat too heavy for the temperature this evening. A glass of wine in my hand, I bring it to my lips and let the sweetness trickle down my throat. I think I've had too much, not because I feel unsteady on*

*my feet but because I feel an unfamiliar boldness. A man walks up beside me and places his hands on the railing.*

*"I'd like to paint you. You're one of the most beautiful women I've ever seen." The words take me by surprise, stealing my breath even as they ignite a slow heat beneath my skin. His gaze doesn't just flatter—it makes me feel wanted in a way I haven't in so long. There's an ease to his attention, an intimacy, so unlike my husband's distant presence, his long absences that have become the rule rather than the exception.*

*"You could give the portrait to the captain, to remember you while he is away," and I wonder how this stranger seems to know my deepest fears. Something in his voice now triggers a familiar terror that takes root in my body as he continues to speak, his words heavily accented. I feel someone approaching behind me; from that direction, I feel safety and a familiar warmth, and I want to turn and run toward it. As if I am cleaved in half, I feel the left side of my body, nearest to the dark-haired man, shiver with fear, but the right side of my body is relaxed as if under warm sunlight, knowing a safe embrace approaches, promising perfect peace. The man on my left, the one with eyes of quicksilver, turns and looks past me and speaks to the man who approaches.*

*"You have a beautiful wife, Captain," the dark-haired man says as he lifts my hand to his lips and places a cool kiss on it, never taking his eyes off the man who stands behind me, then walks back into the party.*

# Chapter Eleven

# Mira

"Wanker!" I shouted to no one but myself, safely enclosed in the soundproof bubble of my car, after someone laid on their horn when I hugged the curb a bit too tightly in the roundabout just outside Kirriemuir. I'd driven in the UK several times over the years, but I was still slightly hesitant behind the wheel—at least by American standards, since everything felt reversed. On major roadways, it wasn't so bad; the flow of traffic heading in the same direction seemed to lull my brain into a state of calm. But the roundabouts? They were my nemesis.

*"Look to the right," "indicate where you're going," "use your signals,"* and *"follow the path"*—I chanted these phrases like a mantra every time I approached one. But after the second nightmare in two days, my focus was frayed and my nerves were shot. I flipped the driver the bird as they sped past, a small, petty gesture to reclaim a shred of dignity.

The drive to Kirriemuir had otherwise been smooth—just over two hours, most of it heading north on the M90. But the unease lingered. I couldn't shake the feeling that the visions and the dreams were connected. Like I was caught between two opposing forces: one drawing me toward safety, the other into something dangerous.

34

I could only hope that meeting the Garvies would help me understand what, exactly, I was supposed to do with all of this.

As I drove through the center of Kirriemuir, it felt like I'd entered a storybook. Whitewashed stone buildings stood shoulder to shoulder, their colorful shopfronts brightening the narrow cobblestone streets. In the village square, a bronze statue of Peter Pan stood poised mid-flight, a tribute to the author, Sir James Matthew Barrie, the town's most famous son.

A couple of miles north of the square, I spotted the hand-painted sign for the farm and turned onto a long crushed-rock driveway, flanked on either side by low stone walls blanketed with moss. I passed a three-sided shed stacked with round bales of silage and a tractor barn that buzzed with activity, a few collies darting around the edges.

Evie George and her aunt, Morag Scott, were distant relations—descendants of Mary Garvie, my grandmother seven generations removed. They'd seemed genuinely thrilled when I first reached out, and even more so at the chance to meet in person. So was I, though a twinge of nerves fluttered in my chest as I rolled to a stop in front of the farmhouse.

Two smiling women stood waiting for my arrival, surrounded by a small parade of animals. Three tabby cats and a terrier of questionable lineage darted in and out between their legs, tails flicking with excitement. Evie, a freckled redhead in her early twenties with a sturdy, square build, smiled at me. Her aunt Morag was an older version of Evie, her frizzy strawberry blond hair streaked with gray, but the same warmth and energy radiated from both of them.

I put the car in park and stepped out.

"Morag and Evie?" I called as I approached, just to make sure I hadn't accidentally wandered onto the wrong farm.

"Yes—yes, Mira?" Morag asked. When I nodded, they both laughed and took turns wrapping me in warm hugs, making it feel as though we weren't practically strangers, as though we were already family.

"Oi...boys! C'mere an' meet the American Garvie lass I telt you'se aboot..." Morag shouted toward the tractor barn, her accent so thick I could barely understand. The three young lads—Finn, Avery, and Jack—emerged from the barn, each offering me a quick, hearty hug. They looked to be somewhere between sixteen and twenty-one, their easy smiles and casual demeanor making me feel a bit more at ease despite the distance I still felt from all of this.

After the round of hugs, Morag and Evie pulled me away, eager to show me around the farm.

"These gals are maiden Blackface ewes," Evie explained as I stopped to pat a couple of soft heads that lingered near the fence, apparently looking for a handout. "Fingers crossed, they will be lambing for the first time come spring."

After the tour, we headed back to the house for lunch—baked lamb chops and something called "rumbledethumps," which turned out to be a comforting casserole made with mashed potatoes, cabbage, and onions, all topped with bubbling cheese. It was as delicious as it sounded, hearty and satisfying, and I dug in with gusto.

Evie, a cheerful chatterbox, filled the room with her voice between mouthfuls. Her sunny disposition was so contagious that I couldn't help but smile. I imagined that no negative thought could ever take root in her brain, and I instantly liked her. Her energy was like a warm breeze, making everything feel just a little lighter.

"You remind me of my dad," I told Evie with a smile. "He had the gift of gab, just like you. He could talk to anyone. I remember going to estate sales with him when I was younger, watching him work his magic with small talk. He genuinely relished pulling out stories from the sellers, like how someone's great Aunt Lillith smuggled emeralds out of Colombia in her socks in 1932, or how exceptional the clarity was on some old mine-cut diamonds in Grandma's platinum earrings. If a seller was hesitant to part with something, he just seemed to know how to make them feel understood and convey that he truly appreciated their heirlooms."

"Is that what yer doin' now? What your mam and da did with the estate jewelry?" Morag asked.

"Sort of," I explained. "I have an Instagram page, and I started designing my own jewelry after college. Now I source vintage and antique pieces and sell those, along with my original designs on our website. Most of the stuff I find, I get at flea markets or auctions; the private sales my dad was so good at are really hard for me. I'm more of an introvert. I struggled for years to fit into my parents' business, and I guess I slowly transformed it into something that works for me."

"Yer not married? No fella back home?" Evie inquired.

"Ha...no. I'm a walking disaster when it comes to men. I have no trouble finding them, but I never like any of them enough to want to keep them around. My therapist says I keep picking the wrong guys..." I shrugged as we started clearing the kitchen table. "Evie," I said, my voice hesitant yet anxious to bring up the real reason I was here. "Do any of you Garvies have what my dad called *the Sight*?"

"Oh blimey, yes! Lass, do ye also?" Curiosity shone brightly in Evie's eyes.

I nodded, "My father did too—he said many of the Garvies did—so I thought I'd ask. Since he's been gone, I haven't really had anyone I could talk to about this."

Evie clapped her hands together in excitement. "Oh, that's nice. Not all of us do, and it's rarer still among the men—the women though are well-known in the area. *'Nae chance, go ask a Garvie woman!'* is what someone from aroun' here might say if asked fer advice. The Sight is a wee bit different for each of us—we don't all see things in the same way. I can see things that's happened in the past, nae sure it's verra helpful." Evie scrunched up her face as if to say she'd been dealt a useless hand.

I exhaled slowly, relieved to finally speak to someone who might understand. "When I touch certain objects, I get these...visions. I see who owned them, or who gave them as gifts long ago. And I feel what they felt too—like their emotions are imprinted on me. But it always comes with this rush of panic first. Does that happen to you?"

"Auch, that's nae but a hint frae above, we all have 'em. I myself get a wicked sore head when it happens. Morag dinnae have the Sight," Evie explained, voice lowered, cocking her head in Morag's general direction. "But 'er sister Molly does, and she get's boky." I had absolutely no idea what 'boky' meant, and it must have shown on my face because Evie continued. "Ah, ye ken...sick at her stomach. Morag's Mam's sister gets sneeshin when she gets the Sight, so everyone knows it's coming!" Evie slapped her knee and laughed before adding, "Do ye see the past or the future, or both?"

"Mostly just the past," I said. "But every once in a while, I'll have a dream about something that's about to happen—like my dad did. I touched a portrait miniature I found in my parents' safe deposit box, and everything changed. I've been having these incredibly vivid visions and dreams ever since...though 'nightmares' is probably a better word for them."

I paused, searching for the right words. "Normally, in my visions, I'm just an observer—silent, detached. But these are different. It's like I *am* Agnes—back in 1785—Agnes Garvie, she's the one in the portrait—and feel everything she felt. There are two men around her—one strong and kind, someone who loves her deeply, but the other one, he's dark, sinister. I get the sense he was dangerous, that he posed a real threat to her."

I watched Evie, trying to read her expression. "That's part of why I came to Scotland. I'm hoping to learn more about who she really was."

It was such a relief to say it out loud—to speak the truth of it—and not be met with the look that usually followed: pity, doubt, or quiet judgment. Evie just listened.

"Well, some of us see the past, and some the future, but a few of us Garvies see both. My Gran has the best Sight of them all; she can read intentions of those around ye, and she can see who ye will fall in love with! But she must lay hands on ye to do so. As ye can imagine, she's verra popular around here with the young lasses."

Evie's face was full of pride as she continued, her words tumbling out even faster. "I was engaged to Jackson Fitzsimmons. I went to secondary school with him, ye know—his family lives right here in the village. But then Gran laid hands on me one day and told me Jackson dinnae love me, said I'd be a better match for his older brother, Davey."

She barely paused to breathe. "I dinnae believe her at first. But then, last year, I burst my appendix—and Jackson went out drinking with his mates instead of coming to see me in the hospital. You know who *did* come? Davey."

She shrugged, as if that explained everything. And maybe it did—for her. Still, the idea of calling off an engagement to one brother and getting engaged to the other felt like it deserved a bit more story. But I didn't pry.

"I wish your granny could tell me something about the two men I keep seeing," I said, a little wistful now, thinking about how even Evie had her love life sorted.

"Well, she lives down the village, we could go see her. Now, dinnae concern yourself when her eyes roll back in her head, she's in no pain. That's her hint frae above, and it scares some people." Evie's infectious enthusiasm quickly turned into action—she grabbed her phone and made a rapid-fire call to her grandmother to let her know we were on our way for a "reading." Moments later, we piled into the old station wagon parked beside the barn.

Morag drove the short two miles back into the village, taking a left at the Catholic church and winding down a quiet lane. Granny Margaret lived in a small two-story terraced house at the end of the block, its stone facade softened by ivy and a crooked garden gate.

When we stepped inside, we were greeted by a plump woman of about seventy-five, dressed in a faded green housecoat, sagging stockings, and black orthopedic shoes. Her white hair was pinned in a loose bun, and she had the kind of face that looked like it had seen—and survived—everything. She smiled, revealing slightly crooked teeth, and motioned us in with a warmth that made the tiny front room feel instantly welcoming.

Morag said in a booming voice, "Mam, this is the American Garvie lass I tol' ye aboot. She's got the Sight too, Mam… She touched a wee painting of a Garvie woman named Agnes from the late 1700s. She keeps seeing two men she thinks were associated with this Agnes from back then. She's hoping you can shed some light on this for 'er. Can ye lay hands on her, Mam?"

"Tog dheth, Morag, I am nae dief!" she said with frustration, which I interpreted as *stop yelling*. She turned to me. "I'll nae harm ye…but I must touch ye face, lass." I approached her to get closer. She placed her gnarled, arthritic hands gently on either side of my face, her palms surprisingly warm against my cheeks. As Evie had warned, Granny's eyes did, in fact, roll back into her head, leaving mostly the whites visible as she slipped into her trance-like state. It was unnerving, to say the least. The room seemed to hold its breath. Time felt elastic—stretching and warping—what was probably less than five minutes felt like ten. I stood frozen, unsure whether to pull away or lean in.

Then, just as suddenly, her eyelids fluttered. She blinked several times, her gaze slowly focusing, and her eyes settled back into their natural position, and she frowned at me in confusion.

"Why de ye ken this was the past, lass? These men are near ye now, in the present! I see it clear as day," Granny Margaret said, her voice low but certain. "The dark one—he's bitter, cruel. Was treated cruelly as a child and grew up twisted by it. But his intentions toward ye…they're clouded. I can't see them clearly, I'm sorry." She gave a small shake of her head, a flicker of apology in her eyes.

Then she raised one bent finger, gnarled at the knuckle, and pointed it at me. "Now, for the ither one—the man with the green eyes—he'll nae hurt ye. True, he carries a great sadness in his heart, and he won't at first know what to do with ye. Ye are a puzzle to him, ye know—but don't miss him when ye find him lass, he's the piece ye be lookin' fer."

I nodded politely, but inside, my thoughts were stumbling over each other like drunks at closing time. God only knew what expression I had on my face—every word she said clashed violently with the narrative I'd been clinging to for weeks.

Now I was really confused.

Before I said my goodbyes back at Morag's, I turned to Evie and asked why she thought the Garvies had these strange clairvoyant abilities. For once, her usual stream of chatter paused. She grew quiet, her brow furrowed as she searched for the right way to answer.

"Weel, ye ken with herds of animals," Evie began, "they can kinda communicate things to each other—like when danger's near, or it's time to migrate, or not to pass up the last good berries before winter. I think humans used to be the same. We had another way to connect before we invented language. But once we learned to talk, most of us stopped relying on that other sense."

She paused, brushing a stray curl from her face. "But some people were always better at it—and their kin, well, they still are. I think that's what it is with the Garvies. We're nae the only ones—there's others out there with gifts like ours. You just hear about us more because we don't pretend we're normal."

She looked at me kindly. "You seem troubled by your Sight, Mira. Don't be. It's there to protect you, to help you understand people and the world around you. If you trust it, it can be a superpower."

The afternoon sun peeked through the misty sky as I hugged Morag and Evie one last time, promising to keep them updated if I discovered anything new about the portrait of Agnes. Then I climbed back into my rental and began the winding drive south to Edinburgh.

Granny Margaret's words looped in my head like a song I couldn't shake. I kept trying to make sense of the reading—cryptic, strange, a little too reminiscent of a visit to a fortune teller. The dreams of the dark man still haunted me, and now this mysterious green-eyed man had entered the picture.

I hadn't seen anyone with green eyes since I'd landed. Who was he supposed to be? And what did she mean by *"he's the piece ye be lookin' fer"*? Did he somehow hold the key to all of this? To Agnes? To the visions?

And if these men existed now, in the present, why did everything I saw—dreams, visions—feel like I'd stepped into the pages of a period novel? The corsets, the cravats, the heavy velvet drapes... Maybe it really was just too much Brontë and not enough reality. Still, the questions trailed me like the fog that had begun to encroach upon the road ahead.

Back at the hotel, I shot off a quick text to Anne, filling her in on my visit with Evie, Morag, and Granny Margaret. When I checked my email, I let out a small squeal of joy—someone had dropped out of the workshop at the Goldsmiths' Guild. A spot had opened up, and I was in. Class started next week.

# Chapter Twelve

# MIRA

The drive to the Isle of Arran was longer than my trip to Kirriemuir, especially with the added hour on the ferry to Brodick and the extra time it took to unload the cars. I tuned in to a local radio station playing a nostalgic mix of late '70s and early '80s music as I made my way down the M8 toward Ardrossan Harbour. It reminded me of my parents—they'd grown up on that music, and as an only child, I grew up on whatever they played.

The scenery along the Firth of Clyde was breathtaking. The road curved past rugged cliffs, wide sandy beaches, and mirror-still lochs tucked into the folds of the hills. I'd booked my ferry tickets in advance, and after a quick lunch at an oyster bar near the harbor, I made it just in time to board the 12:30 p.m. ferry to Arran.

As the ferry neared the port of Brodick on Arran's east coast, two snow-capped mountains rose dramatically in front of me. When we docked, I carefully navigated the Audi A3 I'd rented down the ramp and turned north onto the winding coast road, which circles the island for 70 miles. A few miles past Corrie, heading toward the Inn at Lochranza, I pulled over at a scenic turnout to take in the view.

A sign stood in front of the gravel parking lot, identifying the twin peaks of Goat Fell and Cìr Mhòr, towering near the island's northeast corner. The two mountains were separated by a pass locals called the Saddle, with a deep, jagged gap in the eastern ridge known as *Ceum na Caillich*, or the Witch's Step. I snapped a few photos to capture the moment for Instagram Reels before I got back in the car, continuing on the coast road toward the harbor town where, according to Mr. Blackwell, Agnes Garvie Campbell was buried.

After another thirty minutes or so of driving over the hilly terrain, I started my descent into the valley toward the Inn at Lochranza. As I rounded a bend, a few bars of a familiar song began to play on the radio. The intro, defined by late disco-era synth-pop orchestration, was one I knew by heart. Instantly, tears sprang to my eyes, and my heart shattered into a million pieces. "More Love," written in the 1960s by Smokey Robinson, was covered in 1980 by Kim Carnes, and it was my mom's favorite song. I remembered how she used to belt out that song, full volume, every time it came on—completely unselfconscious, completely herself. The memory hit like a punch to the chest, and suddenly, the grief was too much. It crashed over me, heavy and unstoppable, pinning me in place like my feet were buried in wet sand.

Even through the messy sobbing, through the tears and the runny nose, I could feel her. Like she was still there somehow, holding me up. And without thinking, I started singing—just the way she used to. Lyrics about a love so solid it could endure a hundred lifetimes, joy that can't be worn down, and a heart that stays open no matter what.

A hundred lifetimes, huh? I'd settle for just one if I could find the kind of love my mom and dad had been blessed with. I pulled into the parking lot of the inn and sat there, immobilized for several minutes. The weight of the grief still clung to me, thick and suffocating. Finally, I checked my face in the rearview mirror—red, bleary eyes, mascara streaked down like a raccoon's mask beneath my lower lashes. I looked like a mess.

I dried my eyes with the fast-food napkin I dug out of my tote bag, blowing my nose before grabbing my suitcase, feeling the weight of everything settled in my chest.

The woman at the front desk greeted me with an air of professionalism, but there was a look in her eyes, a subtle shift in the way she held herself, that said she knew I'd been crying. She mentioned dinner would be served in the dining room from 5:00 p.m. to 7:00 p.m., trying to sound nonchalant, but I could tell she felt sorry for me.

The room I booked was small but comfortable, with a window that looked down past the parking lot to the small harbor. A thin jetty of land like a finger bisected the harbor, with an imposing gray ruin of a castle, originally built in the thirteenth century, situated at the jetty's halfway point, a couple of sailboats moored out in the placid waters.

It was a perfect picture.

I made my way down to the small dining room, where a handful of other guests milled around as the innkeeper brought out a self-service buffet of shepherd's pie, homemade rolls, and salad. I was starving now for absolutely no good reason, so I lined up and grabbed a plate, taking a seat at a small table that overlooked the scenic harbor.

The evening sun was low in the sky as I finished my dinner, and I decided to take a walk down the coast road, heading south toward the old graveyard—where Mr. Blackwell's research had indicated an Agnes Garvie Campbell was buried. The road was narrow and winding, but traffic on this end of the island was almost nonexistent, so I walked down the center, the sound of my footsteps swallowed by the evening's westerly sea wind.

After about twenty minutes, the graveyard came into view, perched on a windswept point overlooking the sea. On a hill directly across the road stood an old stone cottage, still in good repair. Dim light glowed behind wavy glass windows, the frames and front door painted a cheery yellow that reminded me of home in Marblehead.

I crossed the low stone fence surrounding the cemetery and stepped inside. There was still some daylight left, but the sandblasted, moss-covered inscriptions were nearly illegible. I pulled out my phone and switched on the flashlight, angling the beam carefully to catch the faint etchings on each weathered headstone. I examined each of the ten graves, one by one, but none bore the name I was looking for. A flicker of doubt crept in. Had I misunderstood Mr. Blackwell's directions? There were other cemeteries on the island, but I was sure this was the one he'd pointed to on the map.

Disappointed, I turned back toward the road—then stopped.

Just beyond the fence, about fifty yards away, under the bowed limbs of a stooped rowan tree, I spotted a small headstone. Lichen-covered, it sat apart, forgotten. I walked toward it, lighting the way with my phone. The inscription was crude, roughly carved, but unmistakable:

AGNES GARVIE CAMPBELL

BORN 1762 – DIED 1785

My breath caught. I had found her.

An overwhelming urge to kneel overcame me, pulling me down into the soft, wet grass. A familiar anxiety surged through me, as if leaching from the earth into my bloodstream.

My chest tightened; I struggled to breathe.

I reached out, fingertips brushing the carved letters—and the world went dark once again.

*I am looking at a man, kneeling in front of the same grave, but the headstone is new; edges crisp and sharp, not worn down by wind and time, and the tree next to it is just a young sapling. He is racked by grief, his body heaving in silent sobs. His linen tunic is untucked and wrinkled, stretched tight across a muscular back, and he wears deep brown breeches and tall leather boots, the soles covered in mud. I want to reach out to comfort him, but it feels like an intrusion. A gentle wind blows in from the sea, and I smell damp cedar, like the forest floor after rain. I walk closer and bend down to touch his back, and he startles briefly, aware now he isn't alone. He slowly turns toward me...*

# Chapter Thirteen

# Mira

I smelled wood smoke before I saw anything, felt the heat of a fire licking at the chill clinging to my skin. My eyes were still out of focus, but shapes began to sharpen. I was lying on a couch, and a man was crouched beside me, close—too close. Behind him loomed a massive, shaggy gray beast of a dog, its eyes trained warily on me. The firelight cast flickering shadows across the room, and in its glow, I could see the man's face—he was staring at me with an intensity that hovered between amazement and confusion. Or maybe both.

Then it all came rushing back—the grave, the name on the headstone, the feeling of my fingers as I touched the inscription. And the darkness that swallowed me whole.

"Where am I? Who are you?" I sat up abruptly, the words spilling from my mouth like an accusation. My head whipped left, then right, as I tried to make sense of where I was.

"You are in my cottage," the man stated, still at my side, his voice low and harsh.

The room was spare but comfortable—slate floors, thick stone walls, and heavy wood beams overhead. The cottage was clearly old, but someone had taken care to modernize it just enough. In one corner sat a tidy kitchen with an old Aga range and a deep porcelain farm sink beneath a window with a yellow casing, soft light cast from a single bulb suspended above it, the wiring exposed in neatly run metal conduit tracing the ceiling. A small wooden dining table stood in the center of the room, and near the fireplace—where the low flames crackled softly—a couch, the one I had somehow ended up on. Two well-worn upholstered chairs flanked a large hooked rug, their presence lending warmth to the otherwise utilitarian space.

"Oh, for fuck's sake. Not again..." I muttered to myself, the frustration sharp in my voice as the reality sank in—there'd been a witness to my latest blackout. My eyes darted toward the man still crouched near the fireplace, and a wave of mortification rose up. This had to be the stone cottage I'd seen earlier, the one perched just above the point—the cheerful yellow door and window frames now a strange contrast to the awkwardness of the moment.

I caught the briefest flicker of wonder on the man's face before it vanished, replaced by a hard-edged seriousness. "I saw someone walking the graveyard with a flashlight while I was standing at the sink. We don't get many visitors on this end of the island—especially not this time of year. I watched ye kneel at the gravestone, then ye collapsed. I ran down, found ye barely conscious, and carried ye back here."

He paused, still crouched by the couch, then added, "My name is Baird, and I believe that answers all yer questions." His eyes narrowed slightly, but one brow lifted. "Now, if ye don't mind, I've one of my own. Who might *ye* be?"

Transfixed by his steely gaze and the closeness of him, I still couldn't quite read this man—or his intentions. I stammered, my voice faltering under the weight of uncertainty. "Um—Mirren—I mean Mira. People call me Mira...Mira Garvie."

As if pushed by an unseen force, he rocked back on his heels and then sat down hard on the rug with an audible thud. For a moment, he looked stunned. Then the tight line of his jaw eased just slightly as he said quietly, "It's a pleasure to meet ye, Mira Garvie."

The massive dog, having apparently decided I was no longer a threat now that introductions were over, padded off to sprawl contentedly by the fire. Baird stood and brought me a glass of water, then returned to the kitchen to retrieve what looked like a neglected tumbler of Scotch. He downed it in one impressive single swallow—and if I didn't know better, I might have thought he was bracing himself, looking for a bit of liquid courage.

"I'd offer ye something stronger," he said, tipping his head toward the now-empty glass, "but seein' as ye just fainted, might not be the best idea. Are ye ill?"

"Oh—no, I'm not ill. That just...happens sometimes. I'll be fine, I promise." I could tell I owed him some sort of explanation for what I was doing down by the graveyard, but I wasn't sure where to start without sounding unhinged. So I stuck to the barest of details.

"My parents died this summer in a car accident," I began, my voice a little steadier now. "I found an old portrait miniature in my dad's safe deposit box—of a woman named Agnes Garvie Campbell. She's some distant relative, I think. This probably sounds silly, but I feel like I need to know who she was. That's why I came...to the island. I'm not even sure if the Agnes buried out on the point is the same Agnes from the portrait, but...I think she is. I don't really know how to explain it."

I stopped there, afraid I'd say too much—visions, dreams, all the parts that would have him calling the authorities to report a lunatic loose on the island. The silence stretched just long enough to make me anxious, so I stood quickly, feigning sudden awareness of the time.

"I should really get back to the hotel," I said, brushing imaginary dust from my coat as I stood and retrieved my cell phone that laid on the couch cushion. "And I'm sorry—for how I sounded when I woke up. Thank you again. For everything."

"Are ya staying at the inn up in Lochranza then?" He asked, eyeing me warily.

"How did you guess?" I replied with an eye roll and a quick laugh, desperate to diffuse the thick tension hanging between us. There weren't many hotels on the island, and mine was the only one within walking distance—hardly a deduction worthy of Sherlock Holmes.

"Would ye allow me to walk ye back to the inn?" he asked brusquely. "It will be dark soon, and seeing as how ye were unconscious not half an hour ago, I'd sleep better knowin' you got back safe."

The offer caught me off guard. I could've sworn he was about to shove me out the door. I should say no, shouldn't I? I'd just spent half an hour alone in an isolated cottage with a total stranger. But if he meant to do me harm, he'd probably have done it already...right?

"Yes...I'd like that." I said hesitantly. He didn't seem to want me around, but something about the man had piqued my curiosity, drawing me in. I couldn't explain it, but I knew I'd just crossed some invisible threshold, stepped onto a path that felt somehow destined. And for the first time in what felt like forever, a quiet sense of peace settled into a small, aching corner of the void inside me.

He kept his gaze mostly on the road ahead as we walked, but I turned to study his face when I answered his questions—when I'd arrived in Scotland, where I lived, what I did for work. The conversation flowed easily, and the pauses between questions felt like natural punctuation, not awkward silences.

He was a big man—at least six foot four, maybe taller, and somewhere in his late thirties or early forties. Muscular in the way men who work outdoors tended to be, not sculpted like a bodybuilder, just solid and capable. He had broad shoulders and a trim waist, and the pair of faded Levi's he wore sat low on his hips. Despite the damp chill in the air, his arms were bare, his upper body covered only by a dark blue cotton T-shirt.

His hair was brown, but in the evening light, I saw the faintest touch of red. The five-o'clock shadow on his strong jaw added to the rugged picture. His skin bore the signs of a life lived outdoors—creases across his forehead, fine lines around his eyes that deepened when he smiled, which didn't seem to happen often. His nose was slightly crooked, like it had been broken once and never quite healed right. But all these imperfections worked together, giving his face a kind of worn, compelling beauty—something far more interesting than perfection.

And then, startling myself, I found myself wondering what it would be like to kiss him.

I was lost in that thought when he stopped suddenly and turned toward me. Only then did I realize we were already standing at the path that led up to the inn.

"So, Mira...when do you leave?" Baird asked.

"I'm planning to explore the island tomorrow, then head back to Edinburgh the morning after," I said.

"You're not going back to America, then?" he asked, trying—though not quite succeeding—to keep the dismay out of his voice.

"No...I'm here for at least another ten days," I said, a little too quickly. "I'm taking a class at the Goldsmiths' Guild that starts next week." I wasn't sure why I felt the need to justify staying in Scotland, but something about the look in his eyes made me want to explain.

He stared at me for a few moments, and then his gaze drifted toward the sea, the fading light casting shadows across his face. For a brief second, I could have sworn I saw something in his eyes—something like sadness, but it disappeared as quickly as it came. When he turned back to face me, the casual lilt returned to his voice, though there was a quiet undercurrent to it.

"Well, enjoy your stay then..." he said, his words now seeming a little lighter, almost as if he was trying to brush away the moment that had passed between us.

I wasn't sure what made me ask, but I wasn't ready for him to walk away just yet. "I didn't catch your last name," I said, my voice a little softer now.

"Campbell... Baird Campbell," he replied.

I frowned, glancing back in the direction we'd just come from. "Campbell?—like Agnes Garvie Campbell? Distant relation?"

Baird scoffed with a dramatic shake of his head. "Nae. Me mam used to say ye can't turn over a stone in this part of Scotland without finding at least two Campbells hidin' beneath," he said, abruptly dismissing any connection. "Baird is another family name. My mother wanted everyone to know I was as much a Baird as I was a Campbell. The cottage belonged to my grandmother once. Locals call it Baird Cottage."

I couldn't help but narrow my eyes at him, trying to parse through the layers in his voice. Something about the way he dismissed the connection between the Campbells and Agnes Garvie Campbell didn't sit right with me. It felt too easy, too quick to brush off.

"You don't seem like the kind of man to forget his roots so easily," I remarked, the words slipping out before I could stop them.

Baird shot me a sidelong glance, his expression unreadable. "Sometimes it's easier to leave things in the past," he muttered, more to himself than to me.

"Well, thank you again. I really appreciate everything you did for me tonight."

With a small wave, I turned and walked up the six steps to the door of the inn. As I grasped the door handle, I hesitated, pulled back to look at him by some unseen gravitational force. I expected him to have walked off, but to my surprise, he was still standing exactly where I had left him—hands at his sides, staring directly at me. I couldn't quite read his expression—whether it was sadness or hope—but the soft sunlight, slanted low across the western horizon, washed his face in a warm, honeyed glow. It was then that I finally noticed the color of his eyes...so green, they almost looked unreal.

# CHAPTER FOURTEEN
## BAIRD

B aird exhaled deeply and raked a hand through his hair as he paced in a tight circle outside the cottage door, torn between storming back to the inn or fleeing as far from Mira Garvie as he could. Unsettled didn't even begin to describe the feeling that had clawed at him since lifting her unconscious body from the gravesite and seeing her face.

He had seen her before—the waking visions that had come to him over the past few weeks. When the visions began, he thought his mind was playing tricks: a face like the one in the old portrait, but clothed in modern attire, with tanned skin and shoulder-length hair. As the images persisted, a creeping dread took hold. He recognized the sensation too well. It wasn't imagination. It was influence. Someone—or something—had planted her image in his mind, just as they had years ago, tormenting him until the visions finally stopped. But now, they were back—and Mira was no longer a figment of his haunted thoughts. She was real. And she was in danger.

He had found her slumped at the grave, not fully conscious but not entirely gone either—caught somewhere between worlds. She had murmured unintelligibly, reaching out with one hand, her fingers grasping at something invisible. He'd carried her to his cottage, placed her gently on the couch, and watched as her breathing shifted from ragged to calm, her heart rate slowing. For a moment, he feared she had fallen under a spell. But as he watched her sleep, he sensed something different. Something powerful—but not malicious.

He'd knelt beside her then, transfixed. Her face was etched with the same features he'd memorized. When she awoke, it was as if life had burst into the room—brash, bold, and unfiltered. She looked him dead in the eye with a spark that both challenged and intrigued him. In those moments, she was electric—alive in a way he hadn't allowed himself to be in years.

He stormed inside now, slamming the door behind him. This—she—was the last kind of complication he needed. But deep in his gut, he knew someone was coming for Mira. And whatever she was caught up in, whatever storm was gathering around her, he had already made his decision.

He would protect her.

# Chapter Fifteen

# Mira

I stepped out of the inn that morning to an unexpected gift—blue skies, bright sunshine, and a warm breeze—unusual for the first week of November. It felt like the island was urging me to make the most of my last full day on Arran. I planned to cram in as much sightseeing as possible before heading back to Edinburgh tomorrow. At the top of my list: Brodick Castle, a hike to the Blue Pools of Glen Rosa, and—if time allowed—a visit to the Machrie Moor Standing Stones and the Auchagallon Stone Circle cairn on the island's wild west side.

Brodick Castle, with its red brick walls and slate-tiled roofs, stood like a brooding sentinel against the bright November sky. Though it looked ancient, most of the structure was rebuilt in the early 1800s, giving it a more polished, baronial appearance than its medieval predecessors. The audio tour I'd selected filled in the gaps: defensive fortifications had occupied this site since the thirteenth century.

"In 1503, King James IV transferred the entire island to the Duke of Hamilton," the narrator explained, his crisp voice echoing slightly in my headphones. "For a time, the site served as a military garrison, until the era of noble feuding faded toward the end of the 1600s. After that, it became a hunting lodge and a summer retreat."

As I wandered through the whimsical gardens on the castle's south side, perfectly manicured even in the off-season, the recording went on to mention that the estate now hosts weddings, private parties, and corporate events in the summer months. The gardens seemed spun from the breath of myths—where forest sprites might dart behind mossy stones and whisper through the fern-thick shade. Sunlight trickled through ancient, towering conifers, their needles glistening with dew like a thousand eyes watching gently from above. Winding paths curled like secrets, each plant or flower a potential crown for a shy woodland fae. I paused by a painted arch doorway, carved into the base of a moss-covered tree, just the size for a forest sprite, and looked back toward the grand terrace, picturing it strung with fairy lights, the sound of a string quartet floating across the lawn. What a magical place for a wedding, I thought. What a place to begin a story.

After I'd returned my headphones to the visitor's center, I made my way down the road to the trailhead that led to the Blue Pools of Glen Rosa.

I parked my rental in the gravel lot just past the campground shown on the map, the lot completely empty except for a dark Range Rover SUV. The pamphlet I picked up at the inn last night had promised "an easy two-mile trek" from the parking lot to the Blue Pools, and for once, the description was accurate. The well-worn trail followed the course of the Glen Rosa water, a stream that meandered through the green valley separating the twin peaks of Cìr Mhòr and Goat Fell. There were few trees in the wide, windswept glen, but the hillsides were still surprisingly lush for late autumn, cloaked in deep green grasses and stubborn ferns clinging to rocky outcrops.

The unseasonably warm day had me toying with the idea of taking a dip—if I found the pools empty, I just might. After crossing a wooden footbridge, the trail curved around a broad rock ledge, and then I saw it—my destination.

Above me, the valley opened up into a stone bowl, where a U-shaped ledge in the stream formed a tumbling waterfall, its clear waters spilling into a series of glassy wading pools below. The smooth stones beneath the surface shimmered like silver coins, and the edges of the pools were softened by feathery ferns and tufts of moss. It looked like something out of a fairy tale—untouched, hidden, sacred. This island was truly a magical place.

I hadn't seen another soul on the trail, so I stripped without hesitation—boots kicked off one at a time, pullover and backpack already abandoned on a sun-warmed rock. I unbuttoned my jeans and shimmied out of them, left in just my bra and panties.

The water was glacial, but it shocked my skin in the best possible way, the kind of cold that made me feel alive and weightless all at once. Goosebumps prickled over every inch of exposed flesh. I waded into the largest pool, the one directly beneath the waterfall, and took a deep breath before plunging under the surface. This was exactly what my soul had been aching for—to be immersed in the quiet solitude of a fairy pool, tucked away on an island off the Scottish coast. What began as a distraction had gently become something more: a reminder that wonder, mystery, and beauty still surrounded me, not just the ache of loneliness and the shadow of grief.

The world fell silent underwater, sound replaced by the rhythmic roar of the falls above. When I surfaced, I flung my head back to shake the water from my hair, the icy droplets flying like sparks.

And then I felt it—someone watching.

I opened my eyes.

Baird Campbell stood on a flat rock above the pool, arms crossed in front of his chest. Long, muscular legs braced his stance, his expression thunderous. The late-morning sun threw him into sharp silhouette, his features obscured—yet the clenched jaw, narrowed eyes, and curled lip left no doubt: he was cross for some reason, and based on the way he was looking at me, it seemed I was the cause.

Maybe it was what I was wearing—or more to the point, what I wasn't. My black bra, with its mesh fabric soaked through and transparent, clung to me like a second skin—thin, revealing, and impossible to ignore. But I stood my ground in the waist-deep water, unwilling to flinch or apologize for the moment he'd walked into.

"You've got a hell of a way of sneaking up on a person," I said, voice steady despite my racing heart.

"What are ye doin', Mira Garvie?"

His voice was stern, but the way he said my name made it sound like a prayer—or a curse. Like no one else had ever said it properly until now. There was something else too, buried under the gruffness—a flicker of amusement. For the briefest second, the corner of his mouth twitched upward in a smirk he clearly didn't want me to see.

This man was a contradiction. Stoic and unreadable one minute, slow-burning heat the next. I couldn't figure out why he worked so hard to seem untouchable.

"Wild swimming," I said, chin lifted in defiance. "That's what they call it here, right?"

"Is that so?" he replied, gaze flicking briefly to the waterline. "Shame ye forgot your swimsuit."

He didn't miss a beat.

"Sorry," I said, not sounding sorry at all. "Didn't pack one."

And then all at once, a hundred pounds or so of shaggy gray beast launched off the waterfall from behind Baird and into the pool, cannonballing with a spectacular splash that drenched every inch of my exposed flesh. I let out a shocked scream. The dog surfaced a few feet away, paddling confidently through the frigid water.

The dog swam up to me with a happy grunt, as if we were old friends reunited after years apart. She nosed my arm once, then promptly began circling like she meant to herd me toward shore.

"Oh, hello there! We didn't get properly introduced last night," I said, trying to stand my ground in the pool.

"This is Bunny. Say hello to Mira."

"Is she an Irish Wolfhound?" I asked, eyeing the enormous dog and wondering if I'd ever seen one quite so large.

"Oof, how dare ye suggest such a thing!" Baird feigned outrage, clutching his chest theatrically. Then he laughed—a deep, unguarded sound—and added, "Nae, but you're close. She's a Scottish Deerhound. They look similar, but Deerhounds are a bit leaner-bodied."

That laugh, and the way it transformed his face, unleashed a flurry of butterflies in my stomach.

"How old is she?" I asked, pressing on with my questions, hoping this lighter version of Baird might linger a little longer before retreating behind his usual reserve.

"I dinnae ken, five now, I think?" he said as he sat down on the edge of the rock ledge above me, deciding to stay for a moment and let Bunny have a swim, his long denim-clad legs dangling just inches above the water. "She's a good lass. A fine companion to me...but she's not much of a conversationalist."

And he had a sense of humor too, it seemed.

Could Granny Margaret have been talking about Baird in her reading? He certainly had the green eyes.

*"You are a puzzle to him, ye know,"* she'd said—and he'd looked thoroughly puzzled last night when I woke up on his couch and introduced myself. And then there was the other thing she'd mentioned—that he carried a great sadness in his heart. He wore that sadness like a second skin, visible to anyone who looked closely enough. But I suspected that getting this mountain of a man to open up, to me or anyone else, would be next to impossible.

"Are ye cold yet? Yer lips are blue and purple, and despite the air temperature, I know for a fact the water is freezing," he said as he stood up, a quick whistle to Bunny signaling it was time to go.

"Well, yes—now that you mention it—I *am* freezing. Can you grab the towel out of my backpack?" I asked as I waded toward the shore, Bunny trailing close behind, giving me a fresh shower when she shook off at the water's edge.

Baird kept his eyes locked on mine when he met me at the shoreline and handed me the towel—an act that somehow felt more intimate, more disarming, than if his gaze had wandered over my half-naked body.

There was a quiet respect in the way he looked at me, but it only made me feel more exposed. I wrapped the towel around myself, chilled more by the intensity in his eyes than by the air.

"What are you doing here?" I wondered aloud. "You weren't...following me, were you?"

"Don't flatter yerself, Mira Garvie." Baird huffed, irritation thick in his voice now, his mood darkening with the same ruthless unpredictability as the Scottish weather. He turned and pointed toward a herd of shaggy cattle grazing in the upper valley, beyond the waterfall. "They're mine. I've a cow that's due to calve soon—late in the season. I was checking on her."

I tried to act unimpressed, but I felt myself soften a little at the way he said my name, even with his sharp tone, like it was something worth holding on his tongue.

"Are ye hungry after yer *wild swimming?*" His tone mocked me as I pulled on my jeans, one leg in, hopping on one foot comically, trying to keep my balance.

"I could eat," I said. "Why?" I asked, my head then stuck inside the pullover I hadn't managed to get on quite yet, trying to sound nonchalant.

"Did ye park in the lot at the trailhead?" he asked, ignoring my question completely, glancing down the trail as I tugged on my socks and boots.

"I did." I nodded.

"I'm parked there too. Ye can follow me. There's a pub in Blackwaterfoot—fire in the hearth, proper food. Ye can warm up."

He and Bunny headed off down the trail, as if the idea of my going to the pub with him was a foregone conclusion. I backtracked a few paces to grab my backpack and water bottle, then jogged to catch up.

# Chapter Sixteen
## Baird

The small pub at Blackwaterfoot was bustling by midday when they arrived. Bunny trotted in behind Baird and Mira as if she owned the place, heading straight for the hearth and flopping down by the fire with a satisfied grunt.

"Baird! Where have ye been, son? I haven't seen ye in a week," the bartender—a thin man with salt-and-pepper hair and ice-blue eyes—boomed across the room. "And who's this wee bonny lass wi' ye?"

Baird offered the introductions tersely. "Robbie, this is Mira Garvie—an American visiting our fair isle. I found her up at the Blue Pools." He kept their initial meeting to himself—the moment he'd found her collapsed at the grave the night before, uncertain whether Mira would want such a vulnerable detail shared with another stranger.

Then, turning to Mira, he added, "This is Ol' Robbie—pub owner, sheep farmer, town gossip, and all-around ne'er-do-well."

"Ye wound me, Baird Campbell." Robbie scowled, though a smile tugged at his lips as he turned to Mira. "So, what'll ye have, lass?"

"What's good?" Mira asked, eyes bright with curiosity.

"I have it on the highest authority that I make the best cheeseburger and chips on the island."

"That sounds perfect. Sold!" She grinned. "And a pint of Stella."

"I like yer style, lass," Robbie said with a wink.

"I'm gonna grab that table by the fire to warm up. Nice to meet you, Robbie." Mira gave a small wave and walked off.

Robbie nodded after her, then leaned across the bar toward Baird conspiratorially, lowering his voice. "Oh, lord...yer in trouble, my boy. Is this the one ye had the visions of?"

Baird frowned and gave a single, almost reluctant nod.

"Did she fall in at the Blue Pools?"

Baird shrugged and turned his head toward where Mira now sat, her profile lit by the glow from the fire, curls wild around her face as her hair began to dry. "She went swimming."

"What then...?" Robbie asked, eyes hungry for the details.

"What then? Nothing." Baird responded harshly. "I told her ye had a fire to warm herself by, and she followed me. And here we are."

Robbie shook his head in mock disapproval. "If that's how it went down, ye've got more willpower—and less sense—than I ever gave ye credit for, Baird Campbell. I suppose ye'll be needing a burger too, just for appearances?"

"Aye, Robbie. I will." Baird's voice was low, almost tired, but his eyes never left Mira.

# Chapter Seventeen

# Mira

B aird returned to the table by the fire with two pints of Stella and sat down, the warm glow of the hearth casting amber light across his face. Bunny snored contentedly a few feet away from us on the stone floor, utterly at home.

"You and Bunny must come here a lot," I said, nodding toward the sleeping dog.

"Oh aye, Buns is a proper barfly—I couldn't keep her away if I tried." His eyes glinted with dry humor, but a shadow of tension lingered beneath the smile.

He reached to hand me my pint, then drew it back at the last second. "Ye're not gonna pass out again, are ye?" A crease of worry tugged at his brow.

"I can assure you, sir," I said, one brow arched, teasing as I tried to peel back another layer of the man. "Yesterday's blackout was neither alcohol nor jet-lag induced."

He chuckled softly and finally handed me the glass, but his voice shifted as he asked, "What was the cause then, if ye don't mind me asking?"

I took a deep breath, surprised the topic had even come up—but for some reason, I didn't want to shy away from it.

"Well," I began, "I expect you might find what I'm about to say hard to believe. And if you think I'm crazy, I wouldn't blame you." I offered a weak smile and shrugged, not sure how else to explain. "Ever since I was thirteen, I've had what some might call...visions. Or maybe it's some kind of clairvoyance."

Baird didn't flinch. Just listened.

"Sometimes I can touch objects and see people from the past—people connected to that object. And sometimes, when the emotions connected to the vision are really strong, I pass out."

I glanced at my drink but didn't touch it.

"When I found the portrait of Agnes Garvie—the one I told you about from my dad's safe deposit box?—I had the most intense vision I've ever experienced." My voice grew softer, tinged with wonder at the power of the memory. "It was extraordinary. I was on a boat with a man—I couldn't see all of his face, but I felt...connected to him. I could feel the wind on my skin, the sunlight, his arms around me. He called me *Agnes*."

I paused for a breath, surprised by my own candor—and how much the memory still stirred something inside me.

"And then at the gravesite...it happened again. I passed out and saw the same man. He was weeping at the grave. At her grave." I swallowed, my voice faltering. "I never really see his face clearly...but I know it's him. Always him."

Baird looked down at his glass, unmoving, unreadable. His face was impassive—stone-still.

I shifted, suddenly self-conscious. "Ugh. I told you it sounded insane. I don't even know why I'm telling you this. I've never told anyone—not even my therapist." I let out a nervous laugh that didn't quite land. "I have no idea why I told *you*, either..."

The silence stretched between us uncomfortably.

Baird set down his pint. "Mira, I believe ye—I do, truly." His tone was grave, his eyes steady and intense. "There are things in this world most people couldn't begin to imagine...not until it happens to them." He turned away then, and I thought I saw it—the wall he used to hide whatever it was he didn't want seen rising back into place.

"Can I ask ye a question?" He stared at the flames dancing in the hearth, hesitation in his voice.

"Of course," I said, though a flicker of unease crept in. I wasn't sure I liked where this conversation was headed.

A storm was brewing, something fierce stirring beneath his calm exterior—his body tense—as if sheer will could silence the wind.

"Why did ye come?" Baird asked, his face still turned toward the hearth.

His question felt like a challenge. I took a deep breath.

"To Scotland?" I asked, unsure that the explanation was even clear to me.

"Aye."

"I told you...to try to learn more about Agnes Garvie, I suppose."

"She died in 1785. What exactly do ye think ye can learn?" There was curiosity in his voice, not accusation, but my own self-doubt was surfacing, nagging at the back of my mind.

"I don't know..." I said, my voice defensive, the same way I reacted while packing when Anne asked a similar question. "Maybe to figure out why I have these stupid visions," I spat out. "My dad told me the Garvies are famous for it, but I've never understood why I'm cursed with this. I met some relatives up near Dundee earlier this week, and it turns out most of them have some form of clairvoyance. But they all act like it's some kind of blessing. A *superpower*, one of them called it."

Baird turned to me, his intense green eyes locking onto mine like a magnet. "When ye touch something and get a vision, what do ye think makes it happen for some objects but not others?"

I sat with the question for a moment, searching my memories for a pattern, realizing I'd never really tried to connect the dots before.

Finally, I spoke. "Love—I think it all starts with love—powerful love. Not just a passing fancy—but big love. I've felt the love between a man and a woman, the sorrow of love lost, the love of a parent for a child. That's the common thread. The object, I think, is just a conduit, or maybe a representation of that emotion."

The silence stretched, and I could almost see him turning the new information over in his mind.

"That makes ye sound like some sort of 'diviner of love,'" Baird said, nodding slowly, as if it all made perfect sense to him. His eyes searched mine, though for what, I couldn't say.

"Yer kin are right. 'Tis truly a gift you possess, Mira."

I just rolled my eyes. These Scots are a romantic lot.

# Chapter Eighteen

## Mira

"So ye're headed back to Edinburgh tomorrow then?" Baird asked as we stepped out of the pub, bellies full, the gravel crunching underfoot breaking the silence that had settled between us. I was off to finish my sightseeing; he—well...to wherever. He tried for casual, but failed miserably—there was a tightness beneath his words, a hesitation that said more than he would.

"Yes" was all I said, watching him, waiting to see if he'd offer any hint of what was really on his mind.

"Well, as it happens, I need to be in Edinburgh later this week—some business I need to attend to..." he said as we walked to our cars, the ligaments in his jaw tightening, like the words were being dragged out of him under quiet duress. "If ye don't have plans, perhaps we could have dinner?"

The look on his face said this was the last thing he wanted to do—so why even ask? It wasn't like Edinburgh was small enough that we'd just bump into each other. And honestly, I wasn't convinced he had any real business there at all. If he didn't want to see me again, we could shake hands and part ways right now.

But Baird Campbell was maddeningly mercurial—tightly guarded one moment, almost irritated that I had invaded his space, then the next, looking at me like I was some magical creature only he could see. And then there was that smirk—the one he tried so hard to hide from me. The smirk that reached all the way up to his eyes and completely transformed his face. The face that had started to settle into my mind, deep and familiar, like an echo of someone I couldn't quite name.

He made absolutely no sense to me...but I was finding it harder and harder to think about anything—or anyone—else.

"Uh... sure, why not?" I said, though I wasn't even sure how to respond—convinced now that something was going on beneath the surface, something I didn't fully understand.

"What's your number?" I asked, pulling out my phone. When he gave it, I created a new contact: *Baird Campbell*.

"Let me know tomorrow when ye get back, just so I know ye made it safely." His mouth set into a hard line.

I found my thoughts wandering back to our walk last night and thought again about what it would be like to kiss those lips, but I quickly pushed it from my mind.

"Aye aye, Captain," I replied with a mock salute, wondering why he was so concerned for my safety. "I'll give you the all-clear signal. Where are you staying?"

"Staying?" he echoed, like I'd just started speaking French.

"In Edinburgh?"

"At my house there," he replied.

"You have a house there?" I said, a little taken aback.

"Yes, Mira," he said, with a note of exasperation, like it was the most obvious thing in the world.

Maybe he really did have business in Edinburgh.

*Don't flatter yerself, Mira Garvie,* indeed.

# Chapter Nineteen
## BAIRD

He knew Mira had seen right through his excuse for being in Edinburgh—she was far too smart to fall for that. It felt like Mira saw everything he was trying so hard to hide from her. It had been so long since he had any use for all these emotions, it almost made him angry to feel them. Being around her was maddening. It wasn't just her beauty; the way she moved through the world, seemingly unaware of the way people looked at her—not just men, but everyone.

It ran deeper than that. She felt like disruption, a quiet force sent to challenge all the rules he'd built to keep others at arm's length, to protect his heart—and protect them from what came with getting close to him. For the first time in years, he wanted to know someone—but he was fighting every instinct not to.

He had lost everyone who'd ever truly mattered. Some to age, yes—but even then, it wasn't death that hurt the most. It was the enforced distance, the inability to say goodbye, the aching silence left in place of a held hand at the end.

It was the island itself that had taken Edan from Baird.

He could still see it clearly, as if time hadn't dulled the edges. He and his brother had been hunting on the rocky slopes of Caisteal Abhail, just two boys left in their grandmother's care for the summer. Baird was thirteen. Edan, only nine. The goat Edan had shot bolted toward the valley, and Edan had followed it, stepping into a narrow gash in the ridge they called the Witch's Step. The sediment beneath him moved like a slow wave, then faster—rocks tumbling, larger stones gaining momentum, until the whole slope gave way in a cascade of noise and dust. Baird had watched it all. Helpless. Edan's body was gone before he could even call his name.

The guilt etched itself into him like stone. For years afterward, he stayed away from the island, unable to face what it reminded him of: his failure, his brother's scream swallowed by the wind, the empty silence after. But after the greatest loss of his life—one even deeper—he returned. Not to heal, but to vanish. To build a world where solitude could masquerade as safety.

And into his world, Mira had walked—bold, brash, vibrant. A storm wrapped in sunlight. Her very presence was on a collision course with something dark and merciless—a monster in human form. A man without a soul, who hunted women that stirred something in him. Always the same type: dark hair, dark eyes...just like Mira.

But Mira was more than just a type. She was a mirror image of another—one who had come to a bloody end.

He would do anything to stop history from repeating itself.

The question was: was he strong enough? Strong enough to alter the ending...before it came for her, too?

# CHAPTER TWENTY

## BASTIEN

He knew she was coming. He'd seen her in his dreams. At first, he thought they were just shadows—echoes of the one he'd once tried to possess. But night after night, she returned: holding a key, unlocking a metal box beneath harsh fluorescent lights, collapsing onto a floor, laughing over drinks on a patio, packing a suitcase in quiet urgency.

She wasn't the same. Not the one he remembered. But she was a version of her, another woman he had tried, and failed, to make his own.

He knew where she was going.

And he was going there too.

This time, it would end differently.

He would finish it. End it.

And maybe then, the black thoughts that haunted his mind—and clawed at what remained of his soul—would finally fall silent.

# CHAPTER TWENTY-ONE

# MIRA

I was so distracted on the drive back from the Isle of Arran that I nearly had a head-on collision in the first roundabout I entered, and I scolded myself for not paying attention. *What is wrong with me?*

But it was so hard not to think about Baird Campbell. I kept telling myself it was just a coincidence that he had green eyes—after all, Ireland, Scotland, and the Scandinavian countries have some of the highest percentages of green-eyed people in the world. Still, he stirred something deeper in me, something I couldn't explain. I was drawn to him in a way I'd never been drawn to any other man. Maybe Granny Margaret had seen a love match for me after all.

As soon as I got back to my hotel, I sent Baird a text, as promised.

> (Me) *This is Mira. Just wanted to let you know I got back to my hotel in Edinburgh.*

He wasted no time responding.

> (Baird) *Glad to hear, I was worried.*

Why was he so concerned? I'd managed just fine for nearly thirty years before Baird Campbell appeared in my life two nights ago. Maybe he was still shaken by finding me unconscious. That had to be it.

> (Me) *My workshop at the Goldsmiths' Guild starts Tuesday, so I'm basically free until then. If your dinner offer is still on the table, let me know.*

The only plans I had before class was to hit some flea markets on Saturday.

> (Baird) *Tonight?*

I hadn't expected it to be this soon—I didn't even realize he was coming to Edinburgh today—but I didn't have any other plans.

> (Me) *Okay. Meet me in the hotel lobby? 7 p.m.?*

> (Baird) *Perfect. See you then.*

I sent him the address of the hotel, and to my own surprise, I was more excited about it than I probably had any right to be. And that excitement raised some nagging questions. I wanted to know more about the man I was getting involved with.

I did a quick search on *Baird Campbell* and found several hits—including a historian—but the photos confirmed they were the wrong man.

I narrowed it down: *Baird Campbell, Isle of Arran.*

Nothing.

*Baird Campbell, Edinburgh.*

A few obituaries came up, some with photos. Not him.

This guy was...completely off the grid.

*Strange.*

I texted Anne to let her know I'd met someone, a *hot farmer* I met on the Isle of Arran, who also happened to be here in Edinburgh this week, and that I was meeting him for dinner—just in case I didn't come back.

I took a leisurely shower, letting the warm water flow over my body. The hotel's grapefruit and bergamot body wash—one of my favorite scent combinations—filled the steamy air with its crisp, citrusy aroma. After toweling off, I smoothed on the matching lotion, layering the familiar fragrance on my skin.

After my shower, I tamed my hair with the blow-dryer. The unruly curls I'd battled all week were gone, replaced by smooth, glossy waves—a small personal victory. Not knowing what to expect from the restaurant, I settled on a silk blouse, black pants, and ballet flats. Casual, but still polished.

Was this a date? I wasn't exactly sure. I guess I'd find out soon enough. I clasped the gold chain necklace with opal pendant I'd made around my neck and checked my watch. It was 7 p.m. on the dot, so I grabbed my jacket and purse and left my room to meet Baird.

I considered texting him to ask for his ETA, but as the elevator doors slid open to the grand marble-floored lobby, my eyes immediately found him—Baird's tall frame, facing away from me, standing out like a familiar landmark. He turned toward me before I even said a word, as if he were somehow attuned to my presence. He wore jeans again, this time darker and more refined, paired with a navy linen dress shirt and a wool peacoat in matching tones. Dark leather boots completed the monochromatic look. Every piece was impeccably tailored, skimming the contours of his muscular frame with effortless precision. God, he looked good.

"I wasn't sure what to wear—hope this is okay?" I said as I walked up to him, but the look in his eyes gave me my answer. For the first time, he was looking at me the way a man looked at a woman—or at least, the first time he'd let me see it. The realization sent a quiet thrill through me.

"You look lovely, Mira Garvie," he said with a reverence in his voice, and I thought again how much I loved to hear him say my name like that.

"You look great too," I said, a little awkwardly—because I meant it, and because I honestly didn't know what else to say. He really did.

Yes—this was a date.

"So...what did you have in mind?" I asked, referring to our dinner plans.

And there it was—that smirk. He leaned in slightly, holding my gaze, his eyes lit with humor.

"I'm afraid ye'll have to be more specific, lass," he replied, his voice laced with the tiniest bit of innuendo.

"Dinner?" I asked, letting a smirk of my own show that I wasn't going to pretend I didn't notice this new side of him.

"Ah, yes. I got us reservations at a nice place a few blocks away. It looks up toward Edinburgh Castle—it's spectacular all lit up at night. And then maybe a walk around town after, if ye're up for it."

"That sounds perfect," I said, slipping my hand into the crook of his elbow as we stepped out the door and headed toward the restaurant.

The quaint Italian bistro sat directly across from Princes Street Gardens, offering a perfect view of the imposing twelfth-century fortress perched on a basalt outcrop in the heart of the city. At night, spotlights bathed the castle in a ghostly glow, breathing eerie life into its dark stone walls and making it easy to imagine the once-bustling community that had thrived there.

When we walked in, the maître d' and the bartender both greeted Baird by name—clearly, this wasn't his first time here. We were seated at an intimate table for two, set apart in a bay window a few steps above the main floor, where flickering candlelight cast a warm glow over us both, and I wondered how much effort he'd gone to in order to secure this particular table—the most romantic one in the place. What spell had come over Baird, transforming him from the gruff farmer I'd met just days ago into someone seemingly intent on impressing me?

Maybe I was reading too much into this.

"Do you like red wine?" Baird asked as he looked over the wine list.

"I do. I've never had much of a taste for white wines. I'm a rule breaker; I even prefer a red with fish," I confessed.

I caught a glimmer in his green eyes when I called myself a rule breaker—almost as if he liked that about me.

"Bottle, then? Any particular varietal ye like?"

"Um...not sure how sophisticated my palate is. But I like cabernet sauvignon, cab franc, pinot noir—I'm sure whatever you pick will be great."

He leaned in just a fraction of an inch closer. "We're at an Italian restaurant, let's do a Barolo, if that's okay with ye."

"I've never had one, but I'm sure I'll like it." A lesson in Italian viniculture hadn't been on my bingo card tonight, but when he leaned in—close enough that his voice curled low and warm around me—I wondered if he had more than wine on his mind.

The waiter brought the bottle Baird had ordered, quietly confirming the name and vintage to Baird, which may as well have been Greek to me with my limited understanding of fine wines. He cut the foil cleanly just below the lip of the bottle, removing it with practiced precision, and then wiped the rim with a clean cloth. He extracted the cork in one smooth motion, then poured a small amount in Baird's glass. Instead of taking a sip, he leaned across the table and handed it to me.

"Ye be the judge. If ye don't like it, we can get something else."

I felt a surprising amount of pressure with him deferring to me on this—especially given my limited wine knowledge. Most of what I drank came from the grocery store and rarely cost more than twenty bucks a bottle. I wasn't sure I was the best judge, but I took a sip anyway. The wine was silky on my tongue, with flavors of dried cherry and plum dancing across my palate. It was bold yet nuanced, with a quiet complexity—something elusive and intriguing that lingered just beyond recognition. It was, without question, the most delicious glass of wine I'd ever had. I was officially ruined for the cheap stuff—there was no going back now.

With glasses of wine in hand, we both settled in. He leaned back in his chair, studying me with a look that suggested he had a thousand things to say—and all the time in the world to say them. I, on the other hand, had a laundry list of questions for Baird Campbell and far less patience. I wasn't about to wait for him to make the first move.

"So, Baird...I suppose I should have asked this before now. Are you married, divorced, engaged, long-term girlfriend?" I asked without beating around the bush.

"No, Mira, none of the above." He chuckled. "But what about ye? I find it hard to believe ye'd be unattached." His eyes convinced me he meant it.

"I'm completely unattached," I assured him. "No husband, no boyfriend—or *girlfriend*, for that matter—waiting back home. I haven't exactly had the best luck with relationships."

"Why is that, do ye think?" he asked, his voice low, laced with genuine curiosity.

I'd only meant to get the practical questions out of the way—were we really free to explore whatever this was between us? But instead, he'd gone straight for something deeper. Who was I, really? At my core. He had a way of asking the hardest questions—the ones that left me feeling disarmed, exposed...vulnerable.

"Well, I know my therapist has a few theories. I might be too independent?" I shrugged. "I'm an introvert—I don't like chitchat. That part of dating is exhausting; I'd honestly rather have a tooth pulled than suffer through it. One blind date recently told me I'm 'too direct...almost abrasive.' So there's that."

He just stared at me, and more words tumbled out before I could stop them. I'd never found it so easy—and yet so hard—to talk to someone. He challenged me on a cellular level.

"My mom and dad were like one soul split in two—they spent every day together. My dad used to say that meeting my mom was like finding the part of himself he hadn't even known was missing. Maybe that kind of love is just too much to hope for."

His smirk was back, the one that reached his eyes and tugged at my heart, and I found myself thinking about doing more than just kissing him.

"Ye don't strike me as someone who gives up easily. Plus...isn't that what we are doing right now? *'Chitchatting,'* as ye call it?" Baird teased, his green eyes alight with humor.

"I find you unusually easy to talk to," I replied with a smile that wasn't in the least bit forced.

# Chapter Twenty-Two
## BAIRD

B aird felt a stab of guilt for deceiving Mira. He could see she was drawn to him—her eyes gave her away. Even after years of his self-imposed, hermetic existence, he hadn't lost the ability to read a woman. So he made the choice to use that attraction, to stay close to her while she was in Edinburgh. It was necessary, he told himself. The pull between them offered a convenient excuse—one he had to remind himself of constantly. Because the way he looked at her wasn't part of the act. That was real. And if his life were anything other than what it was, he'd have made her his without hesitation.

After dinner, they walked around the city for the better part of two hours. Mira opened up about her failed relationship with some architect, about the disconnection she often felt from people, and the things her therapist had said. She spoke about how designing jewelry was the only thing that ever truly made her feel free. She told him how hard it had been to go through her parents' belongings, how the grief still crept up on her at the strangest times—like during the quiet drive to the Inn at Lochranza. Baird listened, patient and still, wondering how anyone could have ever called her abrasive. How some fool back in America—*Michael*—could have chosen anyone else over this perfect, vibrant, intelligent woman. This woman.

He kept one eye on Mira and the other on their surroundings, always alert—always watching for *him.* The one he knew would come. There was something between them, some dark, binding cord that let Baird sense his presence like a storm gathering at the edge of his mind. But tonight, the air was still. He neither saw nor felt anything, and before long, they were back at her hotel. He let himself exhale, just slightly. But then, without warning, a different kind of unease settled in his gut. He had a request for Mira, and he didn't know how she'd react.

"Would ye allow me to see the painting? If ye aren't comfortable with me coming back to your room, I'd understand..." His voice trailed off, uncertainty creeping in.

"Absolutely. Come up," Mira replied without hesitation.

Trusting him seemed to come easily for Mira—too easily. It unsettled him more than he cared to admit. Was she always like this? So quick to believe in someone, to lean in without hesitation?

They took the elevator to her room on the third floor. Once inside, she dropped her bag and draped her coat over a chair before crossing to the small safe. She keyed in the code, opened it, and retrieved the red leather box. Lifting the lid, she handed it to him without a word.

He stared at the painting for what felt like an eternity. The face—one he knew so well—suddenly seemed cold and lifeless when compared to the vibrantly alive woman he'd been watching all night. Mira Garvie's eyes held a spark the painting could never capture.

Baird pulled his eyes away from the portrait and looked back at Mira, then said quietly, "It's beautiful. "

Mira seemed to be searching his face for a reaction when she asked, "Are you surprised to see how much we resemble each other?"

"No," he said simply, giving a slow shake of his head.

The moment shifted. His walls were back up—he felt them lock into place after letting them fall for most of the night. And he knew Mira saw it. She saw everything.

He handed the portrait back to Mira. She took it gently, set it on the counter, and drew in a deep breath—as if bracing herself. Then she turned, walked over to him, and took his hand in hers.

"Baird...I think you know I'm attracted to you. I don't know if you feel the same, but if you do, I'd like you to spend the night with me."

"There it is," he murmured, his voice tinged with awe. "The direct Mira. Not abrasive at all...just clear. Decisive. Honest."

As if accepting the invitation, she stepped closer, her other hand sliding up to the back of his neck, drawing him in. Their lips hovered a breath apart when he stopped just shy of the kiss. His body leaned in with aching need, but his mind braced itself, caught in a silent war. Desire surged hot and insistent, but something deeper held him back—a flicker of doubt, or maybe fear. He hadn't surrendered. Not yet.

"Mira...I don't think ye know what yer asking," he whispered, his breath warm against her mouth.

She inhaled deeply, catching his scent—and he saw a flicker of recognition in her eyes that seemed to throw her off-balance. His hesitation lingered between them sharply.

"I'm sorry," she said quickly, pulling back just slightly. "I misread you. If you're not attracted to me—"

But before she could finish, he caught her hand—gentle yet firm. His other hand found her hip, drawing her in until their bodies met, no space left between them. He pressed his hard length against her, letting her feel the answer. The heat that surged through him was immediate, electric—impossible to hide. Her question had been absurd, but he didn't want to shame her. He only wanted her to understand, in the most undeniable way, just how much he wanted her.

He held her gaze, his voice low and rough with desire. "Does that feel like I'm not attracted to ye, Mira?"

The question lingered in the charged silence between them.

"I don't understand. We're both consenting adults—I'm on birth control, if that's what you're worried about..." Mira said breathlessly.

Baird's cool hands framed her face, his thumbs resting lightly along her jaw, one settling into the soft cleft of her chin. Then, finally, he bent down and kissed her. It was soft, tentative, and far too brief. When he pulled away, he saw disappointment in Mira's eyes.

He exhaled, steadying himself. "I don't think I've ever wanted a woman more than I want ye right now, Mira Garvie," he said, his voice thick with restraint.

He let his hands fall away from her but held her gaze.

"Lock your door. Don't open the windows," he said quietly, his gaze steady. "This city can be a dangerous place." He hesitated, then added, "Can we pick this up tomorrow—after yer flea markets? I was thinking...maybe I'll make ye dinner at my flat. That is, if ye can stand a bit more of this *'chitchat.'*" When he said the last word, he gave her a faint smile, a nod to his earlier teasing. He hoped she'd hear the warmth behind it—and maybe a quiet apology, too.

"Yes," she said breathlessly. "I'd like that...very much."

He gave her a quick nod, and then he was gone.

# Chapter Twenty-Three

# Mira

A nd suddenly, I was alone in my hotel room. Baird had disappeared through the door with a swiftness that seemed to defy the laws of human physics, leaving me just as dizzy and breathless as that kiss had. When his thumb settled into the cleft of my chin, I felt the world tilt—just slightly—as if the ground beneath me had shifted. Maybe I really did need to see a doctor when I got back to Boston. The passing out, I could explain. But the way my head swam, the flashes of disorientation that struck whenever Baird was near...those were something else entirely.

I locked and bolted the door behind him, just as he'd asked. Then I slipped off my clothes and slid into bed naked, my skin still tingling from where his body had touched mine. The cool cotton sheets felt indulgently sensual against my hypersensitive skin. I tossed and turned, unable to settle. Sleep refused to come—my body was restless, aching, pulsing with the tension he'd left behind.

My fingers slid between my thighs, and the wetness I found was evidence of just how deeply his nearness had affected me. I moved slowly, trying to quiet the hunger he'd stirred, but even after, sleep was fitful and shallow.

And when I finally drifted off, it was Baird Campbell I saw in my dreams.

# Chapter Twenty-Four
## BAIRD

He'd left Mira's room quickly—almost too quickly. But he had to. If he'd stayed a moment longer, he wouldn't have been able to leave at all. The guilt sat heavy in his chest. Mira had been so open with him, sharing pieces of herself that clearly didn't come easily. She was an open book tonight, and he knew that wasn't her default setting. Their connection was real, undeniable—and that only made the lies harder to carry.

She deserved more than half-truths and guarded silences. But the truth he carried— it wasn't something most people could accept, especially not from someone she was just beginning to trust. His mission was clear, if not simple: keep Mira close, earn her trust, and then, when the time was right, stop Bastien. Everything else—what he wanted, what he felt—wasn't relevant. Couldn't be relevant.

There was little chance this would end well between them. The truth *would* come out. Baird felt that certainty settle heavier with each passing second. But if Mira could return to America and live out her life in peace—safe, free—then he'd take her anger. He'd risk her hatred. That, he could live with.

Losing her before Bastien was stopped? That, he couldn't do.

After leaving the hotel, Baird made his way to a nearby parking garage and found a lookout point that offered a clear view of the hotel's entrance. He stayed there through the night, silent and still, keeping watch just as he had the two nights before, perched on a rock ledge across from the inn at Lochranza.

Watching. Waiting.

# Chapter Twenty-Five

## Mira

I drew back the curtains to find another sunny day and whispered a silent prayer of thanks. What I had planned would be far easier without the rain—or the relentless drizzle that had defined my first three days in Scotland.

Today was for scouring the flea markets near Ocean Terminal. Baird had called early that morning to confirm our dinner plans—two nights in a row—and said he'd pick me up in front of the hotel around 6:30 p.m.

I got dressed, grabbed a bagel and a latte from the lobby café, and headed out. The walk to Ocean Terminal was just over two miles, and I wanted to be there right when the market opened at 10 a.m.

The first stop was an indoor mall with vendor stalls lining the hallways. I was a little disappointed to find that most of the vintage jewelry sellers knew exactly what they had—and priced it accordingly. Still, I managed to score a small assortment of 14K gold charms, which I planned to repurpose on a chain I'd fabricate once I was back home.

Next, I made my way to a market the locals affectionately called the Pitt. This place was much more my speed—a chaotic, colorful sprawl of pop-up tables, vendor tents, and food trucks. It had everything: tag-sale treasures, bins overflowing with old vinyl, racks of vintage clothing, and a few sellers who dealt in exactly what I loved—old, forgotten jewelry just looking for someone to give it new life.

I pulled up to one booth and let myself pause, taking in the jumble of colors, textures, and forgotten treasures laid out before me.

It was a glorious mishmash—vintage advertising signs, abstract art, empty ornate gesso frames, knock-off Eames chairs, Lucite side tables, and a chesterfield couch that had been reupholstered, regrettably, in a hideous striped velveteen. A lamp with a taxidermy squirrel as its base—standing upright in sunglasses—stood proudly as if it belonged in a gallery of the absurd.

But what really caught my eye were the cardboard trays scattered across every flat surface, overflowing with old and broken jewelry. My heart did a little skip.

The seller was as colorful as his wares—trucker cap perched atop a weathered face that had likely seen a lot of life between forty and fifty years. His salt-and-pepper beard was wild and uneven, longer at the sides than in the middle. His sun-exposed arms were covered in tribal and Celtic tattoos, the ink faded but still bold.

He greeted me with a warm smile and handed me a felt-lined tray without a word, like he knew exactly why I was there. I started picking through the pieces: a few kinked gold chains I could scrap, a large emerald-cut aquamarine, and a well-made gold-filled locket that had potential.

I pulled out my phone and scrolled through an album of reference photos I'd saved—pieces I'd admired, designs I wanted to recreate, fragments of inspiration. When the seller finished up with another customer, I stepped forward and introduced myself.

"Hi, I'm Mira," I said, holding up my phone. "I'm a jewelry designer—I wonder if I could show you a couple of things I'm interested in? I've been looking for a sourcing partner in the UK."

I showed the gentleman a few photos of Victorian-era engagement bangles that had been flying off my website lately, along with examples of the 14K gold charms I was hoping to find more of.

He leaned in, squinting at the screen with interest, nodding slowly as he studied the images.

"Oh yeah, I come across these from time to time," he said, squinting at my phone. "Let me get your contact info, Mira."

I gave him my cell number and email. A moment later, my phone buzzed with a text:

(Unknown): *This is Honey*

"Honey?" I laughed, raising an eyebrow. "I'm sure there's a story behind that."

"Wouldn't ye know it," he replied with a wink so exaggerated it made him look like Popeye. "Name's actually Colby, but everyone calls me Honey."

"Well, all right then, Honey. If you come across anything like this—or anything you think I might like—send me a few pictures. If we can agree on a price, I'll Venmo you and tack on enough to cover shipping to the U.S."

I gestured to the tray in my hands. "What's the best you can do on this lot?"

Honey ran a hand thoughtfully down his beard, eyes scanning the tray as he did a bit of mental math. "I'd let that lot go for five hundred quid."

I didn't need to think long; the aquamarine alone could bring that much, set in one of my original pieces.

"Done," I said, reaching out to shake Honey's hand to seal the deal.

As he counted the cash and began wrapping the pieces in tissue paper, something tugged at my attention. I glanced up—and saw a man standing beneath an awning about twenty feet away, partially hidden in the shadows.

The skin on the back of my neck prickled. A cold ripple slid down my spine.

He was slim, just under six feet tall, with close-cropped dark hair and an olive complexion. Sunglasses obscured his eyes, and he wore a dark raincoat despite the sunshine. Something about him felt...off. It wasn't how he looked—it was the heavy, crawling feeling in my gut, like I'd been seen in a way I didn't want to be.

I stared back for a moment, unsettled. He didn't move.

The irrational urge to get away from him surged in me. I quickly took my package from Honey, thanked him with a wave, and turned away from the market, heading toward my next stop on Dalmeny Street—my pace just a little too quick.

My final stop was just under a mile away—another indoor venue where vendors set up inside a large event space. I spent some time rummaging through bins at a few tables and managed to find two gold-filled Victorian engagement bangles and a handful of loose cabochon stones. But the selection was thinner here, with fewer sellers overall, and not much else caught my eye.

On the walk back to the hotel, I stopped at a street vendor for a gyro. As I tapped my card to the point-of-sale terminal, I glanced up, and there he was again.

The same man I'd seen earlier when I was talking to Honey.

Across the street.

I quickly looked away, tucking my card into my wallet like nothing was wrong. But something *was*.

Same close-cropped dark hair. Same black raincoat. Sunglasses—*still*—even though the sunny morning I'd woken up to had faded into a gray, overcast afternoon.

Twice in less than two hours. That wasn't coincidence.

And he wasn't moving. He wasn't pretending to head somewhere or fiddle with his phone.

He was watching *me*.

When I glanced up again—just seconds later—he was no longer across the street.

Now he was *here*.

Leaning against a brick wall ten feet away. Not walking. Not browsing. Just *standing* there.

Facing me.

Staring.

My head spun. How had he crossed the street that fast?

Something wasn't right.

A primal instinct surged in my chest, slamming into me like a wave.

*Predator.*

*Prey.*

Fear crept into my chest, slow and cold, settling there like something ancient and instinctive. I turned quickly, stepped off the curb, and flagged down a passing cab, giving the driver the name of my hotel as soon as I slid into the back seat.

# Chapter Twenty-Six

## BASTIEN

She should have been more aware. But she was so naive. He'd followed her for hours before he finally let her see him. He wanted her to know he was there. He wanted her to feel it—*fear*. That part never got old. Not even after all these years.

She had no idea he'd been watching until he allowed it. Until he made her *feel* it. The weight of his stare. The presence she couldn't explain.

He knew Baird was crafting some elaborate plan to protect her—always the noble one. And he knew Baird could sense him. That instinct of his was still sharp.

So he stayed just far enough away. From him. From them. He didn't want to tip Baird off. Not yet. He wasn't ready.

He was forcing them together. Guiding it. Watching it unfold. How could Baird *not* fall for her? She was stunning—so full of life it practically spilled out of her.

He wanted them closer. Closer still. Until Baird couldn't deny what he felt.

And then he would use that to his advantage.

# Chapter Twenty-Seven

## Mira

B aird was waiting in front of my hotel at exactly 6:30 p.m.—punctual, as always. I liked that about him. I was grateful for the distraction after the unnerving afternoon I'd had. Still, I pushed it out of my mind.

I *had* to be imagining things.

Had to be.

He stepped forward to open the passenger door of the same Range Rover he'd been driving when we met at the Blue Pools, and I slid into the smooth leather seat. After the modest stone cottage on Arran, I wasn't sure what I'd expected—but it certainly wasn't the elegant three-story Georgian townhouse on Regent Terrace where we arrived less than ten minutes later.

The home was beautiful—warm and authentic yet renovated with care over the years. Tall coffered ceilings crowned a spacious formal dining room just off the wide central hall, where ornately patterned tile gave way to wood floors and antique Persian rugs. Bunny trotted up as we stepped inside, accepting my pats this time with cheerful familiarity.

Baird took my coat and neatly hung it in a small closet tucked beneath the staircase as we continued into the kitchen. The space was tasteful and inviting, with cabinetry and walls painted a muted deep sage. Stone floors grounded the room beneath a broad oak island, and a brass-trimmed zinc range hood gleamed softly above a newer Aga—sleeker than the one I'd seen in the cottage.

A small pantry and laundry nook opened off one end, and I let my fingers trail along the cool Calacatta marble of the island as I took everything in. A wooden trestle table sat nestled in an alcove overlooking the terrace, its surface set for two with slender, unlit candles poised in their holders. On the opposite wall, a pair of framed Kuba cloths added warmth and texture, softening the dark gray-green of the surrounding cabinetry and trim.

If I ever built a kitchen of my own, it would be this one.

Baird paused to slip off the Chukka boots he'd worn, stuffed his socks inside them, and tucked them neatly into the same closet where he'd hung my coat. There was something unexpectedly sexy about watching him pad barefoot through his own kitchen—comfortable, unguarded.

He disappeared briefly into the butler's pantry and returned with two bottles of wine, offering me a choice between a French cabernet sauvignon and an Italian Barolo.

"I liked the Barolo we had last night," I said with a playful smile. "But who knows, maybe we'll drink them both."

"Let's pace ourselves, lass," he teased, the corner of his mouth lifting.

I laughed, unable to stop the thought: I really liked it when he teased me like that.

With practiced ease, he pulled the cork and poured a glass for me, then one for himself.

"How do you like your steak?" he asked as he moved to the stove. "I like mine quite rare, but I can cook yours however ye prefer."

"Medium rare for me, please," I said, stepping up behind him—close, but out of the way—watching as he moved confidently through the space.

When the steaks were cooked to his liking, he topped each with a pat of butter and set them aside to rest. From the fridge, he retrieved a bowl of salad—already assembled—and dressed it with a quick drizzle of olive oil and vinegar. He refilled our wine glasses, then lit the candles on the table, their warm glow casting soft shadows across the alcove. With easy grace, he carried everything over and set the plates down.

I took a bite of the steak—perfectly cooked, simply seasoned with coarse salt and pepper, seared just right on the outside and warm, juicy rare on the inside.

"I don't know what you do for a living," I said as I sliced another piece, "but you could be a chef. This is the best steak I've ever had."

"What do you mean you don't know what I do for a living?" He cocked his head. "I told ye, I raise cattle."

"And that pays for all this?" I asked, trying—and mostly failing—to hide my amazement.

"At one time, I owned a shipping company," Baird said with a shrug, cutting into his steak. "I sold it. I've got some income-producing commercial properties now, but day in and day out, it's Highland cattle and barley crops."

He spoke so offhandedly, like it was the most ordinary thing in the world.

"This house—it's quite a place."

Something flickered across his face. Sadness, maybe pain. I couldn't quite tell, but I knew I'd touched a nerve.

"It's been in my family for well over two hundred years," he said after a pause, his voice even. But the openness I'd seen in him moments ago was already slipping away, like sand through my fingers.

I cleared the table quietly and dried the dishes while he washed, the two of us working side by side in a companionable silence. I hoped that, with a little time, the unguarded version of Baird might return.

When we were done, he opened the second bottle of wine, poured us each a glass, and sat back down beside me at the table.

"So at the hotel, you said you wanted to continue the conversation we were having. If I remember correctly, I had just come on to you, and you turned me down," I said, skipping the preamble.

"Ah...and there's my girl again," Baird said, his voice low and smooth, like good whisky. "The very direct Mira Garvie. Did you know she's my favorite version of you?" He leaned back slightly, a glint of amusement in his eyes. "But I'm not so sure about this whole *'you came on to me'* bit," he said, slipping into an exaggerated version of my American accent. "Makes it sound a lot more aggressive than it actually was."

"How was it?" I asked softly, still lingering on his word choice of 'my girl,' letting it sink in.

"It was the best thing any woman has ever offered me, Mira," he said quietly, tracing the rim of his glass with one finger. "I lost someone, long ago. And since then, I haven't really given my heart to another woman. Sex, sure—now and then. But nothing more. So I hope you can understand my hesitation."

I didn't understand it. "That's what I was offering, Baird," I replied. "Sex. It doesn't have to be more than that."

He looked up then, straight into my eyes, his expression serious and unflinching.

"That's where yer wrong, Mira. I want it to be more than just sex. Yer worth more—deserve more—than casual sex."

Dr. Patrick's words from one of our sessions echoed in my mind: *"Do you not think you are worthy of true connection?"*

Baird made me feel worthy for the first time in my life.

I rose slowly from the table and stepped in front of him. He didn't move at first, and for a moment, I wasn't sure if he would. He looked like he was debating something, caught in a quiet war with himself.

Then his hand came up, resting gently on my hip. He lifted his face to mine, eyes searching.

He stood up slowly, his body filling the space in front of and above me. He touched my shoulder, his cool fingers brushing the wide neck of my sweater, and it slipped lower to expose the skin above my breast. He traced the swell above my bra with his finger slowly, and my skin burned under his touch, blood rushing to the surface, the feeling exquisite. His finger traced my collarbone and then moved upwards until he cupped my face with one hand. He bent to place a soft kiss on my lips, his mouth opening mine, his tongue tentatively exploring inside. Our lips found a rhythm, one that normally takes lovers time to acquire through repetition, but it felt like we were each born to do this very thing.

He bent down to trace the side of my neck with his lips, and I felt the skin there start to tingle and heat, as if molten gold flowed from his lips and moved as a rivulet throughout my body, pooling in my belly and lower still, my limbs suddenly heavy. I had never felt anything remotely like this.

I couldn't take the slow agony any longer. I lifted the hem of my sweater and pulled it over my head, letting it fall to the floor without hesitation.

He stepped behind me, unhooked my bra with a practiced ease, then slipped one strap down my shoulder, letting it slide from my arms and drop at my feet.

His large hands slid around my ribcage, then slowly moved upward to cup my breasts, letting the weight of them settle into his palms. My nipples were already hard—aching—and the contrast of his cool skin against my warmth sent a shiver rippling through me.

He kissed the side of my neck as his fingers found one nipple, rolling it gently between his thumb and forefinger. The pressure was just enough to send heat spiraling through me.

I wondered—briefly, breathlessly—if he somehow knew how much I liked that. How sometimes that one small act was all it took to send me over the edge.

His hands moved to the zipper of my pants, easing it down. When he pushed my jeans past my hips, my panties slipped down with them, pooling on the cool stone floor. I stepped out of my flats, then out of the pile of fabric, and turned to face him.

Reaching up, I began unbuttoning his shirt, my fingers steady despite the rush of heat between us. He didn't hesitate—already working the buttons on his jeans, our movements synced in quiet urgency, the efficiency of shared desire.

His body was muscled perfection—broad shoulders, lean hips, that sharp line some men have that cuts from hip to groin. His thighs were strong, well-muscled, and his cock stood thick and hard between them.

I reached out, brushing my fingers across a soft patch of golden-brown hair on his chest. I traced it slowly as it narrowed into a neat line down the hard ridges of his abdomen, a path that pulled my gaze—and every thought—downward.

I locked eyes with him as I slowly sank to my knees on the cool stone floor. The sharp intake of his breath told me he knew exactly what was coming.

I reached for him, wrapping one hand around the thick length of his cock, feeling him pulse and harden even more in my palm.

Breaking eye contact, I lowered my head and parted my lips, my tongue teasing the tip, savoring the salty taste as I began to take him into my mouth.

I opened my mouth wider, taking in as much of him as I could before pulling back, letting my tongue tease the tip again. Then I ran it slowly along the length of him, savoring the way he twitched beneath the attention.

But then he reached for me—roughly, urgently—and pulled me to my feet. He turned me so my back was to him once more, his hands firm, possessive.

Bending down, he brought his face close to mine, angling it over my shoulder. His mouth found mine in a deep, consuming kiss.

And then he said my name, breathless, desperate.

*"Mira."*

He pressed my upper body down against the surface of the table, right in front of the glass terrace windows. For a fleeting second, I wondered if any of the neighbors might have a view of this scene—but even if they did, it wouldn't have stopped me. Nothing would.

In that moment, I wanted only this—to be claimed by him complete-ly.

Baird slid a hand between my legs, finding the wetness that clung to me. He let out a low, guttural moan, raw and unguarded.

Then he took himself in hand and guided the thick head of his cock to my entrance. I pushed back, meeting his urgency, wanting all of him.

A slow, exquisite pressure bloomed as my body stretched around him, inch by inch. He pulled back slightly—just enough to make me ache for more—but didn't leave me empty.

With a low, frustrated growl, he bent to whisper in my ear. "I wanted to go slow, Mira...but I can't. Please forgive me."

In place of words, I gave him my answer. I braced my arms against the table and pushed back against him, taking in the full length of him, meeting his desperation with my own. His hand gripped my hip, anchoring us to a shared rhythm.

Each thrust was long and deep, gaining urgency, intensity. I moaned—whimpered—lost in the sheer, exquisite pleasure. There was something I loved about being taken like this, about surrendering completely from behind.

Baird's hand slid into my hair—not to pull, just to feel, to let the silken strands thread through his fingers as he moved inside me.

He pulled out of me abruptly.

Before I could fully react, he slid two fingers into my slick heat, then withdrew them slowly. I turned to watch him, breathless, as he stood to his full height and closed his eyes. Then, almost reverently, he brought his fingers to his mouth, taking each one in to taste me.

My breath caught.

In the next moment, I was lifted off the floor, one arm beneath my knees, the other wrapped around my back. My mind struggled to track how I'd gone from standing against the table to being held in his arms, weightless and dizzy—though I couldn't tell if it was the wine or the moment itself that made my head swim.

I didn't want the spell to break. I wrapped my arms around his neck and whispered, "Where are we going?"

He looked down at me, his voice rough and final.

"Bed."

# Chapter Twenty-Eight

# Mira

U p two dark, winding flights of stairs, he carried me, never once breaking eye contact. He walked into his room and laid me gently onto a grand, ornately carved tester bed. Four thick, turned columns anchored each corner, rising to support a flat canopy above. Heavy rails framed the top, from which thick curtains hung, drawn back now but ready to wrap around us like a cocoon. Antique rugs softened the floor beneath his feet, and a fire, already lit, crackled in the corner hearth—casting a flickering glow across the room. Baird laid down beside me, brushing a few strands of hair from my forehead with the pads of his fingers. His expression shifted into something softer. Tentative. Apprehensive.

"Are ye all right?" he asked quietly.

I reached up, cupping his cheek in my hand. My fingers stroked the side of his face with deliberate tenderness, needing him to feel the certainty in my touch. I didn't want to leave even a trace of doubt in his mind.

"Baird, I've wanted you since the moment we met," I said, my voice steady, but soft. "I was trying to answer your questions that first night, when we walked back to the inn—but all I could think about was kissing you."

I paused, my fingers still against his cheek. "I'm a grown woman. I know what I want. And I don't have any expectations beyond tonight...but I don't want it to pass without knowing this part of you. I want you. Take me roughly, make love to me tenderly—use my body for your pleasure, and give me the same. I don't want to wait."

He didn't need any more confirmation. He rose over me, then moved down my body, one hand gently but firmly parting my thighs, his head lowering between them.

His lips brushed softly against my pussy before his tongue found my clit—slow at first, then more insistent. He slipped lower, tasting me deeply, and I arched off the bed, clutching the sheets in both hands as pleasure surged through me.

His pace quickened, his tongue unrelenting, and then he moaned—*moaned*—as if the act of pleasuring me was its own reward. That sound alone nearly undid me.

He slipped two fingers inside me again, curling them upward, and my sharp inhale told him everything he needed to know. He stroked that inner wall, steady and precise, building a pressure so intense I could barely breathe.

My inhales came fast now, erratic, my body flushed and trembling. The climax overtook me like a wave of heat and light, and I cried out as incandescent pleasure flooded through me. Liquid spilled like a fountain against the palm of his hand, and he withdrew his fingers to capture as much as he could in his mouth, tasting me with reverence.

The act shocked me. No lover had ever responded that way before, and I'd always carried a quiet shame about the mess I sometimes made.

Reflexively, I reached up to cover my face, flustered. "I'm sorry," I whispered.

But he gently caught my hand and pulled it away, holding it as he looked into my eyes—really looked, as if trying to see every part of me, even the ones I still tried to hide.

"I don't ken... Why are ye sorry, lass?" he asked, a furrow forming between his brows.

"I can't always control that," I said, my voice small. "And your bed is wet now."

He laughed, low and rough. "Well, Mira Garvie." The smirk I loved pulled up the one corner of his mouth, his eyes glinting. "We're not done yet. And this bed may be wetter still before we're through tonight."

# CHAPTER TWENTY-NINE
## BAIRD

They picked up where they had left off downstairs, but this time slower, more deliberate. Baird wanted to savor her—to taste her again, breathe in her scent, explore the softness of her skin. He took in the perfect curve of her teardrop breasts, nipples still flushed and tender from his teasing mouth and hands.

Mira rolled him onto his back and swung her leg over his hips, straddling him. She took his hard cock in her hand and guided him inside, inch by inch, her breath catching as she adjusted to his thickness. She stilled for a moment, letting her body reacclimate, then began to move—slow, sinuous, more back and forth than up and down, controlling the pace.

He gripped her ass with both hands, grounding himself, giving him just enough leverage to push up into her deeply with every few strokes. Her moans grew softer, more desperate, as her second orgasm began to build. Her breath came faster, shallower, and he watched her reach between them to touch her clit—sliding two fingers along each side and squeezing gently as she rode him.

Baird felt her tighten around him just before Mira cried out, her body convulsing in waves of release. Tears welled in her eyes and spilled down her cheeks—unexpected, raw. He reached up and pulled her down to him, holding her against his chest, their noses brushing.

"That's it, Mira," he whispered. "God, I love the sound you make when you come." She collapsed against him, breathless, letting herself rest there until the storm inside her stilled.

After a few moments, Baird eased out from beneath her, stood, and reached down to offer his hand. He led her across the room to a large picture window, throwing back the heavy velvet drapes. Below them lay the same terrace they'd looked out onto at dinner—now seen from thirty feet above. There was a full-length mirror to the left of them, and the chandelier behind them cast enough light to turn the window glass into a kind of mirror itself—ten feet high, reflecting them both.

He pulled a wide, low stool in front of the window and helped Mira step onto it, aligning their heights. Then he turned her again, back to him, her body framed in the reflection—bare, perfect, powerful.

"Look at me, Mira," he said, his voice rough with need and something deeper—possession, longing. "Look at us. Watch me...*feel* me. I need you to see what this is. What *we* are."

He entered her again from behind, urgent now, his thrusts deep and relentless. Mira braced herself against the window frame, her face transformed—wild, untamed, her skin glowing with sweat and fire, her chest and cheeks flushed with passion. Seeing their bodies reflected back heightened everything.

It was primal. Feral. Sacred.

There was no shame.

She was made for this, he thought. For this moment. For him.

His rhythm began to shift—subtle at first, then more frantic, uneven. His breath hitched, his groans growing louder, his lips pressed to the hollow of her neck—right over the place where her pulse beat steady and strong. He knew that spot, knew the way it sparked a white-hot current between them, energy flowing into both their bodies like fire through a closed circuit. He wanted his lips there—needed his mouth there. To feel how alive she was beneath him, how her heartbeat thudded against his skin. It made him feel alive too, in a way he hadn't in years.

When his climax finally overtook him, he cried out—loud and un-restrained. Waves of pleasure crashed through him, deeper, longer, stronger than anything he'd ever known. It rolled through his body in relentless pulses, as if she'd unlocked something buried—something he hadn't even realized he'd been holding back.

Still deep inside her, he braced a hand against the glass, his forehead resting in the crook of her neck, both of them breathing hard, tangled in the afterglow.

He stayed inside her, unwilling to let the moment end.

He wanted her to see them—exactly as they were.

Together.

And if Bastien had been out there watching, Baird hoped he saw it too.

He watched her sleep through the night, her body limp with exhaus-tion, utterly spent. It had been so long since a woman had slept beside him—he hadn't allowed it. When the need became too great, he took his pleasure in passing encounters, one-night stands that were little more than transactions. A means to an end.

But this...this had not been that.

Not at all.

He wondered why he'd fought it so hard in the beginning. Why he'd wasted even a moment resisting what he was now so afraid to lose. Was this penance? A higher power letting him feel—only to remind him what he could never truly keep?

He'd told himself getting involved with her was the last thing he should do—his role had been to protect her, nothing more. But it hadn't mattered. He was drawn to her like a moth to flame.

And for a man who understood all too well how to wield power, how to enthrall—he now felt utterly spellbound. As if she held an invisible cord tied to his chest, turning some unseen wheel, pulling him closer with every slow, deliberate crank.

Her body had felt like it was made for his—their connection electric, magnetic—but from the very first moment, he'd known it was more than physical.

Beneath the conflict, beneath his half-hearted attempts to keep her at arm's length, there was something else: peace. A quiet, undeniable peace that settled over him whenever she was near.

And it was that peace, more than anything, that terrified him. Because deep down, he didn't believe he deserved it.

The time was fast approaching when he would have to tell her the truth. He didn't know how, or what might happen afterward. So he prayed—quietly, fervently—that when the time came, she would believe him.

# Chapter Thirty
## Mira

I was still asleep in the massive carved bed when something cold and wet nudged me. I blinked my eyes open to find Bunny's solemn face inches from mine, watching me expectantly. I smiled, drowsy and amused—the wiry silver hair around her eyes reminded me of Jonathan Blackwell's unruly white eyebrows. Footsteps echoed down the hallway, and a moment later, Baird appeared in the doorway.

"Oh, Buns...why'd ye wake her?" he chided softly, a tentative, almost shy smile tugging at his lips.

I watched him through half-lidded eyes, trying to read his expression. Something about the way he avoided my gaze made my stomach flutter—not with excitement, but with uncertainty.

Did he regret last night?

He didn't seem cold or distant, not exactly. But there was a caution in him this morning that hadn't been there the night before. I wrapped the sheet a little tighter around myself, suddenly unsure of where we stood now that the fire had cooled and daylight had settled in.

The heavy drapes had been redrawn sometime after I'd fallen asleep, leaving the room in a cocoon of darkness, save for a narrow sliver of morning light pouring through the stairwell window just outside the door. My clothes, which had been left in a careless heap on the kitchen floor the night before, were now folded neatly at the foot of the bed.

"I stopped at the bakery for pastries when I took Bunny to the park," Baird said, his voice casual, kind. "I got an assortment—almond croissant, pain au chocolat, raspberry strudel...or I could fry ye up an egg?"

He gestured vaguely back toward the hallway. "I've got tea on and coffee in the kitchen, and some juice too. Come down whenever yer ready. Bathroom's across the hall." With that, he turned and disappeared down the hallway, Bunny trotting faithfully behind him.

I took a quick shower in a marble-tile bathroom, then pulled on my jeans and sweater, skipping the bra. I towel-dried my hair and padded barefoot into the kitchen, bra in hand, ready to shove it into the pocket of my coat hanging in the closet.

Baird looked up as I approached, taking in the sight of me.

"I like the edit to yer outfit, Miss Garvie," he said with a teasing smile, a lascivious glint in those sparkling green eyes he tried—and failed—to suppress. "I agree—the bra was redundant."

Okay, maybe he didn't regret last night after all. Maybe I'd been projecting.

"Coffee or tea?" he asked, already reaching for the carafe when I pointed toward the coffee maker.

"What shall it be?" he added, gesturing to both the plate of pastries on the island and the frying pan on the range behind him.

I grabbed an almond croissant and bit into the flaky end. "Mmm... I'm ravenous, and this is delicious," I mumbled through a mouthful.

"I'm glad," he said, leaning across the marble island to kiss my forehead. "How did ye sleep?"

"Like the dead. I don't think I've slept that soundly in months."

He stood behind the island like some absurdly handsome short-order cook, but I noticed he wasn't eating.

"Have you eaten?"

"Nae," he said with a shake of his head. "I don't eat much breakfast."

Baird said he had some calls to make and sat down at the kitchen table with his laptop open. "Make yourself at home," he said, his voice casual—but it landed with unexpected weight.

I already knew the layout of the first floor, but up a flight of stairs on the winding staircase, I discovered a formal living room, anchored by an exquisite carved Italian marble fireplace. Wood floors stretched beneath antique Oushak rugs, their patterns softened with age.

A smaller, more casual family room occupied the northeast corner, outfitted with a large television and a comfortable sprawl of furniture. Across from it, a guest bath was tucked discreetly into the wall.

On the third floor, down the hall from the master suite, there were two smaller guest rooms connected by a shared Jack-and-Jill bathroom. The walls in every room were painted in deep, rich colors: a moody moss green in the family room; dark coffee-colored walls in the formal living room. One guest room was done in a muted fawn, with matching painted twin beds, the other in a serene French blue, centered around a brass bed with a wooden trunk at the foot.

Art hung in a curated blend of styles—contemporary works by Elliott Puckett and Caio Fonseca—originals, perhaps?—mixed with traditional Scottish plein-air landscapes. The contrast kept the otherwise classical interior from feeling too formal, too preserved.

There was something strikingly familiar about it all. The way this house had been decorated—layering modern and traditional elements with intent—reflected the very approach I'd used to build my own business. It made me feel unexpectedly at home.

Maybe too much so. And that realization brought with it a flicker of unease. I wasn't sure yet what this was between us, or what it might become. But here, in this beautiful, thoughtfully lived-in space, surrounded by objects and choices that mirrored my own taste so precisely, I felt a strange and growing sense of belonging.

And that scared me just a little.

I wandered back to the master suite and realized just how little attention I'd paid to the room the night before. Every hour I'd spent in it had been focused on Baird—either staring at his face, tracing the lines of his body, or lying face-down under the heavy velvet coverlet in a dreamless sleep.

Unlike the painted walls throughout the rest of the house, this room was wrapped in rich wood paneling, lighter than the almost ebony oak of the carved bed. A large painted wardrobe stood against the far wall, and wide side tables flanked the bed, each topped with a brass reading lamp.

I stifled a giggle as a thought struck me—I couldn't imagine ever using one of those lamps. Not with Baird Campbell occupying the space beside me. Reading in bed seemed laughably optimistic.

I opened the door to a built-in closet tucked into the corner of the room, its interior lined with cedar. I wondered if this was the source of the scent I'd come to associate with Baird—subtle, earthy, and ever-present since the day we met.

Inside, a few pairs of jeans were neatly stacked on a shelf beside folded T-shirts and sweaters, all in the same muted, natural tones that echoed throughout his home. A handful of finely tailored suits and an assortment of crisp dress shirts hung on wooden hangers. Below them, a shoe rack held several pairs: tennis shoes, the low-heeled boots he'd slipped off the night before—now returned to their rightful place—polished black and brown dress shoes that looked rarely worn, and a few pairs of rugged boots that clearly saw regular use.

This was the closet of a man who knew how to dress up but clearly preferred to dress down.

Baird found me about an hour later, curled up in an overstuffed chair in the formal living room, a book open in my lap.

"Do ye have any plans today?" he asked as he stepped into the room.

It struck me then—he might be wondering why I was still here. The warmth of the house, of the morning, suddenly gave way to unease.

"Oh—gosh, I should probably head back to the hotel," I said, already shifting to sit up. "I'll just call an Uber—"

"*Whoa*, lass," he interrupted, brow furrowing as he tilted his head. "Are ye plannin' on doin' a runner?"

"A *what*?" I asked, blinking.

"Unexpectedly runnin' out on me," he translated, lips curving into something halfway between amusement and concern.

"Oh." I hesitated, unsure how to explain what had taken root in my gut. "I just realized I've been here almost eighteen hours—you probably want your house back to yourself."

It sounded flimsy, even to me, but I couldn't ignore the sudden weight pressing in my chest.

"Are ye projecting, Mira Garvie?" he asked, voice light, not unkind. "Does the independent introvert need her alone time?"

His tone wasn't judgmental. If anything, it felt like curiosity, like he was trying to understand me, not push me away.

"I mean, come on," I said, attempting levity. "If I picked up some guy and took him home, I'd absolutely want him gone the next morning."

He stepped closer, gaze steady. "Do ye want to be gone?"

I cleared my throat, the truth prickling just beneath my skin. "No," I said quietly, shaking my head. "I don't."

The admission sat between us like a fragile glass—exposed and delicate.

"You're not tired of having a stranger wandering around your home," I added, glancing down at my feet tucked beneath me, "barefoot and curled up on your furniture?"

"No," he said simply. "If ye want to know how I feel about something, just ask. That's part of getting to know someone—something ye might not be all that familiar with."

His tone was gentle, not scolding, and the honesty in it quieted the storm in my chest.

"Now, if I've calmed your fears," he continued, "I was hoping we could spend the rest of today together. I can drive ye back to the hotel to grab a change of clothes, and then... we could take a drive, go sightseeing, maybe a hike...or," he added, that wicked grin spreading across his face, "we could spend the rest of the day in my bed. Your choice."

Just the look in his eyes made my sex-sore muscles ache for him all over again.

"Hmm...I like these à la carte menu options," I purred, arching a single eyebrow. "I choose a change of clothes...and your bed, please."

"For clarity's sake," he said in a tone that could've belonged to a contract attorney, "I should point out that the term *bed* will not restrict us exclusively to an actual bed. If ye recall, last night also featured the kitchen table...and a window frame."

"Duly noted," I replied, biting my lip.

"Then let's start with a run to the hotel," he growled, stepping closer. "Because once we start the second item on that menu, I don't think we'll want to stop for anything."

And with that, he leaned in and kissed me—savagely, thoroughly—until I forgot where I was, what day it was, and why I'd ever considered leaving at all.

# CHAPTER THIRTY-ONE
# BAIRD

Thirty minutes later, they pulled up to the hotel and handed the keys to the valet. Upstairs, in Mira's room, Baird stood silently as she moved about, selecting a few fresh pieces of clothing and undergarments, folding them neatly into a small overnight bag. He wanted to say something—make a suggestion—but now that he understood more of who she was, he hesitated. The introvert in Mira might shrink from the wrong kind of pressure, and the last thing he wanted was to push too hard.

"Uh...Mira. What if ye brought all your things back to the house? Stayed with me for the rest of your trip?" He rubbed the back of his neck, suddenly nervous now that the words were out. "No pressure, truly—I know your days will be busy with class. But if your evenings are free..." He trailed off, gave a small shrug, and then met her eyes. "I'd love the chance to spend more time with ye. You can drive the rental back and park it at the house."

There was a beat of silence. Then Mira looked up at him—eyes wide, surprised, but glowing—and nodded. She seemed to leap at the idea before hesitation flickered across her face, as if suddenly questioning her own sanity.

But still, she said yes.

And Baird was deeply, quietly grateful.

He could have enthralled her—could have nudged her mind, twisted her will, made her *think* it was her own idea. But the thought of it being anything less than her true desire was abhorrent to him.

# CHAPTER THIRTY-TWO
## MIRA

When I walked back through Baird's front door and dropped my bags onto the floor, Bunny immediately began hopping with excitement—true to her name, tail wagging furiously.

"I think someone's got a fan," Baird said, mock jealousy softening his voice. "High praise, considering Bunny doesn't like anyone but me."

He picked up my bags. "Mind if I put these in the closet upstairs?"

I shook my head, and the three of us made our way up the stairs to the master suite.

As I began unpacking, hanging a few items in the cedar-lined closet, Baird sat on the edge of the bed, watching me with quiet interest.

"So tell me about your class," he said.

"The workshop is focused on gold granulation," I replied, tugging a blouse onto a hanger. "It's this ancient technique where you create tiny spheres of gold—really tiny, like .2 to 1 millimeter—and fuse them to a design. Everyone does a class project, so I brought some emeralds from my safe back home to make a pendant in 22 karat gold."

I pulled a sketchbook from my tote and handed it to him, flipping to a page with the rough design. Then I took out a small box and opened it.

Inside was a stunning oval-cut emerald, at least five carats, its deep green catching the light in long flashes. A few smaller stones nestled around it, loose but already claiming space in the imagined pendant.

Baird whistled low under his breath. "That's not just a class project, lass. That's a work of art waiting to happen."

We spent the afternoon making love and talking—long, unhurried conversations that unraveled between kisses and tangled sheets. By evening, we opened another bottle of wine and ordered takeout.

I was famished, eating straight from the container while standing—naked—at the kitchen island. Baird watched me with something close to reverence, picking at a few bites of his own between my mouthfuls, but clearly more entranced by the view than the food.

"You don't eat much," I noted between bites.

"Aye...I've been a bit preoccupied with a certain Mira Garvie these last few days," he said with a teasing smile. "Dinnae worry about me, lass."

When I held up the container in offering, a silent last call, he shook his head with a lazy grin. I shrugged, popped the leftovers into the fridge, and glanced over at Bunny, who was snoring softly in the corner on her bed, perfectly content.

"I thought it might be nice to have a relaxing soak upstairs," Baird said, rising from his seat at the counter. "Give me five minutes to draw a bath?"

When I walked into the marble bathroom a few minutes later, the lights were low, and candles flickered gently around the room. The clawfoot tub was filled, steam curling softly above the surface. Baird was already there, lounging back with the water lapping around his waist, his arms stretched along the rim like a king at rest.

I slid into the bath in front of him, nestling my back against his chest. His arms wrapped around me as my head came to rest on his shoulder, the warmth of the water soothing every muscle in my body.

Then, in that quiet glow, he said, "Did ye ever think to reframe your view of who ye are? Not as some 'odd girl' who hates people and can't find love, but as a woman with a gift—someone who receives messages from the universe. A woman who won't settle for the wrong partner?"

I groaned softly. "You sound like my therapist."

"She sounds like a smart woman," Baird murmured, kissing the top of my head.

When we eventually climbed out of the tub, Baird wrapped me in a plush towel and dried me off carefully. Then, with a wicked glint in his eye, he spanked me lightly with it and grinned.

"Go on, get into bed, lass. I've not quite finished with ye tonight."

He winked, and in that moment, I knew sleep would have to wait.

And it did—at least for a while. But eventually, I drifted off for the second night in a row, utterly spent in Baird's bed, wrapped in warmth, my back pressed to his chest.

Cocooned. Safe.

*"You know what I am, Agnes... Don't play coy with me," the dark man says, his voice low and cruel. His liquid-silver eyes lock onto mine like a magnet, unblinking.*

*I am frozen, paralyzed by terror, every alarm bell in my body scream-ing—my sympathetic nervous system hijacked, helpless.*

*"Your husband doesn't want you. He doesn't understand your sensitive nature the way I do." His words twist like a knife. "Your father's doctor was wrong—a husband can't fix you. The pain inside you is too great. The captain is powerless to help you—only I can take it away."*

*He pauses, watching me with cold satisfaction. "But you already know that, don't you?" He's toying with me.*

*"Isn't that why you keep coming back?"*

*He tilts his head slightly, already knowing the answer.*

*"It's not for the portrait, Agnes..."*

*He is ten feet from me—and then suddenly, he isn't.*

*He is inches away.*

*Even through the haze of my disorientation, his features begin to sharp-en—like watching a camera lens snap into focus. Blurry lines hardened into shape. And in that instant, horror strikes.*

*I recognize him.*

*I had seen this man just a day ago. The man who was following me.*

*Now, with our faces only inches apart, he smiles with wicked delight.*

*"Or should I call you...Mira?"*

# Chapter Thirty-Three

# BAIRD

He startled awake when he felt Mira's heart racing beside him, her body rigid, eyes darting frantically beneath closed lids. Adrenaline surged through her veins like wildfire—he could feel it radiating from her, every muscle locked in terror.

"Mira...Mira, wake up!" he urged, shaking her gently.

She screamed, thrashing against him. Her hands clawed at his face and arms like a panicked animal, wild and disoriented. He shook her again—harder this time—and her eyes snapped open, wide and glassy, unfocused. She didn't know where she was.

Baird resisted the impulse to pull her into his arms. He knew better. She needed time—to reorient, to recognize him, to come back to herself. Her pulse thundered against his fingertips. He waited, letting the rush of panic ebb as her brain slowly stopped receiving the relentless distress signals firing from her adrenal glands.

Her hair was damp with sweat. He could smell the fear on her skin, and it turned his stomach—not because she was afraid, but because the scent stirred something deeper in him. Something darker.

He was glad the room was cloaked in shadows. Glad she couldn't see how her fear made his pupils dilate.

"Dinna fash, Mira," he said quietly, cupping both sides of her face. "Yer with me."

Her eyes finally focused, and the tears came in a sudden rush. Her breath hitched in shallow, broken gasps.

"Baird..." she choked out. "I've been seeing a man in my dreams. He's different than my waking visions—*darker*. He's the one who painted Agnes, I know it." Her words came in sobs. "But I saw him the other day, at the flea markets. He followed me for hours. I *know* it's the same man."

An ancient, visceral fury sparked in his chest—Bastien was there, following her, watching her. He knew this would happen, he'd just not known when. The dark one was taunting her—both of them, and the rage that grew inside Baird wasn't hot—it was cold, bleak, and black.

"There, there, love...hush now," Baird whispered, lips brushing against her damp hair as he pulled her into his arms. "It was nothing but a bad dream. Nothing more. Lay back on me—I've got ye."

He held her close as her trembling began to ease, as her breathing slowly steadied.

"Yer safe," he said again.

But Baird knew it was the furthest thing from the truth.

He needed to tell her.

# Chapter Thirty-Four

# Mira

I woke to find Baird still in bed beside me, watching me, his eyes clouded with concern. I'd been too shaken to sleep for hours after the nightmare, but he'd held me tightly through the night, anchoring me, until eventually the exhaustion won out. The clock on the nightstand read 8:37 a.m. I needed a shower—my skin still sticky with the cold sweat that had clung to me as I tried to escape the dark man in my dream.

"I'll run the shower for ye, let it warm up a bit," Baird said softly, sliding out of bed. "Come down when yer done, and I'll make breakfast. Ye can tell me more about this man ye saw the other day."

His voice was gentle, but there was a guarded edge to it—something just beneath the surface that didn't sit quite right. It made my stomach twist with unease. He must have thought I was crazy.

As the hot water poured over my face, I let the steam rise around me, hoping it would loosen the grip of fear still lingering in my chest. I couldn't shake the feeling that I'd somehow lost hold of myself.

Was I unraveling?

Had I sounded completely unhinged last night, rambling about strange men and dreams that bled into reality?

Maybe Baird was right to be wary.

Who was I now? This Mira—haunted, reactive, a stranger to her own sense of control—felt nothing like the woman I'd always been. Normally rational. Steady. Unshakable.

Now I felt reckless. Untethered. Taken hold of by something I couldn't define—and worse, something I couldn't deny. It moved beneath the surface of my thoughts like a tide I couldn't swim against, pulling me further and further from the version of myself I used to trust.

I dressed for comfort—old jeans, tennis shoes, a soft T-shirt. I pulled my hair back into a ponytail, keeping it out of my face and out of the way.

When I came downstairs, Baird handed me a cup of coffee without a word.

"Scrambled eggs and toast okay?" he asked.

I nodded absently, still caught in the fog of my thoughts.

He moved about the kitchen, but I could feel the weight in the room before he even spoke again. He looked troubled—more so than when I'd first woken in his cottage days ago. Something was pressing down on him, dragging the spark from his eyes. He looked older somehow. Worn.

"Why didn't ye tell me someone was following ye?" he asked at last, his voice low, rough with fatigue.

"I didn't want to tell you at the time," I said quietly. "At first, I honestly thought I might have imagined it. And then later that night...I was here with you. It felt like the last thing I should bring up."

I hesitated, my fingers tightening around the coffee mug. "I thought you'd think I was crazy."

Baird was silent. His expression had turned to stone—impassive, unreadable.

The walls were back up. Not slowly this time, not subtly. They had slammed into place, locked tight. And somehow, that chilled me almost as much as the nightmare had.

Last night, he'd told me I needed to reframe who I was. He'd spoken like he believed in me—like he saw something more than the broken, haunted version of myself I tried to keep buried.

But now I could see the shift in his eyes, the wheels turning behind them.

I wasn't a gifted diviner. I wasn't some woman touched by the universe.

I was just the cursed, odd, broken girl again.

And this time, I was sure he saw it too.

He turned his back to me, busying himself with cleaning up after breakfast. I could tell he didn't want to talk to me.

I needed to leave. Get some distance from whatever was happening to me.

"Um—I think I should go," I said, rising from the stool at the counter. "These past few days...they've been the best I've ever had. I've never felt so cared for, but—"

Before I could finish, he was suddenly in front of me, blocking my exit.

My breath caught. He'd been at the sink only a second ago.

Another wave of disorientation hit me—like my brain couldn't process the steps it must have taken for him to cross the room. I hadn't seen him move. Hadn't *heard* him—the same way the dark man moved in my nightmare.

My vision shimmered at the edges, a dizzy rush rising in my chest. I felt like I might faint. His face twisted with anguish—anger, pain, sadness all colliding in a storm just beneath the surface. The expression was almost unrecognizable, and for the first time since I'd met him, I was afraid.

"What is happening, Baird?" I asked, my voice barely above a whisper. "What's wrong?"

"You don't really know me," he said, his voice low, heavy with a sadness that felt centuries old.

I didn't understand what was happening, but my fear twisted, calcified—became anger. And what made it worse was the truth in his words. He was right.

But I didn't know who I was more furious with—him for hiding, or myself for letting sex take the place of real questions.

"You know what? You're right," I snapped, arms folding tightly across my chest. "Somehow you know my whole freakin' life story. How did you pull that off in less than a week? I've known people for *years* who don't know half as much about me as you do." My voice rose, heat spilling out now. "But you? You've told me next to nothing."

Baird's jaw tensed. "I know, Mira. I do. And I want to fix that—I *need* to—but I don't know the words to explain what I need to say."

"Oh, let me help you then." My tone sharpened, fury barely leashed. "Here's what I've figured out on my own, just by watching you. You're smoking hot, somewhere between thirty-five and forty. You've got a cottage on an island, a multimillion-dollar townhouse here, and a *giant* dog."

I pointed to Bunny, who was snoring peacefully in her bed, blissfully unaware of the rising storm between us.

"You're obsessively neat. You can cook but barely eat. You collect art—some of it museum-worthy. And you're some kind of tantric sex god or—" I stumbled over my words. "I don't even have the vocabulary for what you are in bed."

He didn't move. He just watched me, silent, taking every word.

"But as for what *you've* told me?" I lifted my hand, fingers counting off. "One: your name. Two: the cottage belonged to your grandmother. Three: you sold a company and now you farm and own real estate. Four: you made some vague reference to losing someone long ago. And five?" I popped up my thumb. "Your dog is five and her name is Bunny."

I stared at him, my whole hand raised. "*That's it.* That's all you've given me."

My voice cracked, but I pushed through. "I've looked for you online, Baird. Tried to find *anything*. A digital footprint. A photo. An article. A *business listing*. But there's nothing. It's like you don't even exist. Like you're just..." I faltered. "Like you're some figment of my imagination."

My anger began to tremble under the weight of something else—something I didn't know how to name. "And yet I know how you make me feel. Seen. Cared for. Safe. Important."

I dropped my hand, the silence between us thick, aching.

Then, Baird's voice broke the stillness, soft and sure.

"Do ye remember when you told me about your clairvoyance?" he asked. "Ye didn't think I'd believe ye, did ye?"

"No...not really," I said quietly, my voice stripped bare.

"I don't think saying words can communicate what I need ye to know, but I've had an idea that may," Baird said, a splinter of hope in his voice. "I need ye to promise me ye won't run away. Ye will have so many questions, and I need to know ye'll stick around to ask them. Just promise me that much." Baird held out his hand to me, and when I took it, he gave it a small squeeze.

He led me up the stairs to the third floor.

With each step, my heart began to pound erratically. Part of me wanted to turn and run—to bolt from whatever this was. But I'd made a promise. I *wanted* answers. Answers to who *he* was...and to what the hell was happening to *me*.

Baird passed the master suite wordlessly and continued down the hall until we came to one of the guest rooms—the one with the French blue walls, the brass bed, and at the foot of it, the old trunk.

The trunk was wrapped in dark, timeworn leather, its edges studded with tarnished brass tacks. The corners were cracked and peeling, like skin too long exposed to the elements. It looked like it had been waiting—patiently, ominously—for someone to open it.

Baird let go of my hand and stepped into the room. He knelt beside the trunk, running his hand over the worn leather before slowly lifting the lid. The hinges groaned in protest, a rusty, aching sound that echoed in the stillness as the top creaked open.

I hadn't even taken a full step into the room when I felt it—that strange, unmistakable pull. There was something inside. *Calling* to me.

Baird looked over his shoulder and saw me still standing in the doorway, frozen.

"Come kneel down with me," he said softly. "I want ye to touch this. I think—I think this is the only way ye'll truly understand, Mira." Something raw flickered in his eyes—hope, fear, a silent plea, maybe. I crossed the floor and sank to my knees, even though every part of me wanted to stay standing. It felt just like that day at the gravestone on Arran—something pulling me down, not just gravity, but something deeper. Older. Winning the battle against my will.

I went down slowly, my body resisting, my face twisted with fear and the bone-deep certainty that something was about to be revealed. Something I wasn't sure I *wanted* to know.

Baird shifted beside me, placing one arm gently behind my back. I couldn't tell if he was trying to protect me—or stop me from running.

Inside the open trunk lay a parcel wrapped in old linen. My hands moved toward it, almost without permission, and as I peeled back the fabric, that familiar wave of anxiety surged through me.

Beads of sweat broke across my forehead, though my skin had gone cold. My breath turned shallow, thin. It was as if I was watching the scene from outside my body—kneeling beside Baird, but also hovering above us, detached, observing.

The panic was recognizable. But this time, I didn't fight it.

Something deep within me whispered that the only way forward was to surrender—to trust this strange ability of mine, whatever it truly was.

Beneath the linen, a dress appeared. Lavish and impossibly old, yet still miraculously intact. Silk, heavy and rippling in deep caramel tones. The bodice was boned and fitted, edged with soft ivory lace at a wide neckline. I reached for it, touched the fabric with my fingertips. It was stiff with age, but the silk still held a ghost of softness.

And as I gave myself over to the darkness rising around me—sinking into it like water—I felt Baird's lips press gently against my neck. Right in the place they always went—where my pulse thrummed just beneath the surface, lifting the skin in tempo with the pounding of my heart.

It was like he could feel it too. As if he knew that spot wasn't just tender—it was *important*. A place where something in me opened. To him.

*I hear Baird's voice faintly in my ear—though I can't tell if it comes from beside me or from somewhere in front of me.*

*"I have ye, Mira... I want ye to see it all this time. See the truth only ye can."*

*Music fills my ears, and suddenly—I am wearing the dress.*

*It swishes and sways with each movement, the fine woolen petticoats underneath trapping heat against my skin, clinging to my legs in the warm night air.*

*I am dancing.*

*My heart pounds—not with fear, but joy. I feel jubilant, alive, spinning through a room full of laughter and music. Men and women in lavish formal attire move in perfect time around me, a choreographed harmony.*

*My body knows the steps of this unfamiliar dance. My right arm reaches for one stranger, then my left for another as we turn, switch, and spin. We all move together like parts of a living clock. I find myself lined up across from a row of men, my eyes drawn to the one directly in front of me.*

*He reaches out his hand. We circle each other, playful, magnetic. His body draws me in like gravity, his nearness heating my skin—not with sweat, but with something else.*

*Desire.*

*Candlelight flickers over us as we move. I finally let my gaze rise to take him in.*

*Tall—at least a foot taller than me. Broad, powerful shoulders. He wears camel-colored breeches, tall boots, a finely embroidered waistcoat, and a deep blue cutaway tailcoat with polished brass buttons.*

*He spins me again, and I laugh—throwing my head back, the sound bubbling up from a place in me I haven't touched in years. I can't remember ever feeling so free.*

*And then I see his face.*

*Suntanned skin, the lines around his eyes deepening when he smiles like this. The strong nose, the square jaw. Those green eyes I know so well.*

*Baird.*

*I am dancing with Baird.*

*I hear his voice again—distant this time, and oddly disconnected from his lips, which aren't moving.*

*"Mira, what do you see? Tell me…"*

*Confusion stirs. My smile begins to falter.*

*A chill gnaws at my spine—cold, creeping upward, unwelcome. I feel eyes on me. Watching. Claiming.*

*I stop moving, lifting the hem of my skirts as I step backward off the ballroom floor.*

*Baird stands frozen, his face a portrait of love one moment, then confusion as he watches me retreat. I want to go back to him. Want his arms, his safety. But something is pulling me away—something I can't resist.*

*I turn.*

*And I know who I'll see before my eyes find him.*

*He stands near the wall of the ballroom, a goblet of wine in hand. His eyes—liquid mercury—are fixed on me, drilling into me like knives made of ice.*

*The dark man.*

*His hair is longer now, curling near the collar of his black and gold brocade jacket. He is handsome—unsettlingly so. Not like Baird. This is a beauty with sharp edges. A dark fox in human form. It hurts to look at him.*

*I try to look away. Try to move. But I am frozen. My body screams to run, adrenaline flooding my veins, but my feet are rooted to the ground.*

*He doesn't speak. Doesn't move. Just watches.*

*And still—I know he is controlling me.*

*"Mira! Mira, come back to me. Talk to me!" Baird's voice calls out, far away now.*

*I turn toward the dance floor to find him, my paralysis loosening just enough to let me look over my shoulder—*

*But he's gone.*

*The guests have vanished. The music has stopped.*

*Only silence remains, thick and unnatural, like the room itself is holding its breath.*

*The ballroom is empty. Except for me.*

*And him.*

*The man with the silver eyes moves toward me—slowly, deliberately. His gaze sweeps over me like a predator assessing its prey.*

*He circles, close enough that I can feel the chill radiating off him. His presence brushes against my skin like a shadow come to life.*

*That psychic tether pulls taut again, locking my limbs in place. I can't move. Can't even turn my head.*

*I'm caught—held fast in his gravity.*

*An impossibly long finger reaches out and touches my cheek, tracing the line of my jaw with excruciating patience. The touch burns—cold and stinging, like dry ice kissed to flesh.*

*He moves behind me. I feel his finger trail along the back of my neck, catching on a curl that escaped my updo, then circles back around, facing me again.*

*He looks into my eyes—searching, debating.*

*And then, in a voice that is somehow both male and female, layered like two tones from opposite sides of the veil, he says:*

*"Baird is the best one to tell you this story, Mira..."*

# CHAPTER THIRTY-FIVE
## BAIRD

Baird cradled Mira in his arms, her body rocking gently against his as he held her close. Tears slid down his cheeks, falling onto her face—tears for what he had allowed to happen nearly two hundred and fifty years ago...and for what he feared she would now see in him. The story was unraveling now, piece by piece.

She mumbled incoherently, starting and stopping, her voice barely more than a whisper. Her eyes were wide, pupils blown, unfocused. Then she began to resist—weakly at first, her limbs trembling against him, then with rising urgency. A muffled cry escaped her, raw, wounded.

And then her gaze locked onto his. He saw the terror in her eyes. He saw the look, like an animal cornered, frantic. Her feet slipped helplessly on the smooth wood floor, struggling for traction as she tried to pull away. Baird released her instantly, his arms falling open the moment she resisted.

He knew better than to hold her against her will.

She crawled backward, dragging herself across the floor, still too shaken to stand. She cowered in the far corner of the room, one arm raised in front of her, palm out—warding him off like he was a fire that could burn her down.

Baird didn't move.

The pain in his chest was sharp, hollowing him out—because he knew *he* was the reason for what Mira was feeling. The space between them was only a few feet.

But to him, it felt like the deepest river gorge.

Uncrossable.

He watched her, unsure of what to do next.

"*Tell me!*" she screamed at him. "Tell me what he *is!*" Her voice cracked, still locked in the grip of panic, as she pleaded through sobs that fell so fast, she could barely see him through the blur.

Baird crawled slowly toward her, cautious, one hand reaching out to brush her tear-streaked cheek. His voice trembled.

"Please, Mira. Please...ye have to know. The man ye've seen in your dreams—and here, following ye through the city—he's undead."

"*Undead?*" she snapped, recoiling, eyes wide with disbelief. "What the hell are you talking about? That's *impossible*. I'm not *stupid*, Baird—"

"Mira," he interrupted, urgent now, his voice raw. "Please. Just listen." He tried to steady his tone, willing her to hear what he should have told her days ago. What she never would've believed—until now.

"Think about what ye've seen. What ye *feel* when he's near. His eyes—how they *glow*. The way the air *freezes* when he looks at ye. The speed...the *way* he moves. Ye've seen him in your dreams, Mira. *Centuries ago*. And again—*this week*. The same face. The same man."

He lowered his voice, trying to soothe her, to call her back from wherever fear had taken her. "Ye *know* he isn't human."

She shook her head, lips trembling, torn between denial and the truth unraveling in her chest.

Baird's voice dropped to a whisper. "He's what you'd call a vampire, Mira." He looked down, unable to meet her eyes. "He has lived for hundreds of years. He's the painter... *Bastien Bethune*."

The name hung in the air like a curse.

Tears streamed down Baird's cheeks as he finally said the words he had never wanted her to hear. Without coming any closer, Baird took both of Mira's hands gently in his own.

"Mira..." He slowed his speech when he said her name, almost in reverence—almost in shame. He knelt there, utterly prostrate before her, and for a long moment, neither of them moved.

Then, slowly, he raised his head. His eyes met hers.

# Chapter Thirty-Six

# Mira

The green irises—so familiar to me by now—were nearly consumed by darkness. His pupils were dilated so wide they left only the thinnest glowing emerald ring around the edge. The effect was inhuman. Mesmerizing. Terrifying.

"Tell me what ye see in *me*, Mira," he whispered, then again louder—pleading now. "*Tell me!*"

His voice was firm but tender, carefully measured. It was like he needed me to *see* him—needed me to understand that the power in this moment belonged not to him, but to me.

He was giving me the truth.

I looked at him—and then quickly turned away, unable to hold his admission, unwilling to admit what my body already knew.

I'm sure the painful recognition was clear on my face. I could no longer deny what I'd seen, what I now *knew*. His eyes, luminous green, pulsed with a glow no mortal man possessed. The way he moved—too fast, almost a blur at the edge of vision.

He was the same. He had *always* been the same.

He had tried to hide it from me, shielded me from the truth of what he was, but a few times he'd slipped, just for a moment. Why hadn't I seen it? Or had I seen it, and simply refused to believe?

When he finally spoke, his voice was quiet, thick with shame. "Bastien killed Agnes when he couldn't have her. I couldn't protect her," he said. "He killed her—forced me to watch as he drained the blood from her body. And then..."

Baird's voice cracked. He was shattered by the remembering. "And then he turned me. Into the same kind of monster *he* is."

A silence settled, heavy as stone.

"Agnes was my wife, Mira," he said, barely audible. "And I failed her."

Baird's shoulders were shaking with silent sobs. The same broken weeping I'd seen at Agnes's grave, only now I understood what it truly meant. The rational part of my brain was lighting flares in every direction, sending up warning shots, begging me to run. And yet...some illogical but deeply rooted *knowing* inside me believed him.

I didn't want to. It would've been so much easier to walk away, chalk it all up to meeting a dangerously attractive man in Scotland, falling into a wildly passionate fling, only to discover he was a complete crackpot.

But I knew better. I *knew.*

I stayed in the corner, silent. Just *watching* him.

I don't know how long passed—maybe an hour, maybe more. The fear ebbed from my body eventually, slipping out of reach like a receding tide—illogical, perhaps, but no less real. In its place rose something far more dangerous.

Anger. Anger at *him.*

Finally, I found my voice. "So...let's say, for the sake of argument, that I believe you. Or...maybe I'm trying to." My tone was sharper now. Controlled. "Can we go back to the part where you said *vampire*?"

Baird looked up, his face pale and drawn, but remarkably calm. "It might not be the perfect word," he said quietly, "but it's the closest I know—for what I am. For what *he* is." He paused, searching my face. "The books and movies...most of it's nonsense. We don't sleep in coffins, we can't fly or turn into smoke. Daylight doesn't affect us. But some of the things they say are true."

He hesitated.

"We need blood to survive. Doesn't matter the source. Animal or human—it works the same. We age slowly...we live for a long, long time."

"But you eat food," I said, folding my arms. "I've seen you."

He gave a small shrug. "It's mostly for show. Part of how we blend in. We're good at hiding in plain sight."

"Garlic? Crosses?" I asked, half a smirk curling my lip.

He shook his head. "No effect."

"Mirrors? Photographs?"

"Ye've seen me in a mirror. And if ye want, grab your phone—take my picture."

"That would just prove you're an *insane human*, not a vampire."

He sighed, the grief returning. "Maybe I just want there to be something for you to remember me by. Like the portrait of Agnes was supposed to be for me."

"So you aren't going to kill me and drink my blood? Isn't that how this ends?"

"Jaysus, Mira, is that what ye think of me?" Baird said in frustration. "If I was going to do something like that, wouldn't I have done it already?"

"Maybe you like to play with your food?" I raised one shoulder in a half shrug, eyes steely in their resolve. And then, unbidden, Granny Margaret's words echoed softly in my mind: *"Now for the ither, the man with the green eyes, he'll nae hurt ye."*

I clung to that. Beneath all my questions, beneath the fury and fear—I knew it was true. But I wasn't done. Not even close. I needed to ask at least a thousand more questions, and I was going to do my best to make sure he was uncomfortable before I was done.

At that, Baird let out a short laugh—but the smile faded almost instantly, pain flickering across his face.

"Touché, Miss Garvie," he murmured flatly. "I see ye've managed to keep yer sense of humor."

"What else?" I asked, my voice low but steady. "What else do I need to know about *you*?"

Baird tilted his head, brows knitted together. "Aren't ye more interested in *him*?"

"Oh, I'll get to him," I said, my tone sharp enough to cut. *"After* I'm done asking about *you*, thank you very much. Remember just a bit ago—when you hauled me upstairs and opened that trunk? What was it you said then?" I cocked my head. *"Oh, right.* You wanted me to promise I'd stay and ask all my questions. Well, I'm just getting started asking the *fucking* questions," I said through clenched teeth. "And *you*, you asshole, are going to sit there and answer every single one of them until *I'm* ready to change the subject."

Baird sat cross-legged on the floor in front of me, hands in his lap like a schoolboy. All his attention was on me as the questions kept coming.

"What else," I said, gesturing wildly between us, "*can you do?*"

"We're unusually strong. And fast." He met my gaze. "I know ye've seen the fast part. A few times, I...I let ye see how I move. Wanting ye to ask. But ye just...didn't."

He shook his head and looked almost confused—by what he seemed to read as my willful blindness.

I laughed, but there was no humor in it. "It's easy to ignore red flags when all I can think about is the next time you're going to slide your cock into me," I snapped.

Baird flinched, just slightly.

"You turn my insides to jelly, Baird. I've been walking around for days like some *dick-drunk teenager*, completely unable to think straight."

"*Dick-drunk*, huh?" Baird echoed, a slow grin tugging at the corner of his mouth. "I like that I do that to ye, Mira."

Something flickered across his face—equal parts amusement and self-satisfaction.

"Wait... *Wait*," I said, my voice tight with suspicion. "Is the...'dick-drunk' thing a vampire power?"

Baird inhaled deeply, his chest rising, then slowly exhaled through his mouth like he was preparing for impact. Clearly, this section of the interrogation was going to get complicated.

"The first thing—*the most important thing*—ye need to know before I answer that," he said carefully, "is that I have *never* used any sort of supernatural power dynamic with ye." His gaze locked onto mine, steady and unwavering. "If this topic ever came up between us, I wanted to be able to say with complete honesty that I've never used anything but the part of me that remains human to attract ye, Mira."

He paused, then continued quietly, with something close to shame curling at the edge of his voice. "But yes, vampires can enthrall humans. We can control behavior, draw someone in—even make them forget. It's done with the eyes."

He let that hang in the air for a beat.

"But I have *never* used that power on ye, Mira. *Never.* I swear it." He leaned forward slightly, his voice softening. "I wanted to know yer feelings for me, physical or otherwise, were genuine."

I rolled my eyes after his statement of wanting to know my feelings, *'physical or otherwise.'*

"But when I put my lips on yer neck," Baird said, voice low and deliberate, "I *know* that has an effect on ye I can't control." His eyes flicked to mine, then lower, his voice dropping further. "When yer blood rises to the surface there, I can feel it...like my mouth opens a vein straight to the center of yer body and lights a fire inside ye."

He took a breath, rough and weighted. "And if ye want to call that *'dick-drunk,'* I can't stop ye." His gaze held mine with such intensity, I thought I might drown in it. "But know this—" he whispered, "it does the same to *me.*"

He leaned closer, his words like a vow.

"Something in *ye*, Mira, *does that* to me. No one else has made me feel that in two hundred and forty years. And it makes me want to possess every part of ye. *Not just* the part of you that sheathes my cock..." His voice caught for just a second, a beat of reverence in the middle of his hunger. "*All* of ye, Mira Garvie."

"Do you want to drink my blood?" I asked, breath catching—his lips still burned on my skin, the ache he'd left smoldering, impossible to ignore.

"Yes," Baird said, ragged. "God help me, yes. But I won't. Ye'll never have to worry about that. When I was first turned, I drank from humans—never enough to kill, never turning them. Then I stopped. Animals were...safer. Cleaner. No worse than eating meat."

He shook his head slowly, then dragged both hands down his face, and then tilted his head back with a strained exhale. He looked like he was in pain. Real, physical pain.

"And just so ye know," he said, voice ragged, "in the spirit of full transparency..."

His eyes met mine, and there was no hiding in them now.

"I can feel what's happening in yer body." He paused—just long enough to make my breath hitch. "Yer desire building...yer pulse quickening. Yer skin flushes, pupils dilate. I *know* ye're wet now." He closed his eyes for a moment, struggling to rein himself in. "I can feel the heat radiating from between your thighs like I'm standing in front of a fire."

His voice dropped to a whisper, bare and wrecked. "I can *see* it. *Smell* it. *Feel* it."

A long silence stretched between us—thick with tension, sacred and charged.

"That's the part I can't deny myself," he admitted finally. "I tried. I tried to resist ye. But in all my years—before and after my human death—*ye* are the only thing I've ever wanted that I *couldn't* deny."

I felt myself pulled in every possible direction at once.

Questions crowded my mind, answers blurred, and for what felt like the thousandth time in the last few weeks, I wondered if I was experiencing a full-blown psychotic break. My emotions were jumbled, overlapping, stepping on each other like dancers out of sync.

I couldn't think straight anymore. I didn't *want* to.

Maybe Baird *was* lying to me. Maybe he *was* enthralling me right now, twisting my mind into knots I couldn't unravel. I still needed to ask about Agnes—why Bastien killed her. How Baird had survived this long. What he *was, truly*.

But all I wanted was for it all to *stop*—the spiraling thoughts, the impossible questions.

I wanted silence. I wanted stillness.

I wanted *him*.

I crawled to him slowly on my hands and knees, my eyes stinging and raw with tears. When I reached him, I straddled his lap, lifting myself up to him, palms framing his face as I brought my lips to his. It was the last thing I should do—I knew it—and yet here I was.

He looked stunned. "What are you doing, Mira?" he asked, awestruck, as I planted soft kisses on his lips.

"I have to know if *this* part is real," I whispered, my tears slipping down onto his cheek.

Baird looked at me—*truly* looked—and whatever he saw there cracked through the last of his restraint. "This is the most real thing there is, lass," he murmured, and in the span of a single heartbeat, I was no longer in the corner of the spare bedroom. He'd carried me—impossibly fast, impossibly gentle—into the master suite and laid me down on the bed.

"How did I get into your bed?" I asked, breathless, not sure if it was sarcasm or awe I heard in my own voice. My stomach swirled like I'd been dropped from a great height.

Baird hovered over me, the shadows softening his features. "Are ye sure this is what ye want?" he asked, his voice low. His expression was a mix of wonder and tenderness—but the desire beneath it was undeniable.

Just like mine. "Ugh—yes—*dick-drunk*. You don't play fair, asshole," I murmured against his lips, my body yielding into his.

The alarm bells in my mind faded, receding like a tide.

All that remained was the pounding of my pulse and the soft, whimpering moans slipping from my lips—hungry, already anticipating his touch, aching for him.

Baird growled low in his throat, fingers threading through my hair as he pulled me closer. "Good God, lass," he whispered, eyes dark with heat. "I love it when ye swear. Did ye know it makes my cock hard?"

I didn't even have words.

But I *knew* it was true.

# Chapter Thirty-Seven

# Mira

Afterward, I lay spent in Baird's arms, my body still humming with pleasure that lingered like an echo in my skin. My head rested at the center of his chest, his arm draped loosely across my upper back—warm, steady, anchoring. I took a breath and began my questions again, careful now, my voice low. I didn't look at his face. Somehow, keeping my eyes away felt like the only way to hold on to my equilibrium, to keep the emotional tide at bay—at least for a little while longer.

"Can you tell me about Agnes?" I asked softly, finally ready to hear the truth.

Baird was quiet for several long moments before he answered.

"She was the loveliest thing I'd ever seen when we met," he said, voice low. "So young—just twenty-one. Not even twenty-two yet when we married a few months later." He paused, eyes far away now.

"I was thirty-seven at the time. Old enough to be settled with a wife, but somehow I had avoided it until then. Her father was one of my biggest clients here—shipping abroad their fine wool fabric from the mill. After I left the Royal Navy, I started a shipping company with a partner. We sailed first out of Glasgow, then later from here in Edinburgh."

He drew in a breath, then continued, slower now. "I was friendly with her older brother, Aillig—he worked as his father's bookkeeper. One night, he invited me to dinner, and I accepted. She lived with them, just up the road. Her mother had died when she was very young."

A ghost of a smile touched his lips. "I knew it was a setup the moment I walked in. But she was so beautiful, I didn't care."

He looked down at his hands for a long moment. "She wasn't the kind of woman I'd been drawn to before. Agnes was quiet...demure. The type who was content to let others decide things for her."

I lifted my head, just briefly, eyes searching his face. "What kind of women *had* you been drawn to?" I asked, unable to hide the curiosity in my voice.

He gave a crooked grin. "Decisive. Assertive. Smart-mouthed."

I caught the edge in his tone. That was directed at me.

"Agnes made me feel needed," he said after a moment. "And I liked that, I suppose. In some ways, she reminded me of my younger brother, Edan. He died in a hunting accident when we were just children. He looked up to me. Always wanted my guidance."

He swallowed hard, gaze distant again.

"Maybe I was trying to prove I could protect someone. I thought...that's what a husband was supposed to do. She was fragile. She needed me."

This was harder to hear than I'd expected. Listening to him talk about Agnes, everything shifted—his grief, his guilt, the way he carried it all so quietly. Suddenly, it made sense. Whatever this was between us, I couldn't pretend she wasn't part of it. The loss of Agnes had branded him, shaped him, molded him into the man lying beside me now.

"I was still traveling then," Baird said, voice distant. "To France, ports in England, Denmark, the Netherlands—trying to secure new contracts. My absences were hard on her, but I didn't understand how hard. I thought she *knew* what it took to grow the company...for our future."

He let out a long, slow breath. "We married six months after we met that night. And shortly after we returned from our honeymoon, I left again—for a month. We were having a ship built near Amsterdam." His eyes flicked to mine, not quite meeting them. "I'd ordered a three-masted vessel with a new design—pear-shaped hull, wide at the bottom, narrow on the deck. Since ships were taxed based on deck size, it was a way to reduce operating costs."

He paused, his voice softening. "But we ran into issues with the shipyard. Delays. And that pushed my return back further than I'd planned." His gaze dropped. "I wrote to her every week. I missed her so."

He went quiet, his hand gently stroking my hair in silence. I wasn't sure who he'd paused for—me, to give the weight of it all a chance to settle...or himself because continuing was too painful.

"I was anxious to return to her," Baird said eventually, his voice low. "But when I did...I didn't recognize the woman I'd married." He swallowed hard. "She was in the library when I arrived—her hair unwashed, her skin so pale she looked like a ghost. Aillig's wife, Mary, was with her, trying to get her to eat something, bathe herself. But Agnes just sat there, staring out the window, rocking softly."

He looked down. "She barely even acknowledged me. I thought she was punishing me for being gone so long. And at first...I was angry." He paused, then continued, quieter. "Mary told me the truth. That Agnes suffered from what they called *melancholia* back then. I'd had *no* idea. Not until that moment."

"I confronted her father. And he confirmed it. Said he'd had a specialist treat her before—someone who'd helped her greatly. I was desperate, so I sent for the doctor immediately."

He took a breath, as if bracing himself. "He resumed the treatments. That's what he called them. *Treatments.* But some of them were...brutal. Inhumane. They submerged her in tubs filled with ice water multiple times a day. Her screams echoed through the halls. She fought them—every time."

His voice cracked. "I felt powerless to help her."

There was a long silence before he continued. "After months, she started to improve...at least outwardly. She began trying to resume her routines. Some days she was animated and lively again, and I thought—*I thought I had my wife back.*"

He shook his head. "But it was a rollercoaster. Her moods would shift without warning. Up and down...up and down again. If she were alive now, I'm sure she'd be diagnosed with bipolar disorder—or something similar. But back then, there were no medications. No lasting treatments."

He looked away. "Her brother finally told me that the doctor had once recommended marriage as a possible cure. That perhaps being a wife and eventually a mother might focus her, take her mind off her sorrows. But marrying a man who was constantly away...it only made her worse. I see that now."

His next words came out as a whisper. "I was helpless. And it *hurt* to see her like that. I hired a full-time nurse. Mary visited daily. And I—" His voice broke.

My heart ached for him, listening to the quiet sorrow in his voice as he retold the story. It wasn't just a tragedy—it was a lesion that could never heal, one that had altered the course of two lives.

He took a deep breath and continued. "I started spending more and more time away from Edinburgh. On business. Just to escape the pain of watching her disappear."

"I left again for a few weeks," Baird said, quieter now, "and when I returned...the woman who met me at the door was someone I hadn't seen in a long time."

He smiled faintly, eyes distant.

"She told me we'd been invited to a ball. Said she'd had a new dress made—fine silk, the color of whisky." He lifted his hand and gestured toward the room down the hall. "That dress, the one in the trunk—it's the same."

His gaze drifted as he recalled the moment. "She was so excited. The night of the ball, she was radiant. Luminous. I let myself believe her troubles were behind us. Foolishly, maybe—but God, she looked so happy."

He paused again, voice thickening. "We danced all night. I couldn't keep my hands off her. Every man in the room looked at her with envy."

His jaw tensed. "But there was a man there that night. French, dark-haired, slim. I noticed him watching her." Baird's eyes clouded, the memory growing heavier. "Later in the evening, I found her on a terrace overlooking the garden. She was speaking with him. Just the two of them."

His lips pressed into a line. "When I approached, he smiled. Said I had a lovely wife. Kissed her hand."

He paused again—then shook his head. "When I turned to ask his name...he was gone."

It hurt—*unbelievably*—to hear the love in Baird's voice. The pain. The memory of someone he'd lost, something he still carried like a wound that refused to close.

My heart broke for him.

But it broke for me too.

For the foolish hopes I hadn't even realized I'd begun to entertain. The fragile, beautiful things I hadn't yet imagined might be possible between us.

So foolish.

Baird traced slow, absent circles on my back with one finger. I'm sure he meant it to comfort me. But each touch only deepened the ache in my chest. It didn't feel like affection anymore—it felt like a memory. A gesture shaped by someone else. Someone he had truly loved.

And I?

I felt like an impostor.

"I took Agnes home that night," he said softly. "Throughout our marriage, she never denied me. But I don't think she ever *enjoyed* love-making—not the way I did."

He paused, his voice lowering just slightly.

"But that night was different." He stared ahead, not looking at me now. "She was like a woman possessed. I noticed, over the next few weeks, she seemed...stronger," Baird said, his voice distant. "More passionate with me. There was a gleam in her eye I'd never seen before."

He hesitated, thumb absently rubbing along my spine.

"She told me she had a surprise for me—something she wanted to give me before I left on my next voyage. One night, she handed me a red leather box. Inside was the portrait."

Now I understood. The portrait—it had been for him. A link in a chain of events that bound Agnes and Baird...and now, inexorably, me to them both. Created by the painter, the one still pulling the strings. A chill crept through me as the puzzle pieces fell into place.

"She was wearing the same silk dress she'd worn to the ball. Her eyes gleamed. She looked exactly as she had that night—cheeks flushed, alive, *happy* for once. It was an exquisite likeness. I asked who had painted it." He dropped his hand from my back, freeing me briefly from the quiet ache of his touch.

But without it, I felt suddenly unmoored. Unanchored.

Then I saw his other hand, clenched tightly in the sheets.

He was fighting his way through the memories, just as I was trying to find my footing inside them.

"She said it was the French gentleman from the party. *Bastien Bethune.*" The hatred in his voice when he said the name filled the room like smoke—thick, choking, impossible to ignore. It clung to everything, lingering in the silence that followed.

"I was leaving again, just for a few weeks. The ship we'd commissioned in Amsterdam was finally ready to launch for her maiden voyage back to Edinburgh. But when I returned...Agnes was in a state I'd never seen before."

Despite the sting of it, I lifted my head to watch his face as he spoke. The love he still carried for Agnes was written there, plain and unguarded, and though it bruised me deep inside to see it so raw, it was the thought of him reliving that pain that unsettled me most.

"She was bedridden. Mary and Aillig stayed with her 'round the clock. She rambled incoherently. Refused to eat. Couldn't sleep. She kept saying she had to get away...that *he* was coming for her."

"I asked who she meant." His jaw clenched. "She couldn't—or wouldn't—say. The doctor prescribed a sleeping draught. We dosed her regularly just to keep her calm. After weeks of this, she regained some clarity and begged me to take her to the cottage on Arran."

He looked at me then, a shadow behind his eyes. "You know it's a humble place. But she seemed...at peace, at first. Just to be away from Edinburgh." He paused. "But then one night, she started panicking again. Then there was a knock at the door."

His voice dropped to a whisper. "When I opened it, it was *him*. The artist."

He stared straight ahead, as if seeing it all again. "I believe now she *knew* what he was. But I didn't. I thought he was just a jealous lover. I accused her of being unfaithful."

His breath trembled. "She dropped to her knees and begged me to believe her. She screamed..." A pause. "That he wanted to take her *soul*."

"I came at him with my blade drawn," Baird said, his voice hollow, "but he moved with a quickness that defied logic. He threw me across the room like I was nothing. A *doll*. I'd never seen a man with such strength."

He swallowed hard. "I got up. Came at him again. And he struck me—across the face. My head cracked against the stone floor." His hand trembled slightly where it gripped the sheet. "I drifted in and out of consciousness. But I heard him speak."

Baird's voice dropped. "He said I was a man just like his father—always believing a blade could solve anything. Always underestimating him."

A long pause.

"He said he wanted me to see how wrong I was."

Another breath. A ragged one. "He drained me. Almost dry."

He closed his eyes.

"And then he made me *watch*...as he killed Agnes."

What followed wasn't just silence—it was weight, pressure, like the air had turned to stone.

"Then I heard him—*Bastien*—telling me to drink. He sliced his wrist and held it to my mouth. I was out of my mind with pain—physical, emotional. I was fading away. I was disgusted by the thought of drinking blood, and what little strength I had left, I used to resist him. But he enthralled me, controlled my actions. And I drank."

His voice broke around the next words. "He said...he wanted me to understand." Baird shook his head slowly, broad shoulders slumped. "But I didn't know what he meant."

Suddenly—shamefully—I needed to get away. I couldn't take any more. I couldn't breathe under the weight of it, the story unspooling in my mind like a film I couldn't pause: the fragile woman who wore my face—the one from my visions, my nightmares—meeting a brutal, bloody end, and the good man beside me now, forced to watch her die, only to suffer the final, exquisite cruelty of having his own humanity torn away.

The story was too vast, too impossible. My mind reeled, overwhelmed, unable to take in another word. I pushed away from him, hands trembling, my entire body screaming for it to stop—for some space, some silence, anything to make it bearable again.

"Please," I whispered, then louder, *begged*, "I can't take any more right now. I need some time. I *won't* leave. But I just...*can't.*"

The sob tore from my throat before I could swallow it down. I grabbed a blanket from the end of the bed, wrapped it tightly around myself like armor, and fled down the hall.

Baird didn't say a word.

He let me go.

# Chapter Thirty-Eight

# Mira

I ran down the hall aimlessly. I didn't know where I was going, but I knew it had to be away from Baird. As I turned down the winding staircase, I remembered the overstuffed chair in the living room and threw myself into it, curling up like something wounded. I yanked the blanket around my shoulders, tight—too tight—but it felt like a shield, the only barrier between me and the cold unraveling of everything.

I couldn't process it. Not really. I thought I could—that I was strong enough, curious enough, open-minded enough. But the truth crashed over me like a rogue wave, dragging everything I believed into the undertow. It felt like I'd wandered into some twisted dream, a half-lit world where nothing obeyed the rules anymore. Not gravity, not time. Certainly not biology.

The air felt thinner. My skin tingled. Was I in shock? I wanted to scream. Or laugh. Or run until the earth gave out beneath me. A Victorian woman locked in a crumbling castle...yes. That's what I felt like—trapped in some ridiculous gothic tragedy where shadows had weight and nothing was quite alive or quite dead.

Disbelief, betrayal, grief—for Baird, for the world around me I thought I understood—each emotion fought for dominance. His lies of omission ripped a hole that ran clean through me. And yet, it wasn't really the lies that undid me. It was the foundation beneath them—my foundation. Science, logic, natural law—his existence warped it all. Was it a lie? Or was this a crack in the universe I'd never noticed before?

My heart was pounding too hard—thudding not just in my chest but in my throat, behind my eyes, rattling the cage of my ribs. I was freezing. Bone-deep cold, like I'd been dropped in the middle of a blizzard with no coat, no skin. My teeth chattered uncontrollably. I couldn't stop shaking. Tremors racked through me in waves, small and violent. My fingers were numb. My lips, I realized, were trembling too.

I rocked back and forth without meaning to, a slow, rhythmic motion I couldn't seem to stop. Catatonic. That was the word. Suspended in a state of not-quite-here. I couldn't process. Couldn't breathe. Couldn't face the look I knew would be on Baird's face—the guilt, the grief, the *truth*.

There was more he needed to say. I could feel it hanging in the air between us like vapor. And maybe I even needed to hear it in some distant, rational corner of my mind. But that part of me was unreachable right now. There was no space left in me to absorb another word.

His story had broken me. I felt small—helpless, like a child. It cracked my understanding of everything I thought I knew wide open and poured in something older, darker, unimaginable. By then, I had no tears left to give. I was empty—wrung out like a rag, hollowed by grief that wasn't even mine.

But even in the state I was in, two truths refused to dislodge.

First, Baird Campbell—*whatever he truly was now*—carried a wound that would never close. He believed he was to blame for Agnes's death, and I saw the love he still felt for her hollowing him from the inside out.

And the second, the one that terrified me more than anything else: I was falling for Baird Campbell. God help me.

# Chapter Thirty-Nine
## Baird

In the days leading up to this, Baird had prayed Mira would believe him. And now that she did—now that the truth was out and laid bare—he found himself wishing she hadn't.

He thought he was prepared for her reaction. Disbelief, certainly. Anger, absolutely. Even fear. But this? This hollow, shaking grief that seemed to come from some place deeper than rage or reason? He hadn't been ready for that. It wasn't just the story—it was what the story had taken from her. Whatever the story had stolen, he didn't know how to give it back—or if he even could.

He stood frozen just beyond the threshold, watching her curl in on herself like something fractured. Her silence was louder than any scream. He could feel it vibrating through the air between them—dense, impenetrable.

He wished he understood. Wished he could offer something, anything, that would ease the pain carved across her face. There *was* a way to know what she was feeling. A path his kind could take.

When one of them drank the blood of someone they loved—*truly* loved—they would begin to feel echoes of that person's emotions. Not the reasons behind them, not the thoughts that shaped them. But the feelings themselves—grief, joy, confusion, terror. A sort of window to the soul, or maybe the heart. A way to see the truth they could never otherwise touch.

He had never done it. Not once in two hundred and forty years. He'd never loved anyone in all that time. But he couldn't bring himself to do it now—not like this.

It would be a violation. Another betrayal.

He'd done enough damage to Mira already.

He desperately wanted to be near her—to touch her skin, see her face—but he needed to honor her request to be alone. So he padded softly past the living room's opening on his way to the kitchen, forcing himself not to linger.

But as he passed, his eyes found hers.

She looked at him, wide-eyed, as if caught in the moment between waking and drowning. And then—

A soft, broken whimper escaped her. Barely a sound at all. Just the faintest hitch in her breath, like the air itself had caught in her throat and couldn't find its way out.

Damn it.

He couldn't leave well enough alone. Not now.

He turned and walked toward her, slow and deliberate, never breaking her gaze.

"I'm going to pour myself a drink—whisky," he said gently. "Can I bring ye something? Anything?"

She didn't answer, just blinked slowly, as if even that effort exhausted her. He knelt beside her and reached out, brushing his fingers across her cheek. Her skin was ice cold.

"Oh, lass...why are ye so cold?" he murmured, more to himself than to her. "I'll build ye a fire. Get ye another blanket—"

"Baird," she croaked, her voice papery, rough from silence. She looked up at him, eyes glassy and rimmed red. "Whisky..."

It was just two words. But it was enough. Enough to tell him she was still with him—somewhere beneath the shock, the fear, the grief. Still there.

# CHAPTER FORTY
## MIRA

B aird returned with two tumblers of Scotch. He set his own glass down first, then crouched in front of me, gently pressing mine into my hands. I was still trembling—fine, involuntary movements that made the ice in the glass clink faintly against itself. Without a word, he wrapped his hands around mine, steadying them, enclosing my fingers in his until I had enough control to hold it on my own.

Then he turned to the hearth. He moved with quiet purpose, kneeling to stack kindling from the brass pail, nestling it into the crisscross of logs he'd already arranged. A single match flared to life, its sulfur scent sharp in the air. He touched it to the kindling, coaxing the fire gently until it caught. The first crackles sparked, and the glow began to build—soft amber light blooming outward, casting long shadows and the first hints of heat into the cold room.

"I'm going to move the chair closer to the fire," he said, glancing over his shoulder.

Now that my mind and body were beginning to settle, I scrambled to my feet, suddenly aware of how long I'd sat there—how much I didn't want to be an inconvenience.

"No, stay put," he ordered gently, the authority in his voice laced with care.

He moved behind where I was sitting and bent down, arms around the chair, and lifted—the chair, me, and all—like it weighed nothing. Like I weighed nothing. Like I was some fragile, precious thing he wasn't going to let slip away.

If it hadn't been so achingly sweet, it would have been absurd. It was absurd—being carried across the room in a huge chair like an invalid carried by a giant—but maybe that was the point. Maybe this was his way of showing me I wasn't crazy. That I hadn't imagined the whole damn thing. That all of it—his story, Bastien, and Agnes—were real.

I sipped my whisky and stared into the fire, the soft pop and hiss of the logs filling the aching silence between us. The fiery sting of the Scotch burned down my throat, grounding me—something real, something I could hold on to when everything else inside me felt like it had come apart in ways I didn't fully understand.

Of all the truths I've been forced to swallow tonight, the hardest wasn't that the man stalking me was a vampire. It was that Baird—quiet, steady Baird—wasn't the reclusive island farmer I believed him to be. He's over two hundred seventy years old, when you count his mortal life and everything after. And even after I'd laid my soul bare to him, he still kept that from me.

Or maybe the hardest part was this: that he might be the man Granny Margaret saw for me—the one she said was my missing piece. But what if the thing growing between us, the thing I felt from the first moment I saw him, was nothing more to him than a way to rewrite the past? A chance to bring back Agnes, through someone who shared the same face?

I didn't want to be a ghost's stand-in—some fucked-up second chance at a love that already died.

I was lost to my thoughts when Baird returned with another blanket, gently draping it over my shoulders, tucking it in like I might break if left exposed. Then he sank to the floor beside me, his back resting against the leg of the chair.

He didn't speak. Didn't press. He just waited. And somehow, that made it easier.

I knew he still had more to say—so much more—but he would let me come to it in my own time. What he didn't know was that I had something to say too. A confession. Not a secret I'd been hiding, not exactly. Just another thing I hadn't let myself believe.

But our fates were intertwined now—threaded together by blood and memory, by secrets and things that could no longer be undone. I couldn't keep it to myself any longer. Not with him sitting so still beside me, his presence comforting me in my tumult.

"Baird," I said quietly, my voice still rough and raw. He looked up at me, his eyes catching the firelight, green and glowing and unmistakably inhuman. And yet, somehow, they held more human connection than I'd ever felt from anyone in my life.

"There's something I need to tell you too."

He turned and reached up to hold one hand. "Tell me, love."

"When I met my cousins in Kirriemuir, Evie said her grandmother might be able to help me understand the two men I kept seeing—what they meant, why they kept showing up. I told her I'd had waking visions and nightmares of them, like they were from another time." I hesitated, unsure how to put the next part into words. "Granny Margaret laid her hands on me, and her eyes rolled back into her head. When it was over—when she was satisfied—she could see and speak again. The very first thing she told me was that both men were near me now, not in the past. Then she told me the dark man—*Bastien*—was treated cruelly as a child and grew up to be cruel too. But she said his intentions toward me were unclear. I didn't believe her; it didn't make sense to me. Not then."

"But it does to ye now, aye?" Baird said, and I could see he thought this was the end of my story.

"Yes. But then she told me about the '*ither man*,'" I said softly. "That's what she called him. '*The one with the green eyes*.'"

Baird stilled completely, the fire casting gold and shadow across his face. I saw the flicker of recognition before I even said the rest.

"She saw you, Baird. Before we'd met. She said you carry a great sadness in your heart." I paused, swallowing back the thickness in my throat. "I knew it the first day we met. I *felt* it. That sorrow, like a living thing around you. But she also said something else."

He was watching me now, not breathing. Waiting.

"She said you would never hurt me. And that part...I don't just believe it, Baird—I *know* it. I feel it deep inside me, as sure as anything I've ever known. I don't know if she knew what you are, but it was as if she knew I'd need to know that at some point. Then she said you wouldn't know what to do with me," I added, a small laugh escaping as I remembered the stunned look on his face when I first told him my name. "That I was some kind of puzzle to you."

He laughed too then—low and warm, a sound that wrapped around me, making me feel suddenly safe. "Aye—ye are that, lass," he said, shaking his head with a smile. "A puzzle and then some."

I shifted slightly in the chair, emboldened by the flicker of lightness that was returning between us. "And finally, she told me, '*don't miss him when ye find him—he's the piece ye be lookin' fer.'"* I said it in my best Garvie accent, mimicking the old woman's lilt.

He froze for a beat. His smile faltered, just slightly, eyes shining with something too deep for speech.

"Evidently, she's also famous in Kirriemuir for being something of a matchmaker," I said shyly, embarrassed.

"And ye didn't think ye could tell me this?" Baird chuckled.

"I didn't believe it myself," I replied.

"But ye know it to be true now," he said, his voice low, steady. "And I'll wager that if ye sit with it—quietly, in that place deep down in yer gut—ye believed it even then. When she first told ye. Maybe not with yer mind, but with that part of ye that knows things before they make sense."

His eyes held mine, unwavering, not demanding—but inviting me gently to the place he was going. "It was just too much for the Mira Garvie who deals in facts and logic, aye? Too wild. Too impossible. So ye tucked it away. Fought it. Like I've seen ye do when somethin' in ye dares to feel too much."

He shifted slightly, drawing just a breath closer. "But this thing inside ye—it's beggin' for ye to lean into it, lass. And ye keep holdin' it at arm's length, like it might burn ye if ye let it in. Yer dancin' around this power ye've been blessed with, and every now and then, I see ye let it in, just for a moment. When ye do, ye almost glow from the inside—impossibly powerful. It's a thing of beauty."

We stayed like that—me curled in the chair, wrapped tightly in blankets, and Baird on the floor at my feet, solid and unmoving. Day had quietly given way to night, though I barely noticed. Sunlight and moonlight had twined together in the hours between, blending into something indistinct, like the border between dreams and waking. It passed beyond the windows, and I registered it only vaguely, like a current beneath deep water.

"Mira," Baird said softly, a small yawn escaping his lips—a sound I'd never heard from him before. It startled me in its sweetness, its simplicity. A human sound, somehow more intimate than any touch. "It's late. Let me put ye into bed. Ye've class tomorrow."

The way he said it—it sounded like he meant to leave. Like he'd tuck me in and disappear into the night. And despite everything that had unraveled between us, I didn't want that. I didn't want to fall asleep alone, didn't want to wake from some nightmare and reach for him only to find emptiness. Even though I had the eerie sense he'd come to me before I could even cry out, I still wanted him near. Beside me.

"You're staying with me, aren't you?" I asked, my voice barely above a whisper.

He turned toward me fully then, his green eyes meeting mine. "If ye want me, I'll be at yer side," he said. "All ye ever have to do is ask."

# Chapter Forty-One

## MIRA

My eyes fluttered open. 4:37 a.m., according to my watch. I was on my stomach, my right arm tangled with Baird's. He lay beside me on his back, eyes closed—sleeping. For the first time, he was truly asleep. I'd never seen it before, not in the nights we'd spent like this, side by side. Then, his eyes opened—sharp, sudden. Something in him had sensed me. Like a creature born of night, he knew the exact moment I stirred.

"I think I'm ready," I said quietly. "To hear more...how he turned you."

Baird shifted, propping a few pillows behind his back as he settled into them. He exhaled, long and low. "Ye know, lass...I don't have to tell ye any more if ye're not sure ye want to hear it." His voice was gentle but laced with caution. "I've wanted for so long to speak it aloud—to let someone truly know. But last night, I pushed too far. I saw what it did to ye. And I never want to see ye like that again."

No matter how confused I was about whatever this was between us, I could see the concern in his eyes—he was giving me an out, a chance to step back before hearing more.

"I'm ready," I said softly. "I want to know everything. And I'll try to tell you sooner if I need a break. Deal?"

A small smile touched his lips as he gathered me into his arms. I settled in to rest against his chest to hear more of his story.

"Ah, where were we last night? In the cottage...after. I woke later—perhaps a day, maybe more, I can't say. Agnes lay dead on the stone floor, her long dark hair matted with dried blood. The pain was so immense, I drifted in and out of consciousness, barely tethered to reality. When I tried to rise, I realized he was still there, watching. He told me what I was now. That I needed blood to survive. I was ravenous. He offered himself to me again—his wrist, the same as before. The thought still repulsed me, and yet I couldn't stop. This time it was different, his blood in my mouth as sweet as wine. And as I drank, the pain dulled just enough to think straight again. Then he left. Left me with nothing..."

I couldn't begin to comprehend what Baird had endured then—what it had cost him to survive it, to carry it. And I, I had only been asked to listen. A flush of guilt rose in me for how I'd reacted last night. He had lived through a nightmare. I had only glimpsed it.

"When I could finally stand, I buried her on the point by the sea. With my own hands."

The image of Baird sobbing at her grave came crashing back into my memory, and my heart ached for him—and for Agnes.

"I stayed in the cottage for weeks, learning how to exist. Survive. Hide. I craved blood. When I was strong enough, I slipped out of the cottage under cover of night. I didn't yet understand what I was, what I had become—no one had explained it to me. I didn't know I was nearly immortal now. I only knew I had to move, to follow the pull in my chest."

"So I went back to the place where my brother Edan died, crushed in a rockslide while chasing a goat he'd shot. I'm not sure why—maybe to grieve, maybe to mourn, or maybe to test whether I could still die there too." He reached and brushed a lock of hair back from my eyes, his touch gentle against my brow.

"But as I moved through the darkness, I began to sense the things in me that were changing. I could see like a wild thing in the night, every detail rendered sharp and silver. My hearing picked up the soft scurry of creatures beneath the heather. I could smell every leaf, every shift in the air. My new strength surged beneath my skin, unnatural, foreign. I felt...feral. Like an animal in a body that still looked human. And then I caught it—the scent. A stag, grazing in the valley below. Something in me stirred. A sixth sense, primal and certain, told me the truth: he was no match for me now. Nothing was. I leapt into the Witch's Step—the same deep, jagged cleft in the mountain where Edan had fallen. A part of me, the part still clinging to humanity, hoped this might be my end too. That I'd fall as he had, and the earth would take me."

My breath caught in my chest—his retelling of the desperation he felt then breaking my heart.

"But my feet were too swift. I was faster than the tumble of loose rocks beneath me, faster than fear. I caught up to the stag, cornered against a sheer cliff wall. He *knew*." The haunted look in his eyes as he remembered that night chilled me to the bone.

"Our eyes locked, and I saw it—acknowledgment. A quiet surrender. He understood his life would feed mine. I snapped his neck with a movement that felt instinctive, effortless. And then, without hesitation, I sank my teeth into the hollow at his neck and drank deeply—draining him, taking what I needed to survive." Baird's shoulders sank with an invisible weight.

This was part of the shame he carried. It emanated from his body just like the sadness he wore.

"Only when I was strong enough did I try to return to Edinburgh. I had no family left of my own; my mother, father, and grandmother were long gone by that time. But I needed to tell Agnes's family what had happened. Or...some version of it."

"So I returned to Edinburgh, but I didn't trust myself. Not yet. I dismissed the servants and locked myself inside the house. I couldn't bear them near me, couldn't risk what I might become in their company."

The tone of his voice had become flat. Maybe he was trying to get some emotional distance from his retelling, but I could see it came at a cost.

"One of them must have told Mary—Aillig's wife. Or maybe she just *knew*. She was a Garvie, after all. Aillig's second cousin—born in Kirriemuir. One day, she came alone. She used a key Agnes had given her, and found me in my room, sitting in the dark, clutching the portrait like it could still hold her soul. She was terrified. I could see it in her face, hear it in her breath. I told her to leave. But she didn't. There was a bravery in Mary I hadn't seen until that moment," he said as he turned to look at me. "*I see it in ye too, ye know*—and she asked me what had happened."

Mary Garvie. My grandmother seven generations back. She'd married Aillig—Agnes's brother. Baird had traced the connection without pause. He knew exactly how we were tied together.

"So I told her. I told her Bastien had killed Agnes, and that in trying to stop him, I had become like him. Like the monster. I told her to explain it however she thought the family could bear to hear it—to say Agnes had drowned in the sea. It wasn't a stretch, given what they knew of her affliction, her storms of the mind. It was a story they could accept. Not the truth. They could never believe the truth. I gave Mary the portrait—I couldn't look at it anymore. Every time I did, all I saw were my failures staring back at me. Agnes's father died not long after that. I always believed his grief played a part in it. The weight of losing her was simply too much. I heard that Aillig and Mary left for America a few months later—to start over, to build something new. That's the line you come from. And that must be how the portrait ended up with your father."

He was quiet for a while, letting the silence hold what he'd said. His eyes stayed on mine, steady and searching, as if trying to measure how deep the damage ran—whether I was truly ready now or just trying to be.

I met his gaze and lifted my chin, doing my best to summon the strength he needed to see in me.

"Ye know what ye told me last night—the part about Granny Margaret?"

I nodded my head.

"Well, there is something else ye should know. The part where she said ye were a puzzle to me. I knew ye saw the shock in my eyes, that first night in my cottage."

"Yes—I saw that." The memory pulled me back to that night just days ago, though it already felt like a lifetime had passed.

He gave a faint, wistful laugh. "At first, I didn't think ye were real. Then ye sat up—like someone had pulled marionette strings—and started peppering me with questions."

He reached out, gently turning my head so I was looking at him now. "And then ye told me your name...and things started to make sense. What I'd been seeing."

"*Seeing*?" I echoed, confusion knitting my brow.

"Aye... We have the ability to see things," he said. "But it's different from your visions. A vampire's maker can send images, thoughts...a kind of dark connection that only exists between them. It's been a long time, but when I was first turned, I began seeing women—women who looked like Agnes. I realized I was seeing through his eyes. Bastien was taunting me with them."

He shook his head slowly. "It drove me mad until I learned to block him out. He tortured me with those visions for years. Then...about forty years ago, it all just stopped. I assumed he was dead."

"Dead?" I asked. "I thought vampires couldn't die."

He nodded. "We live a long time—but we're not immortal. Not truly. Any significant injury to the heart will do it. Dinnae have to be a wooden stake; any metal blade, even hands or teeth, if the attacker's strong enough. We're more at risk from our own kind than from humans. I've never been hunted by a human," he added, almost as an afterthought. "I've passed as one of them easily enough."

He paused, voice lowering. "But it's a lonely existence, Mira. That's the truth of it. Some vampires...they just get tired. Of surviving. Of mourning. Of guilt. They stop feeding. Not like a human at the end, but more like...their will gives out. That's the only release from it—the only way to silence the ache."

His gaze dropped. "I've thought about it myself."

The silence that followed was heavy, unbreathable.

Then he exhaled and lifted his eyes back to mine. "But back to my visions of ye. What I saw was you. Your face. Not a memory. Not an echo. It pushed everything else aside when you were in my mind."

I swallowed hard. "How is that possible?"

"I don't know," he said, his voice breaking slightly. "I always assumed the visions were real-time—Bastien tracking prey, maybe. But now?" He shook his head. "Now I'm not so sure."

His eyes searched mine, raw and anguished. "How are ye doing with all this? I still can't believe ye'd believe any of it."

"I'm not sure what I believe," I said quietly. "Part of me wants to call an Uber and go straight to the airport."

"I wouldn't blame ye if ye did," Baird said quietly. "But I canna guarantee Bastien wouldn't follow. And I won't let him hurt ye—not like he hurt Agnes. Though..." He paused, a shadow crossing his face. "He doesn't seem to have enthralled ye the way he did her. At least, not yet."

"Oh, I'm definitely enthralled by a vampire," I replied dryly.

"I meant what I said," he said, voice firming. "I've never done that to ye. Never used that kind of power."

"Nonetheless...here we are." I held his gaze, steady and unblinking, daring him to understand what I truly meant.

He leaned in and kissed the top of my head. And when he pulled back, that familiar, infuriating smirk had crept across his face.

He understood. Completely.

Sometime later, I climbed out of bed and started getting ready for class. I showered, dressed, and skipped breakfast in favor of black coffee. My stomach was too tangled in knots to eat anyway.

"He wouldn't—*you know*—come after me while I'm in class, would he?" I asked, trying to sound casual and failing miserably as I wandered around the kitchen.

"Nae," Baird said. "He abides by the laws we all must follow. He has to blend in among humans, so he'd never risk hurting ye in public.

Confrontin' ye, maybe—he already followed ye once. But I'll take ye to class, wait for ye, keep an eye out."

"You can't do that. Wait around all day? That's insane, Baird."

He gave me a sheepish smile. "Wouldn't be the first time I posted watch to make sure he dinnae come near ye."

"What?" My jaw dropped.

"Aye," he said, unabashed. "Those two nights ye were in Arran, I watched from the rocky ledge across from the inn. And the first night ye were back in Edinburgh—after dinner at the Italian place—I kept watch from the car park. All night."

I stared at him, uncertain if that was deeply comforting...or just a little unhinged.

"So you *were* following me when you found me half-naked in the Blue Pools..."

"Guilty as charged." One corner of his mouth tugged up, and I broke.

I crossed the kitchen in three strides and threw my arms around his neck, kissing him hard—desperately—pushing him back against the counter with more force than I intended. He caught himself, but barely.

It was the only way I knew to show him what I felt. For the nights he'd watched over me without my knowing, for the quiet way he'd made my safety his mission. Whatever doubts still lingered—whatever fears I hadn't yet voiced about what, or who, might be fueling the depth of his feelings for me—I had to set them aside.

Because this much was true: he was nothing if not devoted.

# Chapter Forty-Two
## BAIRD

B aird drove Mira to the Goldsmiths' Guild in silence. She hadn't spoken a word the entire ride. He guessed her mind was still reeling—trying to make sense of everything he'd told her over the past two days. The impossible questions colliding with the new things she could see. The deep knowing he kept telling her to trust, not shy away from.

When they reached the front of the building, Mira climbed out without a word and retrieved her tote bag from the back seat.

"I'll be nearby," he said gently. "But if ye need me...just call."

Just before Mira shut her door, she poked her head back in. "Bunny...she's just a regular dog? Not a—*you know?*"

Baird blinked, caught off guard. "Regular dog? Ye mean— *Auch*. I don't think vampire dogs are a thing, Mira," he said, rolling his eyes.

"Hey, I didn't think vampires of *any* kind were real a couple of days ago, so pardon me for asking a 'stupid' question!" she snapped as the door slammed shut behind her. The surprise on her face said she hadn't meant to close it that hard. "Asshole," she muttered under her breath, glancing around to see if anyone had overheard.

The window rolled down with an electric hum. "Quite all right, lass. There are no stupid questions here...and why do I love it so when ye curse?" Baird said, smug as ever.

"Don't do that!" she barked. "That *thing* you do with the corner of your mouth."

He was glad to see she was regaining her moxie.

He gave her the look again—*that* look—and this time added a wink. "I was going to play dumb, but I won't insult your intelligence, Mira. I know exactly what that smile does to ye."

And he smirked again.

"How am I supposed to get any work done today?" she muttered before she walked off into the building.

# Chapter Forty-Three

# Mira

As I suspected, concentrating was nearly impossible. Day one of my class started with a demonstration and lecture on the history of gold granulation. A visiting master jeweler was leading the class—a woman with olive skin, black hair twisted into a bun, thick black glasses, and a blistering sense of humor. She spoke animatedly about the early Sumerian and Italian metalsmiths who first developed and refined the technique of creating uniform metal granules. They would affix the tiny spheres to a surface using a non-metallic adhesive, allowing it to dry completely before applying heat, and any premature movement could ruin the delicate pattern. Only then would they fuse the granules to the metal beneath, a painstaking but exquisite process.

The techniques and tools used by modern jewelers to create granulation were, remarkably, not so different from those employed by their ancient counterparts. Each student had a designated jeweler's bench, fully stocked with the necessary tools and materials to practice the technique, and by the final day of the workshop, execute a finished design.

I had my design for the final project—the pendant with the large oval emerald as the focal point. After I explained my concept to the instructor, she offered thoughtful feedback—suggesting the most effective sequence of steps for building the piece, estimating how many fusing stages it might require, and warning me about the common pitfalls I'd need to avoid.

I got to work creating the granules. Starting with gold sheet that I passed repeatedly through a rolling mill until it was a uniform thickness of less than .15 millimeters, I cut a delicate fringe into the edge of the sheet, each cut at the same interval right next to the other, then trimmed off the fringe, creating many small flat squares of gold, the length of the fringe piece dictating the final size of the granule.

With delicate tweezers, I placed each tiny square onto a hard charcoal block at intervals of about a half-inch apart and turned on the oxygen-acetylene torch at my bench. Holding the torch above each piece, about an inch or so away from the surface, the gold curled up as the metal went from yellow to orange, and the surface turned liquid like mercury, spinning and dancing on the charcoal. Once that stage was reached, the metal formed a perfect sphere each and every time, and I moved the flame onto the next square. I kept at it until I had about fifty, divided by the sizes I needed.

It was a relief to be back doing something that could take my mind off the chaos of the situation with Baird. But several times during the afternoon, my brain stopped cooperating, bouncing between the danger I might be in, the fact that no one would believe any of this if I'd tried to explain, and the most infuriating distraction—that every five minutes or so, I found myself thinking about climbing Baird Campbell like a flagpole. That stupid smirk of his had lodged itself in my frontal cortex like a heat-seeking missile.

Focus.

Eight hours later—plus one deep cut on my finger from the jeweler's saw—I'd finished the bezels, fused them to the backplate, and created the bail. The plan for tomorrow would be to create the granulation pattern after gluing the tiny spheres into the pattern I'd mapped out.

Baird was parked next to the curb outside the building when I walked out the door. I jumped into the passenger's seat, apron still on, and leaned over to drop my tote bag on the back seat.

"Well, you look like a different person than the one I dropped off this morning. You look relaxed, your cheeks all rosy... In your element today?"

"I think the rosy cheeks are a byproduct of heating a few dozen tiny pieces of gold to nearly two thousand degrees for over an hour," I said with an exhausted exhale. "But yes, definitely in my element."

"Oh, lass...what did ye do to yourself?" he asked, concern softening his voice when he noticed the bandage on my finger.

Instinctively, I covered the finger with my other hand, defensive. "Is this going to be a problem? Can you smell it... *the blood*?"

"I can smell it, aye," he said. "But ye needn't worry about that. I was just worried it hurt ye, is all." He glanced at my finger. "I can fix that, you know."

"No, I don't know," I said, narrowing my eyes. "What do you mean, *fix it*?"

"My saliva," he said simply. "It can heal wounds—faster than you would heal on your own. When we get home, I can show you."

I narrowed my eyes at him, suspicion still simmering beneath the surface—but I couldn't deny my curiosity. Whatever this ability was that he'd just revealed, I wanted to know more.

"Okay—yes, I want to see that."

I pushed food around my plate, appetite long vanished. It was as if I was split in two—one part craving this strange domesticity with Baird, aching to ask him everything about the two centuries and more he'd walked this earth since being turned. And the other...the other was caught in a relentless loop, circling back to Agnes. To the creeping dread that I was nothing but her shadow. A pale echo reborn in flesh, now tangled in a dangerous, catastrophic sexual chemistry with her grieving husband.

My feelings for Baird were clouding everything. How fitting, really—that the first man I'd ever felt truly connected to, the first who made me feel seen, whole, *human*—had turned out not to be a human being at all.

I looked down at the Band-Aid on my finger. The pad was saturated, dark with blood.

"Aye," Baird said as he came up behind me at the sink. "I told ye I could heal that. Take off the bandage, and let me have a look."

I peeled the damp strip away. The cut was deep but clean, not quite bad enough for stitches. Still fresh, still angry-looking. I held it up to him—then, without fully knowing why, I reached up with my other hand and pressed my fingers on either side of the cut, forcing the blood to bead up again and spill down my finger.

Maybe I was curious. Maybe I wanted to test him. Or maybe it was something darker—a small defiance.

I saw it in his eyes then—fury. Not wild or uncontrolled, but focused, sharp, and directed at me. I didn't understand why. His entire body tensed, every muscle and tendon drawn tight as wire. The look on his face was a collision of anger and hunger...and something else. Hurt. I'd wounded him somehow.

He seized my hand—roughly—and brought it to his mouth. He lapped the blood from between my fingers, then ran his tongue slowly along the length of the cut.

The moment my blood touched his tongue, something in him shifted. His body seemed to expand, subtly but unmistakably—broader, heavier, more powerful. Like the breath he drew came from someplace beyond this world. Some deeper realm. Some darker one. His pupils dilated, swallowing the green of his eyes until there was nothing left but immense blackness—an abyss, devoid of even a trace of humanity.

He was a supernatural animal, feeding. Every muscle in his body was drawn tight, trembling with restrained violence. When I glanced down, I saw it—the unmistakable strain against the front of his jeans. My breath caught.

My blood had done this. Had turned him into this.

In this state, he wasn't Baird Campbell anymore. Not the one I'd come to know.

But within seconds, I could see him force his body to settle. The tension ebbed. His eyes cleared, shifting back to their usual brilliant green. He dropped my hand, and I watched as the skin on my finger knit together, the wound pulling closed like a zipper sliding shut.

I stared at him, my mouth half-open, stunned by what I'd just witnessed—what he had done.

In that instant, I understood: when he tasted the blood, it took everything in him not to lose control. I should have been afraid. Any sane person would be.

But I wasn't.

Somewhere deep inside, beneath all the confusion and fear, I trusted him—not with my heart, maybe, but with my body. And my body...my body was alive. Heat coiled through me, rising with the pounding of my heart. What I'd seen—his power, his restraint—ignited something dangerous and electric in me.

And he felt it. I knew he did.

But he didn't move.

He just stared at me, the betrayal etched on his face cutting deeper than anything he could have said. He looked like he hated me.

And I wanted him anyway.

I needed an exit. Air. Distance. Time to think—about what I'd done, and why I'd felt compelled to do it in the first place. "I think I'll take a bath," I said, and without waiting for a reply, I slipped from the room.

# Chapter Forty-Four

## Mira

After my bath, I pulled on one of Baird's T-shirts—why his, I didn't know. Lately, it felt like every decision I made was guided by something just beyond me, like my will was no longer entirely my own. I walked downstairs to an empty kitchen and heard a strange, rhythmic sound—metal scraping against something hard—coming from another room. Curious, I padded barefoot through the front hall toward the dining room.

Baird was sitting in a chair, legs planted wide, a low table in front of him. Bunny lay curled at his feet, sound asleep. On the table rested a wide, flat sharpening stone, and in Baird's hands was a sword—long, ancient-looking. He drew the blade toward himself in slow, precise arcing movements, the scraping noise almost meditative.

"What are you doing?" I asked.

He looked up for only a second, then returned to the blade. His jaw was tight, his body tense, eyes narrowed and unreadable. "Trying to take my mind off something."

I stepped closer. "What, Baird? Tell me."

He stopped, setting the sword down roughly on the table. Then he stood, the chair creaking under the shift of his weight. His stance was solid, grounded—coiled.

"Why did ye do that, Mira?" he asked, voice low but sharp. There was anger in it—real, unfamiliar anger—and the worst part was that it was directed at *me*.

"Offer you my blood?" I asked, knowing the bath I'd taken hadn't provided any answers that I hadn't already suspected.

"You didn't just want me to heal your wound—you *provoked* me. You knew what it would do. And ye did it anyway." His words were sharp, caustic.

"I—" I started, but he cut me off.

"Are ye happy now?"

I didn't even know how to answer. What I'd done had satisfied a truth I needed to confront for myself—but in doing so, I'd turned Baird against me. The cost of knowing had been his trust.

"Do ye know how disgusted I am with myself?" he growled, stepping closer. "Do ye know how *good* ye taste? I've never tasted anything like it. Yer blood is...it's like a siren's song. A drug. I knew I wanted it—but tasting it unhinged me."

His breath was ragged now, fury and desire entwined.

"All I can think about now is fucking ye," he said, each word landing like a blow. "Coming inside ye, with yer blood on my lips. Feeding from a human has always been arousing—but I've *never* fed during sex. Two hundred and forty years. It was a line I refused to cross. Because if I did...I knew I'd lose another piece of what little humanity I had left."

His voice broke just slightly. "Being with ye makes me feel human again. But in that moment, I wanted to forget it all. To surrender. To possess ye and turn myself over to the monster that I am."

"How could I know?" I asked, not cowering. Holding my ground. I wasn't going down without a fight.

Baird froze, the muscles in his jaw flexing as he looked at me—really looked. His breathing was still heavy, but something shifted in his eyes.

"I'm not a vampire, Baird," I said, voice steady despite the tremor in my chest. "I didn't *know*. I couldn't have. You said your saliva could heal, and I—God, I don't even know *why* I did it. Maybe I was testing you. Maybe I wanted to understand what I'm dealing with. But I know you would never hurt me."

I took a step forward, slowly, refusing to shrink beneath the heat of his anger. "But don't you *dare* throw this all on me like I was trying to manipulate you. You're the one who's lived for centuries. I've had two days to process this. You knew what that would do to you. *I didn't.*"

He stared at me, the tension still rippling through his body, but now his expression softened—not weak, just *exposed*.

"I'm not your enemy," I added, quieter now. "And you don't get to lash out at me because you're terrified of this part of yourself, the part you hate."

His posture faltered, just slightly. He looked away first.

My heart was racing—not from fear, but from something far more dangerous. Hearing Baird describe the bloodlust he felt for me should have horrified me. But it didn't.

It aroused me. God—what had I become?

Heat bloomed low in my belly, flooding through me, telltale wetness between my legs. My breath hitched, shame and desire twisting in equal measure.

Baird's nostrils flared. He caught the scent. I saw it the moment he did—his gaze sharpened, his body going utterly still. Like a predator registering prey.

I was powerless to control how my body responded to him—and he *knew*. God, he *knew*.

My legs felt like water beneath me. I didn't trust myself to move, to speak, to do anything that might tip the balance one way or the other. The air between us thrummed, heavy with all the things we weren't saying.

And then, softly, like a vow, he spoke. "I feel everything you do, Mira. Your desire...your need. It sings to me."

Lust gripped me, fierce and undeniable. I wasn't just reacting to him. My body was *calling* to him.

My legs were unsteady. I didn't trust myself to move.

"Do it then," I said, my voice low and trembling—part challenge, part plea. I was pushing him, testing him, daring him. Asking him to stop holding back. To lean in to what he was now, not just the man he'd once been. "Take me."

His eyes locked onto mine, wide with something between shock and hunger.

"You know I want it," I went on. "I can't hide it from you. I want to deny you my body, but I *can't*. And that makes me angry—*furious, even*—that I have no control over how I respond to you."

I stepped closer, or maybe he did—I wasn't sure anymore where he stopped and I started.

"But more than anything...I want to feel what you feel for me." I was drunk on it—on his desire, on the way he craved me, the way he tasted my blood like it was sacred.

"You want me to feed from you." Baird growled, deep and low, a statement of fact rather than a question.

"Yes," I whispered, breathless. "Do it. Do it now."

He closed the space between us in a blur—so fast it stole the breath from my lungs. One moment he was across the room, the next he was right in front of me, body radiating hunger, restraint held together by threads.

His hands gripped my hips, his touch possessive, claiming. I could feel the strain in him, his last grasp on control slipping away.

My body answered him without hesitation—softening, opening, *wanting*. I wore nothing beneath his T-shirt, and his hand slid along the bare skin of my thigh as he lifted me effortlessly. I wrapped my legs around his waist, instinct taking over thought. He popped the button on his jeans and pulled down the zipper with one hand, freeing his cock. My slick pussy was a homing beacon for him, and he rammed it home with a single thrust. He gave me no time to acclimate to his girth; it felt like he was tearing me in two.

But the pain was ecstasy, and with each deep thrust, all I could think of was opening myself more fully, wanting him buried as deep inside me as he could get. It was so deep, so fast—creating the most intense mix of pain and pleasure I'd ever felt.

He pressed me savagely against the wall, the force of it stealing my breath. I could feel every tremor running through him—his control fraying, unraveling as the inevitable grew closer.

His mouth hovered at my throat, breath ragged, and his hand came up to the base of my neck, not choking, but pinning me—holding me still.

"I can't take just a taste," he said, voice hoarse, almost broken. "Not with you."

"Then don't," I said, tilting my neck. "Take what you need."

His groan deepened into something vicious—a growl torn from somewhere primal. And then I saw it.

Fangs, lengthening where moments ago there had been only teeth. He hadn't wanted me to see this part of him—not truly. The part that was still Baird Campbell had recoiled from it, ashamed of what he was.

But that part wasn't in control anymore.

The creature had risen to the surface, and it was the creature who wanted me to see. All of him. Every dark, inhuman edge.

He bent his head to my neck, and I felt the sharp sting—then quickly something far more overwhelming. Pleasure surged through me, hot and electric, curling through my spine and bursting behind my eyes. My body convulsed in response, not from pain, but from the exquisite rightness of it, as if every nerve had been waiting for this exact moment to come alive. Each time Baird's lips had touched that spot on my neck, it had woken, sparked, heated. Now, at last, I understood what it had been waiting for.

With each pull of blood from my neck to his lips, I felt more undone—more lost and found, all at once. Baird was grunting with each thrust, trying to merge our two bodies, like a demon trying to possess me. He was relentless, claiming my body and every breathless response. The rhythm of our bodies—carnal, pounding—echoed like an animalistic bassline beneath it all, until the hardest, most brutal climax tore through me and I screamed his name, my pussy spasming around his still thrusting cock, the sound of it raw, erotic, resounding with each stroke.

At the moment of his release, he tore his mouth from my neck as if something unseen had yanked him back. His cry—a raw, strangled sound—spilled into the room as he came inside me, his body shuddering with the force of it.

His hands still gripped me, crushing my flesh. He didn't let go. Couldn't.

And in that instant, we both knew—there was no going back. Not to who we were, not to what we'd been before this. He panted against me for several minutes as he struggled to regain control.

When he finally bent again to my neck to close the wounds there—I saw it. The shame on his face was unmistakable.

Baird Campbell, the man, had returned.

His body softened against mine, the white-knuckle grip he had on me loosened, and he slipped from within me, the connection between us suddenly tender, exposed. One arm still cradled my back, holding me up. I wasn't sure I could stand.

Not from blood loss—but from the sheer force of him. From the way his body had battered mine, from the blinding orgasm that had left me trembling, adrift, every muscle still quaking in the aftermath.

I didn't fully understand what had just happened between us, only that something had shifted—something vital. The divide between us hadn't closed, as I'd hoped. It had widened.

What had I done?

# Chapter Forty-Five
## BAIRD

"Go to bed, Mira! I won't let any harm come to ye—but I canna sleep beside ye. Not tonight..." His words left no room for protest. No space for softness. He was drawing a line. And he needed to remove any opportunity for Mira to cross it. He bolted through the house, leaving Mira standing frozen in the entryway, wearing a mask of shock, and slammed the front door, the sound echoing through the quiet night air like a gunshot.

He'd seen it in her face before he'd walked out—the lingering hunger. And he could smell it on her, thick in the air between them. Her desire hadn't faded, not even after his brutal claiming of her body just moments before.

If anything, it had grown.

She was still aching for him, still trembling with need. Worse than before.

Baird needed to distance himself from her, to sit with the consequences of the act he'd performed, waiting to see if their bond grew—this connection, this new *thing* that could take root between them.

He had no experience with this.

Robbie had warned him once about what happened when a vampire took the blood of his true mate, from the neck or the heart vein, and by doing so, created something *new*.

The thing he'd called Sanguis Amantium.

A bond forged in blood and love. Ancient. Irrevocable.

It was more than instinct, more than lust. It was an unbreakable chain.

But the bond would only form if both were deeply in love. Not infatuation, not fleeting passion—something ancient, something true. He loved Mira. He could admit that now, in the quiet of his own mind. It wasn't just the way she looked at him, or the way her body fit so perfectly against his—it was her fire, her curiosity, her boldness.

Baird bowed his head, full of shame, as he paced the road in front of the house.

What remained of Baird Campbell—the man—was slipping. And the creature he hated, the one he swore he'd never let himself become, was rising. For *her*.

The monster inside him hadn't wanted her to know. Did the monster need her to love him the way the man inside him did? He wasn't sure. He felt the monster wanted only to possess and would use whatever means were at his disposal to do so. But that wasn't enough for Baird.

His shame was sharp, suffocating. What hollowed him out was the gnawing suspicion that it hadn't only been the monster who'd kept that truth from her.

That what was left of *him* in that moment hadn't wanted to give her the choice. Maybe he needed to know if there was a chance—and the man in him knew this was the way to find out.

The Sanguis Amantium had the power to steal something from her the moment it was created—not just her body, but something more sacred.

The privacy of her inner world. But only if she loved him in return.

He didn't know how quickly the connection could take root, and he was sick with worry. Worry that he'd discover she didn't love him, and sick with worry about how she'd feel if she did love him, knowing he'd taken something from her, not given her the chance to choose.

Robbie had said it was like an intravenous line threaded straight into the nexus of the mate's emotions. The one who drank was no longer limited to reading the biological rhythms of their mate's body. It went deeper—embedding itself into the hidden chambers of the heart.

A parasitic telegraph, wired to the soul.

Happiness. Sadness. Longing. Loneliness. Pride. Hatred.

He thought about what it would feel like if the bond formed between them. Every emotion she felt would pulse through him, broadcast in whispers and surges.

No matter where she was.No matter how far she ran.Regardless of time, distance, or will.

The Sanguis Amantium was one of the many things Robbie had explained to Baird over the years they'd known one another. After Baird had been turned and returned to Edinburgh, a memory surfaced—something his mother had once whispered to him when he was a child. A cryptic, haunting tale passed down through generations.

It was something *her* mother had told her, and hers before that. A piece of island lore everyone seemed to know but no one dared speak aloud.

There was a man on Arran who never aged.

A man named Robbie.

They said he wasn't to be feared—he wasn't evil—but it was wise not to get too close. That he drank blood to survive. That he could make ye forget.

For centuries, the islanders had lived quietly beside him, never confronting what they could not explain. He was simply *there*—a fixture, a shadow at the edge of everyday life.

Baird remembered seeing him once, as a boy. He had the strangest blue eyes—shimmering like twin kaleidoscopes in the sunlight.

And then, Baird couldn't stop wondering.

Was Robbie like him?

Baird had sought him out the moment he returned to the island, and the recognition between them was instant. Robbie had just come in from the water, pulling his small fishing boat up to the dock at Lochranza, a bucket of fresh catch swinging in one hand, destined for the fishmonger.

Baird stood at the edge of the dock, watching.

Robbie looked straight at him—his pale, iridescent eyes catching the light—and nodded once.

"Ye own Baird Cottage, no?" he asked, calm and certain.

"Aye," Baird said.

"Good. Go back home now. I'll finish up here, and then I'll come talk with ye." He paused, eyes narrowing just slightly. "I can see ye have questions... I'll bring a bottle."

# Chapter Forty-Six

## BASTIEN

Her image had come to him, a stabbing vision where he could feel her. The look on her face, hungry with need for Baird, the all-consuming desire that only intensified with every passing second. But beneath that longing, there was something else written on her face—confusion and doubt. And he was certain it had nothing to do with Baird being a vampire. He felt deep in his bones it was Agnes that haunted Mira.

Stupid, silly girl.

Ignoring what was right in front of her.

But in addition to the strange connection he had to Mira, his maker's bond to Baird was also strong, and it was upon this connection he felt it. He knew the moment it happened. He recognized the signs. The Sanguis Amantium—the blood bond of lovers. A connection as old as their kind.

And Baird? Baird was still a virgin to it, in every sense that mattered. Bastien felt a swell of twisted pride. His child—*of sorts*—was finally tasting the brilliant pull of power, that intoxicating force he had spent centuries denying himself. The universe had broken Baird's will at last, dragging him down into the grip of the very monster he'd fought so hard to suppress.

And unless Baird was willing to let that monster win—with Mira—he would never know the full extent of it: the deepest pleasure, the rapture that hovered just beyond reach. All he had to do was surrender. Reach out. Take it. Follow the path laid before him.

The Sanguis Amantium was the path.

# CHAPTER FORTY-SEVEN

# MIRA

I woke alone in bed. Sleep had come in fragments—brief stretches of darkness interrupted by long, restless wakefulness. The bed felt too wide, the air too quiet, the space beside me hollow. His scent still clung to the sheets, a cruel reminder of his absence. Without Baird beside me, I never sank into that deep, anchoring sleep I'd come to crave.

I got dressed for class and headed down to the kitchen. A fresh pot of coffee was on—but Baird was nowhere in sight. I sat at the counter, hands wrapped around a warm mug, waiting for him to walk in. Hoping he wouldn't shut me out. Praying he didn't still hate me.

But sitting there wasn't enough. I couldn't let the silence between us stretch into something worse. I needed to find him—needed to face what had happened—before class, before the day swept me away and left this unresolved.

"Baird," I called out as I moved through the first floor, peering into each room. No sign of him.

I started up the stairs—but then I heard the front door open and shut. I froze mid-step and peered over the railing. His tall frame filled the front hall, and he came into view as I stood on the second step of the winding staircase.

His face was grim. His eyes unreadable.

I wasn't sure how to start this conversation now that I'd been presented with the opportunity. Everything I'd planned to say went right out the window. But I swallowed my pride.

"I'm sorry." My words were quiet, but it was the truth. "I didn't know I'd hurt you by doing what I did—what I asked of you. I just wanted to know all of you, for you to stop hiding that part from me."

"Ye were never supposed to see that, Mira. And I hate that ye did." Baird said, matter-of-factly, clinical. No acknowledgment of the connection we'd felt, the power that existed between us.

"I just don't understand." I was unable to leave it alone—still poking the bear. "You told me to be who I am," I said, breath catching, eyes locked on his. "To stop denying it. So why can't you take your own advice?"

Baird looked away, jaw tightening. "This thing I am—the inhuman part...that's the thing that will keep you from being mine. *Truly* mine."

I didn't understand what he meant, what he was trying to say.

"Do ye not understand, Mira?" he said, frustration making his voice raw. "I love ye. That's the truth of it—from the first moment I laid eyes on ye. And last night only proved I can never truly have ye."

"No," I whispered, shaking my head, a quiet protest slipping out before I could stop it.

Love me? That couldn't be right. It wasn't possible. Whatever he thought he felt—whatever this thing was—it had to be tangled up in his grief for Agnes. In the past. In the echo of someone else. He couldn't separate me from her. He *thought* he loved me, but it wasn't real. Not really.

His eyes flicked back to mine, a question rising in them. He didn't look away.

"This isn't what will keep me from being yours, Baird. Not this part of you." I needed him to hear it—that what he'd endured, what had been forced on him, didn't make me turn away. If anything, it pulled me closer.

And as he held my gaze, something in him shifted—subtle, almost imperceptible. But I couldn't tell what it meant...or why it made my chest tighten the way it did.

"It's something else that comes between us," I said, finally giving voice to the thoughts that had haunted me for days. "Something I can't compete with."

He was still, too still. "Agnes."

He said her name flatly, almost without feeling—but something flickered in his eyes. A strange light. Something I couldn't name.

Her name hung in the air like a ghost, as real and cold as the memory itself.

"You loved her," I said. "And you always will. But I can't live in the shadow of the woman you couldn't save."

A long silence followed. The kind that either shatters or cements something between two people.

Then, softly, Baird said, "I don't think ye are her, Mira. And what I feel for ye is real."

He stood two steps below me, and the man who had looked so grim just moments ago now seemed...peaceful. Almost happy. He reached out his hand. I took it and stepped down to his level, and he pulled me into his arms.

My heart was still splintered, tugged in a hundred different directions—but for this moment, the ache softened. In the quiet shelter of his embrace, everything else fell away.

I wanted to believe him.

God, I wanted to.

But some part of me, buried deep and raw, still wouldn't let go of doubt.

"I don't know how I'll do it yet, Mira Garvie, but I swear I'll prove it to ye," he whispered softly against my hair.

Something had shifted between us—something that felt important, though I couldn't quite name it. I pulled back slightly and looked up at his face, searching for answers I didn't have the language for. But whatever had changed wasn't written in his expression—it was in the air between us, in the way his anger, his self-hatred, all that buried bitterness seemed to lift, swept away by something unseen and inexplicable.

It hadn't been the words that changed things. It was something else entirely— deeper, beyond my understanding. And whatever it was, the weight of what I'd done last night slipped from my shoulders, and I could finally breathe again.

# Chapter Forty-Eight

## Mira

The second day of class passed without incident. After the glue had fully dried, I successfully completed the granulation pattern on the gold backplate, carefully arranging each detail before moving the piece into the kiln to bring the surface to the correct temperature. The final day would be devoted to setting the emeralds and polishing the piece to completion.

Anne had texted me midday to see when I'd be coming back, and I was a little evasive.

> (Anne) *How's Scotland? Class is over soon, right?*

> (Mira) *Yes, tomorrow is the final day. May stick around for a couple more days?*

> (Anne) *How's it going with the hot farmer?*

> (Mira) *Still hot, still a farmer...*

I struggled with how much I could actually tell Anne. Part of me wanted to spill everything, but no rational person could believe this—not the vampire part, at least.

As a sort of consolation prize—or maybe just to soothe my guilt for keeping her in the dark—I sent her a few pictures of the pendant I was working on. Mostly so she'd know it was really me texting back, and not, say, a serial killer who'd buried my body in his garden and was now politely responding to messages in my voice.

> (Anne) *Wow—that's beautiful. Can't wait to see you when you get back.*

> (Mira) *Miss you! Gotta run. When I get my return flight details, I'll let you know.*

Ugh...why did I feel like I was cheating on my friends back home, carrying all of this in silence? But what else could I do? How could I possibly explain any of it? I needed something—something solid, something I could hold on to to prove it had all happened. That I hadn't imagined it, dreamed it. That this place, this life, this version of me...was real.

Maybe Baird was right. Maybe I *did* need a picture of him, or of us together. Something I could show them. Proof that this was more than a story I'd spun for myself, more than a romantic fantasy built on mist and myth.

Proof that *we* had existed.

Before I went home.

Before I returned to the version of my life that had come before all this—before Baird—and left it behind.

◈

When Baird picked me up, that strange look in his eyes from this morning hadn't gone away. It lingered—like he knew something about me that I didn't—and it was starting to grate on me.

Back at his place, he pulled out ingredients for dinner and set two bottles of wine on the counter.

"Do ye like *cacio e pepe*?" he asked, already moving around the kitchen, sleeves pushed up, focused on the task.

I sipped a glass of Italian Primitivo—which I found out was what we call zinfandel back home—watching him from my perch at the counter, feeling more like a character in a play than a person—except I was the only one who didn't know the script. He wasn't jolly—no, it was more like he had a calm purpose, working toward some end goal I couldn't see.

But there was something else too, something restrained. Like a cat with a bird in its mouth, he was being careful with me—watchful, deliberate, as if he knew one wrong move might shatter whatever this was between us.

"Are we going to talk about this morning? Or last night? Or whatever this *thing* is with you suddenly?" I blurted out, unable to hold it in any longer.

He didn't even pretend not to know what I meant, and I had to give him credit for that, at least.

"What is there to discuss?" he said evenly. "I told ye I loved ye. And ye said some nonsense about how ye thought I didn't really mean it—that I was just using ye as a stand-in for Agnes. That about sum it up?"

No anger, no sarcasm. Just calm, like we were discussing what to put on the grocery list.

I, however, was becoming less calm by the minute.

"And I told ye before—if ye want to know how I feel about something, ask me. Don't make things up in yer head, don't project yer own hang-ups onto me."

"*Hang-ups?* My hang-ups?" I snapped. "What about *yours?* You hated yourself until this morning. I want to know what changed."

"What changed?" He took a breath, his voice quiet, steady. "I let ye see all of me—every dark bit. The bad, the bloody, the monster Bastien made me into. And I let *myself* see it too—through *yer* eyes. Ye didn't flinch. Ye didn't run. That's what changed. *Ye* changed me, Mira."

I rolled my eyes. "But you can't really *love* me—you barely *know* me. And just because I can accept something you have imagined that Agnes couldn't—something that you could *never* know, by the way—that's not enough of a reason."

He shook his head, exasperated. "Good God, yer stubborn—stubborn as a *mule.*"

He turned back around to the task of finishing dinner, no artifice now—this was now and would always be dinner for one. Wine, whisky or ale for two—yes—but dinner for one. Just another bizarre routine we'd settled into. Still, I couldn't exactly complain about having someone cook for me every day—especially when the cook was as skilled in the kitchen, and as undeniably hot, as Baird.

"Tell me—why do ye question the depth of my feelings for ye? Why do ye believe it's nae genuine? I need to understand that part," he said, sliding the plate of pasta toward me. The spaghetti swirled in an elegant mound, cracked pepper dotting the surface, a generous snowfall of shaved pecorino romano crowning the top.

Honestly, I didn't have a real answer to that—so, as a delay tactic, I lifted a forkful to my mouth. The sound I made after that first bite was embarrassingly close to the ones I'd made in bed with him. Sublime didn't even begin to cover it.

"Umm...I'm going to eat my feelings for a bit, if that's okay," I said as I continued eating.

"Ye asked what changed, and I dinnae want to keep secrets from ye. Not anymore," he said, determination settling in his features. He let out a long exhale.

"Last night, when I drank from ye, something new was born between us. I can do more than read yer body now—I can feel what ye feel. It hit me this morning, seeing ye on the stairs. I felt it inside ye...a tiny flicker of happiness when I told ye I loved ye. A spark, buried under all the confusion and disbelief inside ye. And I'm going to hold on to that memory, that glimmer. Because if ye were truly incapable of loving me, ye'd never have felt it at all."

I set my fork down with a sharp clang. "Did you *know* that was going to happen?"

"I'd heard it could," he admitted sheepishly. "Ye remember Robbie? At the pub? He's like I am, like Bastien. He helped me when I was first turned, helped me figure out how to craft a life of sorts. He explained this to me once. But I've no direct experience, ye see. He said it only happens when two people are in love. The Sanguis Amantium, they call it—'the blood of lovers.'"

I sat there, dumbfounded. The bartender was a vampire too? These things really were living in plain sight.

"I suppose it was a test of my own," he said. "So now we're even." His arms were folded over his chest, but his eyes held an apology.

We weren't even—not even close—and I *wanted* to call him an ass. But he had a point. Instead of arguing, I stuffed another forkful of cheesy deliciousness into my mouth, letting the food do the talking. Better to keep chewing than say something I couldn't take back.

"Ye love me, ye know. Deep down, whether or not yer ready to admit it. And that"—he tapped a finger lightly over his heart— "that's the hope I'm holding on to now."

I felt violated and exposed, and it was infuriating. I didn't want him to be right, but deep down, the part of me that had visions and nightmares knew it might be true.

"And now yer mad," he added.

"Can you read my thoughts too?" I asked, wondering just how far this Sanguis Amantium thing went.

He let out a low laugh. "Nae, I can't read yer thoughts. But honestly, this new ability would be far more intrusive if ye didn't already wear every feeling plain as day. Ye've no future as an actress, lass."

I took another bite as Baird silently refilled my wine glass. I hadn't eaten much in the last two days, and now that I'd started, I realized just how hungry I was. Hungry and angry.

Then came the soft chime of a text notification. I glanced at my phone as the screen lit up—a number I didn't recognize. And then the photos started coming in. One *ding*. Then another. And another. Ten in total.

All of them were of me and Baird.

The first few showed us walking together, the night after we'd eaten at the Italian place. Then a few of him dropping me off at the Goldsmiths' Guild. But the final images...they were of us inside the house, taken from outside, through the window. One showed me standing in front of Baird at the kitchen table—just seconds before I'd lifted my sweater and given myself to him. Every image crisp, precise. Telephoto lens.

(+33 7 12 55 21 41) *Will you go home when this is over, Mira?*

A chill sliced down my spine. That kind of cold that makes you feel *watched*, vulnerable, *hunted*. My hands trembled, and the phone slipped from my fingers, clattering onto the counter.

"What is it, Mira?" Baird's voice was sharp now, alarmed, as he crossed the room to me.

I picked up the phone and handed it to him, my voice unsteady.

"He's watching us—Bastien."

# Chapter Forty-Nine
## BAIRD

He was caught off guard by how effortlessly Bastien had shifted from the realm of the supernatural to something as cold and calculated as cyberstalking—but at this point, nothing about him could be dismissed. He had felt Bastien closing in over the past twenty-four hours, knowing it wouldn't be long now. The night before, he'd taken down the sword from above the hearth. It had hung there for over a century—a relic of another life, another world. A keepsake. Nothing more.

But now, he'd need it.

He was done hiding in the shadows. Done playing Bastien's twisted game of cat and mouse. It ended here. For what Bastien did to Agnes. For the life he stole from Baird.And for the quiet, cruel torment he now inflicted on Mira—an innocent caught in a centuries-old feud that should have died long ago.

Baird wondered what kind of coward he'd been all these years. He could have gone after Bastien. Could have made it his purpose to hunt him down, to end this blight once and for all. But instead, he'd hidden on the island, buried himself in silence, in guilt, in memories. Waiting for...what? Redemption?

And yet now—suddenly—he felt it. Conviction. Purpose. A calling he'd never known pulsed in his blood like fire. It startled him, this sudden certainty. This vocation that had never once stirred in him now roaring to life.

But he shouldn't wonder. Not really.

It was Mira.She was the reason.

Her presence had changed something in him—resurrected a strength he hadn't known he possessed. The need to protect her had given him courage. And the love he dared not speak until today had given him clarity.

He would face Bastien. And this time, he would not run. Baird replied to Bastien's text:

> (Baird from Mira's phone) *Ye are nothing but a coward lurking in the shadows. This ends tonight. Come now...or I'll hunt ye down myself.*

# Chapter Fifty

# Mira

And then, in just moments, as the darkness thickened around us, a shadowy figure appeared on the terrace—not there one moment, and there the next—standing motionless, watching through the kitchen window where Baird held me in his arms.

I froze.

That silhouette—I knew it. The same dark man who had followed me. The one who stalked the edges of my sleep, haunting every nightmare. My skin crawled with the familiar dread, my heartbeat hammering in my ears like a war drum. Bunny crouched next to us, her low growl reinforcing my fear. I pressed myself deeper into the safety of Baird's embrace, willing myself to disappear into his solidity.

But Bastien was still there. Unmoving. Unblinking. Staring.

He seemed smaller now, somehow less imposing with Baird's arms around me. And yet I knew—it was a lie. He was no less dangerous. His stillness was not passivity but provocation.

"Stay inside," Baird said, his voice low but unshakable. "Keep Bunny with you. This is my battle, Mira—not yours."

And before I could stop him—before I could even beg him not to go—he stepped away from me, grabbed the sword he'd sharpened the night before, and walked out the door. Bunny pressed closer to my side with Baird's absence, her growls rising in intensity, and I was oddly flattered that she seemed ready to defend me too.

Terror bloomed in my chest. What if Bastien killed him? What if I was left alone? I would be at Bastien's mercy, no match for his twisted gifts of enthrallment—the ones Baird had warned me about, the ones I didn't understand.

And then, it happened.

A voice, sudden and unmistakable, coiled inside my head—not mine. Not Baird's.

Bastien.

The same voice from my nightmares. Smooth. Icy. Familiar.

*Come to me.*

At that same moment, Bunny fell silent, then sat back on her haunches, dazed—like she didn't quite know where she was. I stared at her, unsettled, and wondered if *he* could speak inside her head too. The thought sent a chill through me.

Her confusion became mine in an instant, as my feet began to move of their own accord—carrying me to the door, then across the threshold, and out into the night.

Inside, I was trembling. Terrified. But outside, I was calm.

Composed. Controlled.

Anyone watching would think I was walking out of my own free will.

They wouldn't see the war inside me.

They wouldn't hear me screaming no.

"Thank you for joining us," Bastien said, his voice disturbingly calm. "I was just telling Baird I need you to be present for this. There is so much you need to learn—both of you, really…"

I looked toward Baird, just twenty feet or so away from me. He stood rooted, unmoved, his gaze locked on Bastien with the cold clarity of a man who had already decided how this would end. The power I'd seen in him the night before—that wild, thrumming energy just beneath his skin—was back. But now it was different. Stronger. Hardened. No longer restrained by guilt or doubt.

The will of steel I'd glimpsed in moments past was fully forged now, sharpened alongside the blade he had readied. He wasn't merely reacting—he was resolute. Every line of his body, every breath he took, told me he'd stepped into something irreversible. Not just a fight. A reckoning.

He no longer feared Bastien.

But I still did.

To my left stood the figure from my nightmares. His beauty was sharp—dangerously so. Features that hovered somewhere between male and female, symmetrical yet strange, as if nature had over-perfected him. There was a grace to him that didn't belong to humanity at all. It was fluid, primal. The kind of elegance born not of refinement, but of instinct—an animal's grace, poised and predatory.

When he'd followed me, he'd been wearing sunglasses, hiding those uncanny eyes. I hadn't realized how much they unsettled me until now, seeing them fully.

Liquid silver.

His eyes were beautiful, hypnotic. They flickered like candle flames, shimmering faintly, then growing brighter, then dimming softly again. The fear inside me grew each time Bastien's eyes began to glow, as if he were drawing power from somewhere—or someone. There was something storm-like about him, but not the kind that brings life with rain. Bastien was the cold, brutal kind—the kind that destroys.

His power was deadly, relentless, and icy to its core. So unlike the white-hot surge I felt from Baird when his eyes changed—his power burned with purpose, with heat. With *heart*.

Despite the power that had pulled me outside, I found my voice. "Why are you doing this? Is this some kind of sick joke?" I demanded, despite my fear, unwilling to be a damsel in distress.

Bastien laughed—a sound that began sharp and bitter, almost cruel, but as it faded, it thinned into something hollow. "It's not a joke," he said quietly. "I'm here to try to make amends." His eyes moved from mine to Baird's, and a strange stillness settled over Bastien. "Because what I did to Agnes...and to you...still haunts me. And I want it to stop. I want it all to stop."

If Baird was caught off guard by Bastien's speech, he didn't show it.

"I'm tired, Baird. Tired of this life I've led. Ashamed of it, from the moment I was sired by a vampire named Magda—*no, truth be told, even before that*—right up until the day I was saved—if you can call it that—by a woman named Clémence, forty years ago."

It was then that I noticed the vibrant darkness that had cloaked him like a second skin was thinning. He looked...tired. Not frail, not weak, but weathered. As if centuries had finally begun to weigh on him.

Bastien was looking for something in Baird's eyes, something small that said perhaps he understood, but if he did, Baird gave nothing away. So Bastien continued. "My greatest regret—and there are many—is what happened that night. I never meant to hurt Agnes. I wanted to help her. I saw more than her beauty. I saw a kindred spirit. Someone wounded.

Fractured. And I let my ego convince me I could fix her—that I alone had a power no one else did. Not you. Not the doctors. Not even her family."

Bastien's expression shifted, softened—no longer the predator, but a man desperate to be understood. Desperate for another man to see *why*. To know *who* he had once tried to be.

"I thought I could take the pain from her mind. So I used what I had—my power. I enthralled her, clouded her thoughts. Not to harm her, but to soften the jagged edges inside her. To give her something that felt like joy, even if it wasn't real. Even if it only lasted a moment."

I watched Baird, trying to see how he'd receive this. At first, he was unreadable—still as a statue, composed, that same unflinching resolve etched into every line of his face. But I knew him too well now to be fooled. Beneath the surface, I saw it—the flicker in his eyes, subtle but unmistakable. Pain.

Not new pain. Old. Deep. Reawakened.

The pain of watching the woman he loved unravel, powerless to stop it. Of standing by as she crumbled, needing him—and him not being there. Whether by fear, by shame, or the twisted logic of self-preservation, he'd stayed away. And that absence, that failure, had carved a wound in him he still carried. Raw. Bleeding. Close to the surface, even now.

He wore armor forged of duty and purpose, but guilt lived inside it undiminished. And yet he didn't look away. He stood in it, bore it, let it burn. Because this time, he wouldn't turn his back.

"She didn't know what I was—not at first. Just like you didn't." Bastien's voice was soft, almost reflective, but there was no warmth in it. Only weariness, and something darker beneath—contempt, perhaps.

Then a brittle, mirthless laugh slipped from his lips. *"No one ever does,"* he said, almost to himself. His eyes flicked toward me, and his tone shifted—cooler now, more deliberate. "How well you know that now." He gave a small nod in my direction, the gesture so slight it could've been mistaken for something casual.

But it wasn't. It was dismissive. A mark of derision. *Another stupid human*, his gesture seemed to say.

"But then her sister-in-law, Mary—*another Garvie with the Sight*—saw through me. She warned Agnes—told her what I was. That's when she ran. That's when she begged you to take her to the cottage." His voice dropped, thick with memory. "She thought she could escape me. But there was nowhere she could have gone that I couldn't follow. And I did. Because I still believed—I *needed* to believe—that if she just let me in, she'd see it. That I could be the answer."

Bastien looked down at the stone under his feet, as if debating something with himself. "You should know something else, Baird—Agnes was never untrue to you. I don't know whether that makes this easier to hear or harder. But it's the truth."

Baird's face twisted with rage, and he began to pace back and forth. "I don't want to hear your words! Whatever this is—whatever you are trying to do—it's meaningless to me now."

Bastien ignored Baird's protests as if he were a petulant child. "I was unwilling to let her go," Bastien said quietly. "I wanted Agnes to come to me *willingly*—something I think you understand. You feel that way about Mira."

His silver eyes flared, catching the light, glowing just a little brighter—fueled, it seemed, by the truth he dared to speak aloud. "I've seen the way you look at her," he said, turning to me then. "And the way *she* looks at *you*."

My stomach twisted. The air seemed too thin. That he would bring up Baird and me—*us*—in this moment, in the middle of his confession, felt like a blow. Because the truth was, what I felt for Baird *was* complicated. And now Bastien had dragged it into the open like it was just another chess move in his game.

"There's a difference, you know," Bastien said. "You didn't understand Agnes—not truly. But Mira...you understand her better than she understands herself."

What did he mean by that? How could he possibly have seen so clearly what I could barely admit to myself? How Baird always seemed to *know*—the exact moment I wanted to shut down, to disappear into myself. How he never pushed, just offered his presence like a lifeline. How, with a look or a word or the gentlest touch, he coaxed me back into my own skin. Back into the world. How he made me see feelings were something that tethered me to life instead of something I had to survive alone. His words had been meant for Baird, but his eyes were still fixed on mine, sharp and searching, waiting—almost *daring*—me to react.

"He loves you, Mira. Baird loves you." Bastien said this simply, as if it were some universally acknowledged fact. His eyes glowed more faintly now than they had earlier, as if his power was diminishing, fading somehow. "It's plain to see—it doesn't take Sight or any special gift to know it. It's written in the way he watches you, the way he breathes when you're near. He loves you more than life itself. And there should be no shame in that. No shame in what exists between you."

"You can't know that—you can't know what he feels," I said, my voice too sharp, too quick. I was trying to convince him. Trying to convince myself. Because if Bastien was right—if Baird was right—then the truth was too big, too wild to hold. Letting myself believe it, even for a second, felt more impossible than anything else that had happened since that moment I'd touched Agnes's portrait and my world cracked in two.

All the visions, the voices, the strange pull toward Baird—it could be explained away. My clairvoyance. Rationalized. What I'd felt in my visions? Those were Agnes's emotions. But this? This idea that this something that existed between Baird and me could actually be love? A love destined by something outside of our understanding?

That was terrifying.And far harder to believe.

I turned toward Baird—searching for something, confirmation or denial, I wasn't sure. But what I saw instead was the crack in his resolve. The weight of unspoken questions darkened his eyes, and when he spoke to Bastien, his voice was raw.

"Why did ye turn me?" he asked hoarsely. "What was I to ye?" There was desperation in his voice, a jagged edge that sent a chill up my spine. It wasn't just a question—it was a wound laid bare. And I wasn't sure which answer would hurt him more: the truth...or the lie.

"Why did I do this to you? I was punishing someone. A man who looked like you—acted like you did then...maybe still do," Bastien replied.

It was Bastien's face now that looked haunted, his expression flickering with something almost human. He was somewhere else—reliving a past that clung to him like ash, just as Baird had. For a brief, jarring moment, they weren't enemies standing on opposite ends of an ancient feud. They were two men carrying the weight of two separate ghosts.

"I can't blame you for trying to protect Agnes," Bastien said quietly. "But when you came at me with that blade...something in me snapped.

Snapped back almost 150 years before that night—to when I was just a boy."

He paused, as if the memory itself was something he had to push through physically. And for a moment, the mask slipped. The predator faded, and in his place stood something raw and broken. A glimpse of the boy he had been—and the monster he was destined to become.

"There was a man then—my father." Bastien looked down, his jaw tight, and nodded to himself, as if granting permission to revisit the place he'd buried for centuries. "Same height. Same frame. Same coloring as you." He swallowed hard. "He beat my mother. And he beat me—for the smallest sins. For loving art. For quoting poetry. For not being like him. For not *looking* like him."

The words hung heavy between them, a confession long unspoken. Not as an excuse, but to lay bare the lesion in his soul, still raw beneath the centuries.

Bastien's eyes held Baird's, wanting—no, *needing*—him to understand. "When you lunged at me that night, I didn't see you. I saw *him*. I was sixteen again, in the barn, with his blade at my throat after I tried to shield my mother from another one of his drunken rages."

This revelation slammed into me like a freight train, and I gasped when I heard it. This wasn't part of some grand plan. Baird hadn't been a target—he'd been an unlucky bystander. Caught in the blast radius of someone else's tragedy, someone else's obsession. A casualty of a past that wasn't his but had claimed him all the same.

Tears glistened in Bastien's moonlight eyes as he continued. "In that moment, in your cottage, there was no logic. No reason. No clarity. Only rage inside me. Someone coming between me and a woman I loved—*thought I loved*—I'd felt so little of it in my life. I wasn't striking at Baird Campbell—I was striking at *him*, my father. I was making him pay. Holding him responsible for the monster I became after I ran away."

The eyes of the monster were gone—replaced by the eyes of a broken man. And in them, I saw something I hadn't expected, nor would have believed.

An apology.

Not spoken. Not begged for. But there, all the same. Worn and wordless, heavy with the weight of everything he couldn't undo. I looked to Baird and saw him take a step back, as if the weight of Bastien's words had physically struck him. He didn't speak—just staggered slightly, caught between rage and something that looked like it might be pity. It was the kind of truth that didn't rewrite the past but instead cracked something open in the present.

"But it wasn't him. It was you. A man with the same eyes. The same hands. The same damn blade. In the wrong place...at the wrong time. And I realized only after that I had become just like my father."

I saw Baird's shoulders slump, the weight of it all settling over him like heavy cargo on a beast made to bear more than its share. He looked like a man bowed not just by grief or anger, but by the sheer burden of understanding—of knowing too much, too late.

I could only imagine how many times he'd asked this question to the universe, over decades, centuries—desperate for an answer that never came. And now, at last, the only one who could answer was standing before him...and giving up his terrible secrets.

"I know you saw me drain Agnes. But I didn't do it to punish you—not really. I did it to free *her*."

I saw them then—tears, barely held back, glistening in the corners of Baird's eyes. Not from fear. Not even from anger. But from memory.

The memory of this beast draining the life from his wife as he lay helpless near her, dying himself, powerless to stop it. That helplessness had branded him. And now, faced with the monster who had done it, those long-buried tears rose—not just for what had been taken, but for the man he had been and the man he couldn't be in that final moment.

"Can you imagine what her mind would've become if she'd woken to see what I'd done to you? To see the man she loved, broken and bloodied, because of *me*? No...I still believe what I did was a kindness. Twisted, perhaps. But mercy in its own way. For her. And, in a small way, for you."

Bastien stood taller now, somehow freed by speaking this truth. "I don't expect you to understand that. I don't expect forgiveness. My sins are far too great for that."

"Why did the visions stop? Why, after forcing me to witness the long line of women ye targeted to feed from and kill—why did it stop?" Baird demanded. It was as if there was a need in Baird, a need for all the answers he'd been plagued with for 240 years, and he'd pushed it to the surface.

"Oh my, Baird, you've really made me out to be a monster, haven't you? I didn't kill those women—fed from them, yes. Made them my lovers, yes...until I grew bored and moved on. Until I realized, one by one, that they were powerless to fill the void inside me. But you asked why it stopped—it stopped because I met Clémence."

I saw the confusion in Baird's eyes, but Bastien continued.

"It was Paris, 1981. We met in a painting class. I still painted then—it was the last joy I had left in this cursed life. I noticed her immediately; a natural platinum blond, curls so fine and wild they formed a halo around her head, a cherub straight out of a Renaissance fresco."

Bastien's mercury eyes lit up once again as he spoke, stronger this time, the way they glowed in my nightmares. A strange and eerie beauty, lit seemingly by his memories of this woman. "One day in class, she approached me—calm, direct. Told me she'd painted me from memory the night before. No pretense. No flirtation." He gave a faint, almost regretful shrug. "She wanted me to come to her studio. To see the portrait. She wasn't really my type. But she was beautiful, in her own quiet way. And I hadn't fed in weeks." His voice lowered, the next words stripped of sentiment.

"I thought—maybe she was a means to an end." The shrug came again, softer this time. Almost an apology. Not just for what he did, but for what he *was*. "The portrait was unfinished. Like many of the pieces in her studio, it seemed abandoned mid-breath—paint only in the center two-thirds of the canvas, the edges left bare. But in the center...was *me*. My face, my shoulders, rendered in thick, expressive strokes—her Impressionist hand capturing what seemed, at first, like a true likeness."

His story was pulling me under, drawing me in like a tide I hadn't noticed until it was too late. I could see this woman—Clémence—through his eyes, like a silent film flickering across the inside of my mind. Every brushstroke, every glance, felt vivid and close. I didn't know if it was my imagination or some power of his, working subtly as I stood there in the cold night air. But either way, I was caught in it.

"But her painting—it wasn't me. Not really. He looked like me, yes—but there was something else. A quiet dignity in the eyes. A beauty not of youth or perfection, but of *soul*. A human soul. Courageous. Redeemable. And I knew, standing there, that I was none of those things." He drew a ragged breath, his composure unraveling as the weight of memory eclipsed him—dragging him backward into the place he had never truly escaped.

"I told her that. Said the man in the portrait wasn't me. Maybe he was who I *could* have been, had my life taken a different path. She just smiled and said, 'No. He *is* you. I see what you truly are. You are not the things you've done.'"

I felt a kinship with the woman in Bastien's story. Another woman, like me, burdened with a knowledge that defied logic or fact. But unlike me—still tangled in doubt, still fighting what couldn't be measured—I wondered if she had resisted it too. Or had she always known to trust it? That strange, unexplainable knowledge the universe sometimes offers—not as proof, but as truth.

# Chapter Fifty-One

## BAIRD

B aird listened in silence as Bastien unraveled a tale so different from the one he'd carried for centuries—so far from the narrative he had built, believed, since 1785. He'd lived with that version of events like a scar carved into bone, a cavern he'd shaped his entire life around. And now, hearing the truth at last—the truth Bastien had chosen, finally, to share—he couldn't help but wonder: how different might his life have been? Not the events themselves, perhaps, but the way he carried them. The way he survived them.

If he'd just known. If someone had told him.

But no one had.Not until now.

More of Bastien's story spilled from his lips, words unwilling to be contained a moment longer. "I was furious. Violated. Exposed. And yet...no one had seen me like that since my mother, when I was a child. Clémence told me that no soul was beyond salvation. And in time, she became mine. She said she knew what I was the first day she saw me in class. But that didn't matter to her."

Tears flowed from Bastien's eyes, and Baird wondered for the first time if he and Bastien were more alike than they were different. "From that day forward, I was hers—for forty years. Until she died last spring. Cancer. I wanted to turn her. Begged her. But she refused. Said one lifetime was enough for her. She was the love of my life..."

Bastien dropped to his knees on the stone terrace in front of Baird, his moonlit eyes dimming by the second, like the last embers of a fire losing their glow. Anguish and exhaustion were etched into his enigmatic face, softening the sharpness that once made him seem untouchable. He looked tired. Diminished. As if something essential was draining from him.

"I didn't come back to ask your forgiveness, Baird. I don't deserve that." Bastien's voice was raw now with desperation. "I came to ask you to end this. To use your anger, your pain, your revenge—whatever it takes—to rid the world of me—and to release me from the weight of losing her."

"Wait!" Mira said, the words escaping her lips sharply. "I need to understand."

"Stay back, Mira," Baird warned, but she stepped forward, toward Bastien, surprise on her face at the fact that she again controlled her own movement. Perhaps Bastien had released his hold over her some time ago, but she hadn't tested it until then.

"How—how were you able to see me and put my image in Baird's head?" she asked, wide-eyed.

Baird could see this piece of the puzzle was something she desperately needed.

"My mother—she was a Seer, just like you. Like your father. And I was one as well. Another thing my father hated about me. Another piece of me he couldn't understand, couldn't control."

Baird envisioned Bastien as a child then—the one Granny Margaret had told Mira about, the boy treated cruelly, shaped by pain until he twisted beneath it. It wasn't sympathy he felt—at least not entirely—but recognition. He knew it deep in his bones: no one was born a monster. Not even Bastien.

"When I was turned...I retained that gift. That doesn't happen often. The Sight doesn't usually survive the change. But in me, it did. When your parents died, the pieces began to shift. Fall into place. The universe—whatever power governs it—began moving you, guiding you. Bringing you here. To *him*."

Baird saw the confusion in Mira's face slowly turning to anger.

"And I *saw* it. I saw you as my chance. As a thread I could pull, a tool in a plan. I won't pretend I didn't use you." Bastien's voice was softer now. "But even if I hadn't—*even without me*—your power would've brought you to Baird eventually. That was written in the fabric of the world. That was always going to happen."

Bastien stared at Mira, willing her to understand, but Baird knew her too well, he could feel her emotions—and she was fighting against this too.

"You were destined to find him. As only you could. You felt it in your very first vision after touching the portrait...the connection between the two of you. Not Agnes...it was always you."

Baird saw Mira's face harden into a mask of defiance, her irritation with two men speaking over her—telling her what she felt, what was real, what to believe—emanated from her, and he felt it viscerally. And then she turned on Bastien, her voice low but sharp as glass.

"How do you know what I feel? What *he* feels?" she demanded, pointing directly at Baird.

He flinched—just barely—not out of guilt, but from the sheer weight of being seen, named. And in that moment, he couldn't tell whether she was defending him...or accusing him.

"You're wrong," she said, her voice steady, breathless with conviction. And unlike Baird's or Bastien's, her breath still fogged in the cold night air—warm, human. A reminder that she didn't belong to their world.

"Tell her how wrong she is, Baird—or have you kept this from her too?" Bastien's voice cut through the night, sharp with accusation, as if he thought Baird hadn't told her about the Sanguis Amantium. He turned his gaze from Mira to Baird, eyes still glittering softly in the low light.

Mira looked between them, confusion flickering across her face. The silence was heavy, alive with things unsaid.

Baird's jaw tightened, his hands clenched, and when he finally spoke, his voice was low, rough—almost broken. "Aye, I've told her. But there are things she doesn't yet want to know." Baird said at last, his voice gravel-low, worn from holding too much for too long. "Doesn't yet want to believe."

Baird turned toward Mira, not in frustration, but in a quiet plea. "I canna convince her. I've tried," Baird said, his eyes never leaving Mira, waiting to see what she would do with the pieces now laid bare between them.

A small, knowing smile crossed Bastien's lips as he looked up at Baird. "She'll come to it when she comes to it," he said gently. "*Oh ye of little faith.*" He shook his head, slow and solemn, the weight of hard-won wisdom in every movement. "Don't lose faith in her. I haven't. I believe in her...just as I believe in you—to do what must be done."

Then, without flourish or resistance, Bastien clasped his hands in front of him—not in defiance, not in prayer, but in quiet surrender. The silence that followed pressed down around them, thick and unrelenting. The kind of silence that comes before a reckoning.

Baird knew it was time. He expected Bastien to close his eyes, to brace for the end. But he didn't. He looked up instead. And in his eyes, Baird saw shame, yes, and sorrow—raw and unguarded. But also something else. Hope.

Not hope for forgiveness. Not even for mercy.

Hope for *release*. For closure. For an end to the long penance of his existence.

Baird didn't believe Bastien *deserved* release. Not after what he'd done.

And yet...

There was Mira.

She was here—alive, radiant, sharp with purpose. Bastien had brought her into his life. And Baird, for all his anger, knew that mattered. He would *never* forgive the past...but Mira could be his future. And for that, he owed something. Perhaps not to Bastien, but to fate.

He stepped back, circling the vampire slowly across the broad stone terrace, sword held low but ready in both hands. The blade was heavy, forged for battle—but Baird held it like it was an extension of himself.

Baird glanced to Mira, needing to see her face. Needing to know what this looked like through her eyes. He expected fear—of the violence, of *him*. But there was none.

She stood tall, unmoving, her arms at her sides, fists curled not in tension, but in resolve. There was something almost otherworldly about her—like the universe had placed her here for this exact moment, a silent arbiter of justice and mercy, and after fighting so hard, she had accepted her role in this. As though she was meant to bear witness. To hold him accountable, or perhaps...to set him free.

She didn't speak. She didn't need to.

Her eyes found his—steady, unwavering—and in them, he read the unspoken truth: *Do what you must.*

It was then that Baird truly understood. This act would not undo the past. It would not erase the pain. But it might close a door that had remained open too long.

Baird said a prayer in Gaelic, his grandmother's tongue, just before he pressed the tip of the blade to Bastien's chest, directly over his heart. With a cry of anguish, both hands on the blade, Baird used all his strength to force the blade home. When the blade slid through Bastien's body, he felt the brief resistance, then reverberation of the blade fully cleaving Bastien's chest, and then sword hitting stone, shock waves radiating from the ground up Baird's arms. He heard Mira gasp but didn't turn to look at her. Instead, he kept his gaze on Bastien.

And in that moment, Bastien turned to black dust. A swirling cloud rose where his body had been, twisting in the rough shape of a man—then unraveling, thread by thread. There was no scream. No final plea. Just silence.

Then, a sudden gust of wind—unnatural, sharper than the already frigid night air—swept through the terrace. It gathered the ash in one violent breath and carried it off into the darkness, as if the earth itself had waited long enough to reclaim him.

Baird remained where he stood, both hands still gripping the hilt of the sword. He didn't move. Couldn't.

Then, slowly, the weight of it all—tonight, and 1785, and everything between—came crashing down. His knees finally buckled, and he sank to the ground, his head bowed. The blade, now motionless and blood-less, bore his sagging weight as he knelt in silence beneath the stars, breath ragged, shoulders heaving with the burden of everything he could never undo.

# Chapter Fifty-Two

## Mira

The enormity of what had just happened crashed down on me. Bastien turning to dust—swept away by a wind that didn't belong to this world—was something I would never forget. No matter what he was, no matter what he'd done, in that final instant, he was a man to me. And watching his life end with a blade through his heart made me shudder—not with fear, but with grief. Grief for the boy beaten by his father. Grief for the centuries he wandered, clinging to power, mistaking control for love. And worst of all, grief for the man who had finally found what he'd always searched for—only to lose it, not to violence or vengeance, but to the quiet, inevitable frailty of human mortality.

I turned toward Baird, wanting to run to the safety of his arms, but I stopped short when I saw the price he had paid. What I saw reminded me of my vision—the one of Baird kneeling at Agnes' grave. His body heaved in anguish then, just as it did now, and for a moment, I felt like an intruder all over again, as though I was witnessing something too private, too raw.

But this time, I wasn't an intruder. This time, I was *part* of it. Despite the ache in my chest—for the shadows still clinging to him—I couldn't walk away. I couldn't leave him to face this alone.

It wasn't fair. Not after everything.

He would need someone tonight. And I wanted that someone to be *me*.

I walked to Baird and sank to my knees beside him. He didn't react. His eyes were glassy, distant—fixed on something far beyond the terrace, or maybe buried deep inside it. If they'd glowed black with hatred when he drove the blade through Bastien's heart, I hadn't seen it. All I saw now were those brilliant green eyes, dulled and clouded by the weight of what he'd done, of all that had passed.

Gently, I raised a hand to his cheek, my fingers trembling as they brushed the stubble along his jaw. I turned his face toward mine, not forcefully, just enough to bring him back to the present.

To *me*.

I needed him to see that I was here. That I hadn't left. That whatever darkness I'd just witnessed, I didn't fear it—and I would never hold it against him. He turned to me then, and I pressed my lips to his—softly, gently. A kiss not of passion, but of presence. At the touch, his hands released the sword. It fell with a metallic clatter, skittering across the stone before coming to rest beside us, forgotten.

His eyes widened, as if only now truly seeing me. Then he pulled me into him.

His arms wrapped around me with a desperate strength, clinging as though I were a lifeline, as though I were the only thing anchoring him to the world.

"Dinna fash," I whispered, repeating the strange, comforting phrase he'd once said to me on a night filled with fear and dreams I hadn't understood. "I'm here. You're safe now. It's over."

As we passed together through the threshold of the patio door, I felt one weight lift from me entirely—Bastien was no longer a threat. That particular fear, sharp and looming, was gone. But in its place came another weight, heavier somehow for having always been there, now pushed to the forefront where I could no longer ignore it.

Baird thought he loved me.

Truly believed it. I saw it in his eyes, in the way he looked at me as if I were the reason he'd survived everything that came before. But I still couldn't believe it—not fully. Not in the way he meant it. It felt impossible, unreal. And worse, I didn't know what I believed about my own feelings for him.

I wanted him. I needed him. But love?

That was murkier. Slippery. Tangled in too many things—gratitude, survival, the adrenaline of shared danger. And something older, something I couldn't name. Something ancient and strange that seemed to live between us, unseen but always there.

And then there was Agnes.

The ghost of a woman, the one he had loved—still loved. A mirror image of me, whether by fate or some cruel cosmic joke. Could I trust that what he felt was truly mine? That it was for me, and not the echo of someone long gone?

No matter what Baird said, I didn't believe it. Not yet.

And maybe that was the truth I feared more than any danger Bastien ever posed.

Baird stopped in the kitchen and pulled two glasses from the cabinet, moving with a quiet efficiency that said everything he wasn't saying aloud. He opened the pantry, reached for a bottle of Scotch, and poured a generous amount into each glass.

With his back still to me, he downed his in a single, practiced swallow. Then he poured himself another.

Only then did he turn, walking toward me with the second glass in hand. He passed it to me wordlessly, his eyes shadowed but steady. Bunny padded between us, her nails clicking softly on the stone as she circled. The paralyzing force Bastien had wielded lifted the moment the wind took him, and now she moved freely again—weaving in and out between us like a question with no answer.

She looked up at each of us in turn, her gaze shifting, searching, as if trying to make sense of what had changed. She knew something had. So did we.

I should have been a wreck after what I'd just witnessed—but I wasn't. I felt oddly numb, like my body had wrapped itself in gauze, protecting me from what I couldn't yet process.

Baird still said nothing. He just held out a hand.

I took it and followed as he led me up the stairs. He walked into the bathroom across from the master bedroom and set his glass down on the counter. Then he gently took mine from my hand and placed it beside his. Wordlessly, he began unbuttoning his shirt.

I watched him, uncertain what came next, but he didn't hesitate. He turned on the shower, letting the water warm, and then stepped toward me. His hands lifted the hem of my T-shirt and pulled it over my head. I kicked off my jeans and stripped naked as he did the same, and without a word, he stepped into the shower.

He held out his hand again. An invitation. A quiet insistence.

*This is where you belong.*

With him. In the warmth. In the stillness.

I stepped in.

He wrapped an arm around me and slid his back down the tiled wall, taking me with him, until we were both sitting beneath the spray. The water poured over us—hot, steady, cleansing. Neither of us spoke. We didn't need to.

We let it wash over us, down our shoulders, between our fingers, into every hollow space. Washing away what I'd seen, what he'd done. The weight of what we'd just endured.

Washing us clean.Making us new.

I don't know how long we sat there, wrapped in silence and steam. Time lost its meaning, melted by the rhythm of the water and the weight of everything we didn't say.

Eventually, we left the shower and made our way to the bed.

We clung to each other through the night—not in hunger or passion, but in something deeper. Of being the only two people who could understand what had just transpired. Participants in an event that didn't occur truly here, nor in a shadow realm, but between them, in the convergence of them. We needed to feel the other's skin, breath, touch—proof that we were still here. In the now. Still *us*.

No words passed between us. None were needed.

Tomorrow would be the day for words.

My class was ending, the emerald necklace nearly complete. And soon, I'd have to tell Baird. But somehow, I didn't think he'd ask for an explanation. He would understand—perhaps more than I wanted him to.

In the morning, I'd book my return flight. I'd leave in a day or two, slip back into the life I'd stepped out of like a dream. But that was tomorrow's burden.

Tonight, I let it go.

Tonight, I stayed here—in this moment, in this bed, with the only person who could meet me in the in-between.

We held on, our bodies tangled together out of a quiet, aching need to *be present*. To bear witness to each other's existence in that fragile moment. And sometime before dawn, wrapped in the hush of shared grief and the comfort of skin on skin, we finally drifted off to sleep.

# Chapter Fifty-Three
# BAIRD

H e rose before Mira, padding quietly through the house to put the coffee on and start breakfast. He remembered how ravenous she'd been last night just before Bastien arrived. He smiled faintly at the memory and set about cracking eggs, slicing bread, the motions familiar and grounding. He realized how much he enjoyed taking care of her. Not because Mira needed looking after—she was sharp, capable, and fiercely independent—but because it gave him a way to show her how deeply woven into his life she had become. He wasn't sure if that helped or hurt his case with her.

Mira had a way of turning everything over in her mind, poking holes in kindness, tracing the edges of her own uncertainty. He was sure she'd find fault in it somewhere—read it as overstepping, or worse, as some attempt to bind her to him. Still, he did it anyway. Not to prove anything. Just because he wanted to.

When she came downstairs dressed for class, he could see something weighing heavily on her. He didn't have to guess what it was.

"Out with it, Mira Garvie—when are ye leaving then?" he said, wanting this discussion out in the open. Better to have the truth of it between them than to let it linger and waste another second of their remaining time together.

Her eyes widened—shock flickering across them at the fact that he'd confronted her so directly. He wasn't going to let her drag this out.

"The day after tomorrow—it's an early morning flight," she said softly, with something in her voice that sounded like guilt.

"Ye could have left tonight after class, or tomorrow even—are ye giving me that extra day?" Baird asked lightly.

She wasn't running, not exactly. But she wasn't staying, either.

"Yes— What can I say?" she muttered, the words awkward and quiet, as if she were speaking to both Baird and herself. "I need to get back...get some distance from whatever *this* was, back to my real life. But the thought of doing it sooner—it felt like a knife in my chest."

Baird exhaled, slow and steady. He didn't want her to hurt, not for a second. But still, he felt a small relief in her confession. She wasn't as detached as she tried to seem. Her words may have been guarded, but the feeling behind them wasn't. She felt something for him—more than she was ready to admit.

Yet, anyway.

But he felt it. It was there—quiet, fragile, but real. And it grew a little more with each passing day. The confusion and disbelief that shadowed it hadn't lessened—if anything, they clung to her more tightly now, a protective layer she wasn't ready to shed.

But still, he could feel her trying to accept this thing inside her, growing more comfortable with the idea of Baird occupying that space in her heart—what she might finally admit was love for him. And for now, that was enough.

"Well," he said, injecting a little warmth into his voice, "I'll take the extra day and make the most of it."

He didn't want her to feel guilty for leaving. He wouldn't ask her for promises. He just wanted to make what they had—this small, strange, beautiful interlude—end on a note of joy. Something she could carry with her. Something that might make her want to come back.

"Would ye be interested in going for a sail with me tomorrow for a few hours?" Baird asked.

"You have a sailboat?" she asked, her brow creasing as her gaze locked onto his. There was curiosity there, yes—but also a flicker of something else. Bewilderment. Maybe even a trace of worry. He recognized it instantly, the dawning weight of all the things she didn't yet know. Not just about the boat, but about him—about the life he led before she stumbled into it.

Baird shifted slightly, reading her expression like a map. She wasn't afraid, not exactly. But he could see her mind working, recalibrating. And it struck him—how much trust she had already given him, and how fragile that trust still was.

"I do, in fact. I think I told ye I made a living at it at one point—*sailing*, that is," Baird said, his smirk on full display. "Still enjoy getting out on the water. The boat is docked here in Edinburgh, although I've had it docked on Arran too. Ye don't get boky on the water, do ye?"

"Seasick? No. I learned that word—*'boky'*—from Evie the day before I woke up on your couch."

Mira looked pale and distant, the usual spark in her eyes dimmed by whatever storm she was quietly weathering. Baird hated seeing her like this—drifting in a current he couldn't pull her from—but he understood, at least in part, that this was something she had to move through on her own. No words or the comfort of his arms could untangle what was going on inside her. Not this time.

"I guess I don't need you to drive me to class today—or keep watch," she said, her voice flat, almost hollow.

"Nae, lass—ye don't," Baird replied gently, his chest tightening. "But I'd be happy to drive ye."

He tried to keep his tone light, but the truth was, the thought of her going off on her own—of no longer needing him—settled around him like rain clouds. For one short week, his entire focus had been narrowed to keeping her safe, close, and he realized they'd been the very best days of his life. Now, with that purpose fading, he was left with a hollow ache and the creeping realization that he might need to start figuring out how to live without her again.

Even if he wasn't ready. Even if he didn't want to.

# CHAPTER FIFTY-FOUR

## MIRA

Every moment—every breath—of my final day of class, I hovered on the edge of tears. It was absurd, I told myself, to feel this fragile. Even in the raw, disorienting days after my parents died, I hadn't unraveled like this. I'd held it together then. But now, in this quiet goodbye to a place and a man who upended everything I thought I knew, I felt like I was splintering.

I tried to reason my way through it, blaming exhaustion, upheaval, the sheer weight of everything I'd faced since my parents had died, since I'd touched the portrait. Of course I was emotional—it was the cumulative effect of grief and danger, of these revelations that rewrote my understanding of the world. I missed my quiet life back home. I missed the person I used to be—logical, rational, grounded. The girl who had a plan, who always knew the next step.

So why, then, did leaving feel like a loss I couldn't quite bear? Why did the thought of walking away from all of this—chaotic, strange, extraordinary—leave me feeling more hollow than whole?

I still had a long day ahead of me, and no time to fall apart. So I did what I'd always done when emotions threatened to overwhelm me—I pushed them down, willed myself into focus, and turned to the work. The pendant sat before me, nearly complete, waiting for its final details. There was comfort in the precision of it, in the quiet ritual of the bench.

I began by heating the thermal plastic fixing compound until it softened, the scent of it rising faintly in the air. Once it was pliable, I pressed the pendant into the warm material, shaping it around the edges until it cradled the piece snugly. As it cooled back to room temperature, it hardened just enough to hold the pendant firmly in place without damaging the delicate granulation pattern I'd spent hours perfecting. Carefully, I set the whole piece into a pin vise, securing it with gentle pressure. Only then, with the piece steady before me, did I allow myself to breathe deeply, to lose myself in the meticulous rhythm of setting the stones—one by one, in silence, as if anchoring myself with each deliberate touch.

I started with the largest emerald, the heart of the piece, cradling it gently between my fingers before placing it into the bezel. The green shimmer caught the light, vivid and deep, like something alive. My tools of choice for this part of the job—the old-fashioned hammer and bezel pusher—felt like an extension of my hands by now, and I began the delicate work.

I bent the edge of the bezel over one long end of the oval stone with a measured tap, then spun the vise and repeated the process on the opposite side. Each movement was deliberate, precise. I alternated sides methodically, always working directly across from the last point of contact, ensuring the stone settled perfectly level, perfectly centered. It was slow work, demanding full focus—exactly what I needed.

Once the emerald was seated just right, I continued with what felt like hundreds of tiny, careful taps, working my way around the edge of the bezel. The soft, rhythmic sound of gold yielding beneath the pusher echoed in my ears like a heartbeat. With every tap, I tightened the lip of gold around the stone, securing not just the emerald but, in a way, myself, if only for this moment.

With the main stone secured, I turned my attention to the four smaller round emeralds that encircled it, each one a delicate echo of the centerpiece. I picked them up one by one with fine-tipped tweezers, their facets flashing as I nestled each into its waiting seat. My hands moved with calm precision, years of practice guiding me through the sequence—set, check, tap, repeat. These stones didn't require the same weight of force as the central emerald, but they demanded just as much care. Each had to be level, each perfectly aligned, their symmetry vital to the pendant's balance and beauty.

Once all four were in place and snugly secured, I reached for my graver, the small tool gleaming in the overhead light. With patient, practiced pressure, I traced along the inner lip of each bezel, refining the edges that held the stones. The graver left behind a crisp, clean line—a subtle brilliance that caught the light just so, making the settings gleam with a professional, finished sharpness.

Satisfied at last, I powered on the heat gun again and gently warmed the thermal plastic until it softened. Slowly, I pulled the pendant free, lifting it from the vise like a precious relic. The gold was warm to the touch, the emeralds glowing like embers caught in sunlight.

The last step was always my favorite—the transformation. With the stones set and the form complete, it was time to bring out the true beauty of the piece. I set the pendant aside briefly as I prepared my tools: the bench polisher, the flex shaft grinder, and an array of polishing compounds laid out in their familiar order. There was something meditative about this part, a rhythm I could lose myself in.

After covering the delicate emeralds with some protective tape and cutting around them with an X-ACTO knife to expose the metal, I began with the brown compound, pressing the pendant gently against the spinning wheel of the bench polisher. The abrasive grit worked quickly, buffing away any fine scratches left from setting and handling. Then I switched to the red—jeweler's rouge—a finer polish that smoothed the surface and began to coax out a warm gleam from the gold. With the flex shaft, I worked into the tighter spaces around the bezels and filigree, careful not to overheat the metal or mar the sharp lines I'd worked so hard to create.

Finally, I turned to the blue compound, the last and most delicate of the series. As the soft wheel touched the pendant, a mirror-like shine began to emerge, the gold coming alive beneath my hands. The emeralds sparkled, their clarity enhanced by the crisp, flawless settings. By the time I was finished, the pendant gleamed with a brilliance that made my breath catch for just a moment. It was complete—perfect, even—and for the first time all day, I felt the faint flicker of pride break through the heaviness that had lingered since morning.

With the final polish complete, I peeled away the now blackened protective tape that had shielded the delicate stones during the polishing process. I carried the pendant to the sink and gave it a gentle but thorough cleaning with a soft toothbrush and warm water, working carefully around the bezels and under the settings to lift away any remaining polishing compound. When I was satisfied, I patted it dry with a soft cloth, my fingers tracing the smooth curves of the metal like a quiet goodbye.

From my bag, I retrieved the 18 karat gold foxtail chain—substantial, sinuous, almost serpentine in its texture. It was the perfect match for the pendant's weight and dimensionality, each link catching the light in a subtle dance that echoed the flicker of the emeralds. I threaded it through the bail at the top of the pendant, the motion slow, deliberate.

Then I sat back and simply stared at it. The finished piece shimmered in my palm, a perfect union of my vision and the new technique I had learned. Pride bloomed in my chest—sharp and bright—but it was tangled with something heavier. Accomplishment warred with sorrow, and the ache of what came next.

It was beautiful.

It was done.

And I was miserable.

# Chapter Fifty-Five

## Mira

I walked through the door and was immediately wrapped in the warmth of Baird's home. Something smelled incredible—roasted garlic, maybe, or rosemary—and Bunny trotted up to greet me, her nails clicking softly on the floor as she pressed her nose into my leg. I dropped a hand to scratch behind her ears, already feeling the tightness in my chest start to ease. Down the hall, I could hear Baird in the kitchen, humming low under his breath between the sound of pans shifting and cupboard doors swinging open and closed. I followed the sound, dropping my bag by the stairs, and made my way to the counter, where I pulled up a stool and let myself breathe in the scent and the comfort of him.

"Well...where is it?" he asked, not looking up right away but grinning as he stirred something in a saucepan.

"Oh—the necklace," I said, surprised he'd been waiting so eagerly. It hadn't occurred to me that he might care quite so much. I reached into my tote bag and pulled out the leather box. Something about it reminded me of the one that held Agnes's portrait. Maybe it was just the gravity of it—what it contained.

I flipped the latch and popped the lid open, and there it was: the pendant, glowing with the rich, impossible green of the emeralds against the buttery gleam of the gold. It had turned out better than I'd imagined—somehow brighter, deeper, as if the emotion poured into it had become something tangible. I turned toward him and held it out.

Baird took it in silence, his fingers brushing the edge of the pendant like he was afraid to disturb it. He didn't speak, didn't smile, just stared at it—his face unreadable but intent. I saw something shift in his expression, something deep and reverent, like the look he'd given Agnes's portrait that night in my hotel room. He nodded silently to himself, as if confirming something. And then he looked up at me—expectant, yes, but with something more.

"What do ye plan to do with it?"

"Originally I'd planned to sell it," I said. "But I can't now. I knew before I even finished it. It's too personal—maybe the most personal thing I've ever made." It had become a gold and gemstone archive of everything I'd been through.

"All that happened since I came to Scotland is tied up in this piece somehow—it's all in here, like it got pressed into the gold along with the stones." I gave a small, almost sheepish laugh. "Maybe I'll make others like it, now that I've learned the technique. But that one? No. It stays with me."

"Good—I was hoping ye'd say that." Baird smiled. "I want to see this on ye. Will ye wear it for me later?" he asked, eyes hopeful.

"Yes, I haven't even tried it on yet," I said. "What are you making? It smells delicious."

"Ah, just a roast chicken and some vegetables," he said casually, as if he hadn't put thought into every detail. "Maybe leftover chicken sandwich for ye on the boat tomorrow? Whatever is left, Bunny can have," he added, his voice trailing just slightly at the end.

Then he said it—quietly, almost too casually. "Ye know—after ye leave."

The words hung there. He didn't look up from the cutting board, his knife slicing through a carrot with practiced ease, but I felt the shift in the air. The way he tucked that final phrase in like it was nothing, when it was everything. *'After ye leave.'* As if he hadn't just held the most personal thing I'd ever made in his hands with a look that nearly undid me.

He poured me a glass of wine without asking, and I took it gratefully, the warmth as it went down softening something tight in my chest. I sipped in silence while he worked, watching the ease of his movements—how he slid the cut carrots and potatoes into the roasting pan with the chicken, the way his broad shoulders moved beneath the soft cotton of his shirt. It felt so domestic, so ordinary. And yet nothing about it felt small.

"How did you learn to cook? It seems an odd skill for a man born when you were," I asked, sipping my wine.

It was a question that came out of nowhere, and yet, one of the countless things I felt I should have already asked. A thread among a million, and I was grasping at it, aware—painfully aware—that my time with him was running out.

"I suppose that's true. My granny used to let me help her prepare meals when I spent my summers with her. Then when I lived on my own, before Agnes and I married, I cooked some. Just enjoyed it—*forgot how I enjoyed it*," he said, and I wondered if his mind was in the past as he shared this detail. "Probably thirty minutes or so still until it's ready."

"I think I'll grab a quick shower, put something clean on," I replied, holding up my hands to show him the stubborn black smudges still clinging to the creases of my fingers. "The polishing compound gets into everything—it's like ink. I scrubbed at the Guild before I came back, but it's going to take a bit more work to get it all off."

He gave a small, almost amused nod, his gaze briefly drifting to my hands before returning to the task at hand.

After my shower, I padded back downstairs with damp hair clinging to my neck, dressed in clean jeans and a soft T-shirt that smelled faintly of lavender soap. The kitchen was warm with the scent of roasted garlic and rosemary, a few candles on the table, their soft glow flickering against the glass, casting long shadows that danced across the walls. Two glasses of wine were already poured. He sat at the table, cradling his glass, eyes distant as he stared out over the darkened terrace. I didn't have to ask what he was thinking about—I knew. He was remembering the night before. So was I.

When he heard me step in, he looked up, and something softened in his expression.

"Sit. I'll ready yer plate..." he said gently, rising from his seat.

I slipped into the chair across from where he'd been, the candlelight catching the droplets still clinging to the ends of my hair. I looked out toward the terrace too, where the night pressed close, thick and quiet. The memory of it all was still chasing me, like a breath on the back of my neck.

I tried to make sense of what had happened—what it meant, what we were supposed to carry forward. Bastien had spoken in riddles and truths too heavy to hold. Was it a warning? A blessing? A passing of something ancient from one soul to another? I couldn't tell. I only knew that something had shifted in both of us. And now we had to decide what to do with it.

I ate in silence, and Baird's gaze moved from me to the terrace and back to me so many times, I lost count. It was almost as if he were looking for something in me that he couldn't find now, and it made me anxious. I thought about that first night we'd sat in this spot and drank, a different kind of tension between us then. The silence tonight was deafening and made me claustrophobic.

"I feel like we're strangers all of a sudden," I said, the words slipping out before I could temper them, raw and unpolished. I wasn't trying to wound—I was just trying to name the ache that had been threading through me all day.

Baird set down his glass and looked at me with that steady, unflinching gaze. "Nae, lass. Not strangers," he said softly. "Yer guard is up now, is all. That first night..." A crooked smile tugged at the corner of his mouth, and the glint in his eyes made the meaning unmistakable—he'd been comparing the nights too. "Ye were wide open to me," he said, voice low.

Heat flickered through me despite the heaviness of the moment, and he saw it—of course he did.

"My guard's up too," he continued, more serious now. "Not the same way as yours, but...it's there. We're both carryin' something we weren't back then. And it's weighin' on us."

The chicken really was perfect—tender, rich, fragrant—but I could only pick at it, distracted not just by the tension between us, but by the memories he'd so deftly stirred. That first night had been reckless and breathless and real. I wanted that back—wanted to crawl out from behind this grief and uncertainty, just for a little while. To feel him again, to remind myself of what we were before the truth had come out.

Maybe I needed to let go. To stop guarding myself like I was already gone. Because I wasn't—not yet. The thought echoed through me like a vow, quiet but firm. I rose from my chair and walked slowly toward him, so much like that first night—how I had gone to him without hesitation, without second thoughts—but tonight, every step held weight. I was slower. Softer. A little afraid. But I moved anyway.

When I reached him, he looked up at me, and I saw it—the flicker of relief in his eyes, like he'd been waiting, hoping, not sure if I'd come. And maybe neither of us had been sure what we needed until now.

It had only been two nights since we'd last been together, but the distance between then and now felt enormous. So much had happened—too much. Pain I had caused him, truths that had wounded us both. And the deep, dark rupture someone else had carved into us. We were still bleeding from it in places unseen.

I moved closer, swinging my leg over his and settling into his lap, straddling him in the chair. My hands braced lightly on his shoulders, and I felt the shift in his breath, the way his body tensed, then softened beneath me. For a moment, we just stayed like that, eyes locked, the air between us thick with everything unspoken. This wasn't about desire. Not just. It was about needing to remember who we were when all the rest had fallen away.

He leaned in and kissed me—softly, slowly—each brush of his lips deliberate, solemn. Too slow for me. I ached for the rush, for the desperate, hungry part where we lost ourselves in each other. But when I opened my eyes and looked at him, I saw it clearly: that wasn't what this was going to be. This time, it wasn't about escape—it was about being here and now. About choosing tenderness when everything else had been chaos. So I let him lead, and I followed willingly.

It wasn't hesitation in him—not even close. His desire was unmistakable. I could feel his hardness through his jeans, pressing against me, right where I already burned for him. My breath hitched at the contact, and a quiet gasp slipped from my lips, but he didn't rush. He deepened the kiss, one hand splaying wide against my lower back, the other curving around my hip before settling on my ass. In one smooth motion, he lifted me, and I clung to him, legs wrapping around his waist like it was second nature.

He started toward the stairs, and just before we reached them, he paused, bent slightly, and picked up the tote bag I'd dropped earlier. Then he carried me upstairs, the steady strength of him grounding me in a way nothing else could. I buried my face in the curve of his neck, breathing him in, letting the thud of his heart against mine drown out everything else.

He set me down gently at the edge of the bed, his hands lingering at my waist as if reluctant to let me go. But then he stepped back slightly, his gaze sweeping over me with something deeper than hunger—veneration. There was no urgency in his movements, just intent. He reached for the button of my jeans and unfastened it slowly, the zipper slipping down with a soft hum. Then he crouched, easing the denim over my hips, down my legs, his fingers trailing lightly against my skin as he went.

When he stood again, his hands found the hem of my T-shirt. He lifted it over my head in one fluid motion, his knuckles grazing the undersides of my arms as the fabric slipped away. I shivered—not from cold, but from the quiet intensity of his attention. He didn't speak, didn't rush. Just watched me, as if committing every detail to memory.

And then I was standing before him in nothing but my bra and panties, the soft rise and fall of my breath the only sound between us.

He still hadn't moved to undress. He just stood there, his gaze roaming over me slowly, observant, like he was memorizing every contour of my skin, every curve and hollow. It was more than desire—it was as if he was studying me like a map, one he never wanted to lose. The silence between us pulsed with something electric, something sacred.

"Necklace..." he said softly, the single word thick with meaning.

I followed his eyes and realized what he meant. He wanted to see me wearing it.

I turned and picked up my tote, fingers fumbling slightly as I searched for the leather box. My hands were trembling—not with nerves, exactly, but with something deeper. I'd never felt this kind of weight before when putting on something I'd made. This wasn't just gold and emeralds. It was a vessel of everything I'd lived through, every shift in who I'd become.

I handed it to him without a word, and he stepped behind me. His fingers brushed my nape as he opened the clasp, then a subtle pull as he fastened it at the base of my neck. The pendant dropped against my skin with a cool kiss, the weight of it settling just above my cleavage. I inhaled sharply—not just from the temperature of the metal, but from the intimacy of the moment. Of his touch. Of what this meant.

His hands didn't leave me right away. They rested on my shoulders, grounding me. And in the mirror across the room, I caught a glimpse of us—me, half-naked and adorned in something I'd poured my soul into, and him, still fully clothed, standing behind me like some immovable force. Like this was a ritual. A claiming. A goodbye. Or maybe something else entirely. I turned to face him and stood there, one hand against his chest.

He began unbuttoning his shirt with the same unhurried deliberateness he'd used to undress me—as if every movement was its own promise. One button, then the next. My breath caught with each one, the anticipation itself a kind of exquisite ache. The somber look he'd worn for most of the evening had softened, replaced now by something deeper, more certain—a quiet, knowing smile that told me he was fully here, fully with me.

He unfastened the waist of his jeans, then slowly slid the zipper down. The sound alone made my pulse stutter. When he let them fall to the floor, he didn't rush to step out of them. He just stood there, watching me with that steady intensity, like I was the only thing in the world worth seeing.

When he was fully naked, his fingers found the strap of my bra. He hooked one under it and let it slide slowly down my arm. I reached behind me to unhook it, the clasp giving way with a soft snap. The fabric fell away, and the look in his eyes as he took me in made me feel bare in more than body—like he saw all of me and wanted it anyway.

He pressed me gently back onto the bed, his hands sure but tender, and then he slid my panties down my legs with the same adoration he'd shown every other part of me. There was no rush, no urgency—only the deep, quiet intensity of two people choosing each other again. Choosing connection, even knowing the end was near.

His body loomed over mine, solid and warm, and I parted my legs in invitation, welcoming the weight of him as he settled between them. He propped himself up with one hand, the other trailing slowly up my neck and back down again, his fingertips grazing the chain until they found the pendant resting just above the swell of my breasts. He touched each emerald in turn, and then the gold, as if reading a secret message etched into the metal.

He bent to kiss me—first my mouth, deep and sensual—then lower, his lips moving to my breasts. He worshipped them, sucking softly, first one nipple, then the other, lingering at the sides and undersides with a devotion that made my breath hitch. When his mouth drifted across the pendant, he paused for a beat, eyes closed, his lips pressing against it like he was kissing a rosary. Something sacred.

Then he moved lower, his kisses trailing down my belly, growing more urgent as they reached the place I needed him most. His mouth found the wet heat between my legs with a hunger that unspooled me completely. His tongue moved in slow, deliberate strokes, teasing and tasting, until I was writhing beneath him, soft cries spilling from my lips as he drew my clit into his mouth and sucked, sending shudders through me so sharp I thought I might break.

I needed more. I needed him inside me—needed that deep, perfect joining that felt like being made whole again, like a key slipping into a long-locked door. He must have felt it too, because he pulled back with a murmur and rolled onto his back, taking me with him. I moved with instinct, reaching between us to guide him, his thick length pulsing in my hand. I positioned him at my entrance and pushed back slowly, taking all of him, inch by inch, until he was fully seated and I was filled.

A cry tore from my throat—half relief, half ache. I closed my eyes and let my body mold to his, knowing that in this moment, nothing else mattered but the way we fit. Like two halves reunited.

I was so close—had been for what felt like an eternity. My body was strung tight with need, trembling at the edge, every nerve lit and waiting, every movement stoking the slow burn inside me. I moved above him, rocking steadily, feeling the stretch and fullness of him deep inside, grounding me, unraveling me. The rhythm built in waves, and

I let it—surrendering, clinging to the sensation of being completely possessed, completely *seen*.

He reached up again, fingertips grazing the pendant that now lay between my breasts, and then he trailed them higher—over my sternum, my throat—until he cupped my jaw, guiding my face down toward his. His eyes were locked on mine, unwavering, demanding something I didn't fully understand. *Don't look away*, they said. *Stay with me.*

And I did.

Something passed between us then—something that wasn't just physical. It felt like worship, yes, but not just of the body. Like he was trying to show me something beyond either of us, some truth too deep for words. And though I couldn't grasp it, I let myself be open to it, let it wash over me.

My climax hit not just from sensation but from *that*—the raw, soul-deep connection blazing in his eyes. It pushed me over the edge, white-gold pleasure searing through me in waves, starting where we were joined and radiating outward—north, south, east, and west—until I was nothing but light and sound. I cried out, the sound torn from somewhere primal, but I kept my eyes on his, even through it—*especially* through it—and what I saw there made my heart ache. His joy, his awe, the trembling devotion written so clearly across his face. I wanted to give him that same unraveling. That same holy undoing. I wanted to see him come apart the way he'd just watched me. And I wasn't going to stop until he did.

Despite feeling boneless and undone, every muscle still quivering from my release, I kept moving. I rode the edge of that afterglow, hips rolling in a steady rhythm, my palms splayed against his chest to anchor me. His heartbeat thundered beneath my hands, matching the rush still echoing in my own veins. The pendant swung slightly between us, catching the light, and he reached up and cradled it in his palm, as if it had a role in this act between us.

I felt the shift in him, the subtle hitch in his breath, the way his rhythm faltered just slightly—his tell. I'd come to know it, to anticipate it. The moment before he gave in.

He let the pendant go, and both hands came to my hips, gripping tight, grounding us both. He thrust up into me with raw urgency, his hips lifting off the bed to meet mine, pushing me down harder, deeper. I gasped as he cried out beneath me, the sound low and rough, torn from someplace buried. His head tilted back, lips parted, but his eyes were still locked on mine as he surrendered to his release, and I drank in every detail—his voice, the tension in his arms, the way his body arched into mine as if it was the only place he belonged.

I wanted to burn that moment into memory. Not just the look on his face or the feel of him pulsing inside me—but the truth of it. That something had passed between us that was more than want, more than pleasure. It was a connection I'd never felt and didn't expect to feel again. Whatever happened after this, I would carry *this* with me. Always.

I collapsed onto his chest, our bodies still tangled, my skin damp from the shared exertion. He wrapped his arms around me without hesitation, one hand stroking slowly up and down my back, the other holding me close. We laid like that for a long while, the rhythm of our hearts and breathing gradually syncing, slowing, returning to something like peace. His lips brushed against my hair now and then—soft, tender kisses that seemed to say *this matters too*. This quiet after, this stillness between us—it was just as sacred as everything that came before.

Eventually, he shifted beneath me and sat up, and I followed, reluctantly pulling myself upright.

"Let me take that off you…" he murmured, his fingers reaching behind my neck to unclasp the necklace. I lifted my hair for him, and he removed it with care, catching the pendant in his hand as it fell forward. He paused, cupping it in his palm as if weighing it—its meaning, its memory. Then, with a tenderness that undid me all over again, he lifted it to his lips and kissed it once more, a final seal, before rising from the bed.

He crossed the room in silence, placed the necklace gently back into its leather case, and then tucked it into my tote as if returning a relic to its resting place. When he came back to the bed, he slid in beside me, stacking pillows behind him, and laid back, his body a familiar fortress I sank into without hesitation. I curled into the space he always made for me, under his arm, my head resting against his chest. Neither of us spoke. We didn't need to. We simply breathed together, wrapped in the warmth and quiet of what we'd reclaimed.

We made love again, and then again, as if repetition could stretch time, could anchor us in this quiet cocoon where nothing else could intrude, but before we finally drifted off, he made a request.

"Mira," his voice low, breath soft against my forehead. "I hope you'll wear it—*the necklace.*"

"It's not very practical," I said with a small laugh. "I can't imagine finding an occasion to wear it—where I'd need something that special."

Baird made a soft sound of disapproval, that familiar rumble in his chest. "Nonsense," he said, gently but firmly. "I hope ye wear it every day. And think about yer time with me—the parts that were good. I want ye to remember only that."

His words wrapped around me like a security blanket, and for a moment, I let myself believe it could be that simple. I thought back over everything—every wild, tangled moment since I'd arrived in Scotland. The fear, the uncertainty, the things I'd learned about the world and myself that I could never unlearn. But when I tried to hold on to the bad, it slipped through my fingers, dull and distant, already softening at the edges.

What shimmered instead were the bright pieces: the laughter, the way Baird looked at me, the touch of his fingers on my skin, the wicked smirk that completely undid me each and every time I saw it, and the sound of my name when he said it. Somehow, impossibly, those moments outshone everything else.

The only darkness that lingered, sharp and immovable, was the one still ahead—the day after tomorrow, when I'd leave Baird. Leave Scotland. And the ache of it was already growing, solid and cold in my chest. Because no matter how many good memories I carried with me, I knew I had to leave this behind.

# Chapter Fifty-Six
## BAIRD

A s Baird guided the thirty-seven-foot sailboat out of the marina, his hands were sure on the wheel, movements measured and precise. The early morning light cast a golden shimmer over the water, and the air was thick with the scent of salt and seaweed. He kept a slow, steady course, steering with the patience of someone who understood the rhythms of the harbor—the tide, the currents, the dance of vessels coming and going. He nodded to a passing skipper on a fishing boat returning from a long night offshore and gave them a wide berth, letting their wake roll past harmlessly beneath the hull.

Once they cleared the last of the buoys and the harbor fell behind them, he brought the bow head-to-wind. The mainsail went up first, lines taut and snapping, the canvas billowing briefly before catching. Then the headsail unfurled, crisp and white against the pale blue sky. He reached down and cut the engine, the hum falling away to leave only the sound of water against the hull and the gentle creak of the rigging. Sailing was second nature to Baird. It steadied him, gave him a sense of control and quiet power all at once. And more than anything, he wanted Mira to see him like this—in his element, as the man he used to be.

The boat heeled softly as the wind filled the sails, and Baird adjusted his course, easing them into a clean tack. The bow sliced through the swells, steady and true, the sea opening wide before them. Ahead lay nothing but open water and a distant horizon.

He stood at the helm, legs planted wide for balance, facing east as the first blush of sunrise painted the sky in soft pinks and golden light. Cotton candy clouds stretched across the horizon, their edges glowing, and the sea mirrored it all in gentle ripples. The wind tugged at his hair, the sails hummed with tension, and beneath his feet, the boat moved like a living thing—responsive, steady, free.

Baird loved it out here. Always had. There was a clarity on the water he couldn't find anywhere else, a peace that came not from silence, but from a kind of honest motion. And yet somehow, over the years, he'd let this part of his life slip away slowly. Maybe because this had always brought him joy—and for so long, he'd convinced himself joy was something he didn't deserve.

But this past week had cracked him open.

Mira had cracked him open.

The joy had come back, not as a whisper but as a roar, a desperate, exhilarating rush that had reminded him who he used to be—who he still was, underneath all the guilt and the grief. He could feel it now, stirring like wind in the sails, impossible to ignore. He'd been empty too long. And now that he knew what fullness felt like again, he couldn't bear to go back.

Mira stood with her back to the sunrise, its golden light turning the tips of her dark hair to fire. She wasn't watching the dawn—she was watching him. Her arms were folded loosely across her chest, her body swaying gently with the motion of the boat, and her gaze stayed fixed on

Baird at the helm. There was a smile on her lips, soft and steady, and it reached her eyes in a way that told him something had shifted. She was seeing a part of him she hadn't seen before.

And that scared him just a little.

Not because he had anything left to hide, but because he knew Mira's mind—sharp, relentless, always reaching for the deeper layers. She questioned everything, doubting before she dared to trust. It was part of her nature. He loved that about her, even when it unsettled him. But standing there, feeling her eyes on him, he couldn't help but wonder if her thoughts had drifted to all she *didn't* yet know about him.

She had a way of taking the unknown and wrapping it around the things she refused to see, obscuring what stared back at her too plainly. That was how she held the thing between them: not with open hands, but with caution, with the kind of careful distance a person uses when they're afraid to hope.

It wasn't that she didn't *feel* it. He knew she felt it, and he held on to that knowledge. But believing it? Trusting that it could be real, enduring, meant letting go of the part of her that clung to logic and control. No, he saw how hard that was for her.

He beckoned her over with a tilt of his head and a soft lift of his hand, the invitation clear and wordless: *Come here, lass.* He needed her close—not only for himself, but for her. He knew her too well. Knew how silence gave her mind space to spiral, how she could take a rare moment of peace and twist it into doubt. But when she was in his arms, the spinning slowed. And maybe—just maybe—she could *feel* what she still struggled to believe.

She crossed the deck, and he stepped back from the helm, pulling her into him with practiced ease. One arm wrapped firmly around her upper back, anchoring her to him, while the other hand stayed steady on the wheel.

"Will ye take a picture with me? I want one of ye to remember this—remember *us*," he said, his voice low, thick with emotion he was trying hard to steady.

She nodded, the answer clear in her eyes. He could see she wanted that memory too. Something tangible. Something to hold on to.

Baird pulled out his phone and raised his arm, angling it above them. They both leaned in, trying for smiles—shaky, tender, the kind that held more sorrow than joy. A bittersweet snapshot of a moment they both knew they'd never want to forget.

When it was done, he put his phone away and pulled her back into his arms, holding her close like he could imprint her shape into his memory more surely than pixels ever could. He kissed the top of her head, lips brushing her hair, damp from the sea spray. He moved his hand from the back of her neck, fingers trailing along the curve of her jaw until his thumb found that familiar dimple in her chin.

He lifted her face gently, urging her to look at him—not with words, but with touch. Her eyes met his, and for a moment, she let it happen, her features open, searching. But then something shifted. A flicker of something behind her eyes—a flash of confusion or fear—and a look of shock crossed her face.

His heart dropped.

He held her tighter, suddenly unsure what he'd triggered. What unseen battle she was waging inside that beautiful, relentless mind.

"Mira—*what is it*?" he asked, his voice low, threaded with concern.

She didn't answer right away. Her lower lip trembled, and then a single tear slipped free, carving a slow path down her cheek. Without a word, she pressed her face against his chest and clung to him, her arms wrapping tight around his waist as though bracing herself against a storm only she could feel.

He held her close, resting his chin lightly against the top of her head, one hand stroking slow circles across her back. But the silence stretched, and the ache in his chest deepened.

"What is it? Tell me..." he whispered again. When she still didn't speak, he tried to lighten it, just a little, his voice tilting into warmth. "Don't tell me yer seasick after all."

She let out a quiet sound—not quite a laugh, not quite a sob. Her grip around him only tightened.

"It was just—standing here with you, with your hand on my chin like that, it reminded me of something—that's all," she said into his chest, wiping her eyes, the wind whipping her hair, her words stopping briefly before continuing. "It reminded me of the first vision I had, the one when I touched Agnes's portrait, the way you touched my—*I mean, her*—chin. It was like it was replaying in my head. Everything—the way you smell, the sun on my face, I don't know. It's silly, I know." She trailed off.

He hated himself a little now for suggesting the sail in the first place. At the time, it seemed like it might be something quiet and beautiful to ease the ache between them, to create one last memory that wasn't heavy with endings. But he hadn't considered how easily the memory of Agnes could slip in like a shadow beneath the sunlight.

He tightened his arms around Mira as the realization settled in, the guilt creeping in slow and sharp. He hadn't meant to bring her pain—not again. But maybe he'd misjudged her strength or misunderstood what she still carried. Agnes's ghost wasn't gone. It lived in Mira in all the quiet moments. The single touch of a portrait that had turned Mira's world upside down.

"Dinnae fash," he whispered, head bent so she could hear. "Today is no' for cryin', lass. There will be time for that, but let's not waste a moment of our last day together on tears."

He swallowed hard, pressing another kiss to Mira's hair, and said no more. Just held her tighter, wishing he could pull her far enough into his chest to protect her from every ghost, even the ones he'd unwittingly summoned. He wondered if Mira's tears weren't just for what she was leaving behind but for what she might never truly be able to make peace with. For the space Agnes still occupied—uninvited, unresolved—between them. But he hoped, with everything in him, that someday she'd come to understand what he already knew deep in his bones: Agnes had never stood between them. Not really. Not in any way that mattered. Because what he felt for Mira had never been a shadow of the past—it was its own light, fierce and hot. And he needed her to see that, even if it took time. Even if it took letting her go.

Trying to hold on to her now would be the worst thing he could do. She needed space, time to make sense of it all. Time to breathe. So he would let her go, even as every part of him wanted to try to make her stay. And he hoped—whether through fate, or divine mercy, or some quiet whisper from the universe—that she would receive the one message he couldn't give voice to: That his love for her was hers alone. Singular.

That she was not merely someone he loved—but the one he was *meant* to love. The missing piece that made him feel whole for the first time in his long, fractured life. And in the strange symmetry of it all, he found himself clinging to the words of the man he had hated for so long.

Bastien had said Baird knew Mira better than she knew herself.

And God help him, he hoped that was true.

# Chapter Fifty-Seven

# Mira

We got back to Baird's house in the early afternoon, sea salt still clinging to our skin. I felt tired in that satisfying, sun-kissed way that only comes from being out on the water. But more than that, I felt...grateful. Grateful that I'd gotten to see this part of him.

Watching him on the boat had been like watching a memory made flesh—some version of Baird from long ago surfacing through the present. The way he moved with the vessel, sure-footed and instinctive, it was as though the boat was an extension of him, a forgotten limb he'd only just remembered how to use. I saw a flicker then of the man he must have been nearly 250 years ago, before time and grief and Bastien had taken so much from him.

I felt a pang of guilt for breaking down in his arms, for letting the déjà vu wash over me and steal the moment—when really, I should have been holding onto it with everything I had. But I couldn't help it. The feeling had hit me like a wave, so eerily similar to the vision I'd had in my dining room back in Marblehead. Baird's arms around me, the sea behind us, the weight of something ancient and invisible pressing close—it had all come flooding back, too much to carry without cracking a little.

But even through the guilt, I knew something else: that moment, that vision—it had been a gift. From the universe, from Agnes, from something older and wiser than I could name. Without it, I never would've come here. Never would've stepped into this strange, beautiful, terrifying world. I wouldn't have had the last week with Baird—the laughter nor the heartbreak. I wouldn't have had last night—the way he'd touched me like I was something sacred—or today, watching him reclaim the sea that still belonged to him.

And for that, I would never be anything but grateful.

After dinner and a shower, we settled in front of the fire, tucked into a chair just big enough for both of us, our bodies curved together in easy silence. The fire crackled softly, casting flickering shadows across the stone hearth and warming the air with a slow, gentle heat. I curled into Baird's side, my legs draped over his, a glass of wine cradled in my hand, the stem cool against my fingers.

He held a tumbler of Scotch, the amber liquid catching the firelight like liquid gold. I'd come to recognize that as more than just a drink—it was his crutch when the world pressed in too heavily. A way to withstand memory, or the past, or an uncertain future that weighed on him in moments like this.

I felt the words pressing against the back of my throat—things I needed to say, questions I wasn't even sure how to form, let alone expect answers to. Maybe neither of us had them. Maybe some things weren't meant to be resolved. But still, holding them back felt like holding part of myself back from *him*, and I didn't want to do that. Not now. Not after everything.

The truth was, the new parts of me—the ones I barely recognized, the way his eyes saw through every wall I'd ever built—those parts only existed because I'd let him in. Because I'd let myself *be* with him, fully, vulnerably, without pretense.

And if I walked away without giving him all of me—the messy, unfinished thoughts, the fears, the raw hope—I'd be carrying a version of myself forward that wasn't whole. So I took a breath, gathering the courage to speak, to let the unsaid find its shape between us. Because this—whatever *this* was—deserved nothing less than honesty.

"What's wrong with me?" I asked. "Why can't I believe this—that it's really for me?"

He sat with that for a moment, his thumb tracing idle circles against my arm, and I could see the thoughts flickering behind his eyes—see him reaching for the words that might explain it all. Explain *me* to me, as if he understood something I hadn't yet unraveled. But whatever clarity he had faltered before it could take shape, and instead, he let it slip away in favor of something easier. Safer.

"Beyond ye being a stubborn, obstinate, headstrong thing?" he said, lips curving into a crooked smile, that teasing lilt softening the weight of everything he didn't say.

I rolled my eyes, but I couldn't help the smile that tugged at my mouth in response. It was his way of pulling me back from the edge—of reminding me that even in all the uncertainty, there was still this: the banter, the warmth, the knowing. Still *us*.

"I canna explain this fear ye have. I loved Agnes. I'll never deny that," Baird said quietly, his voice steady but thick with something deeper. "But I've lived two lives—thirty-nine years the first time, and two hundred and forty since that life ended. And in neither of them...neither...have I ever felt what I feel when I am with you, Mira Garvie."

He paused, searching my face, trying to gauge if I truly heard him this time—if I *believed* him.

"I've tried to show ye, to convince ye," he continued, softer now. "But maybe it's not just that ye canna believe I love ye enough—for who ye are, all the stubbornness, and fear, and doubt and boldness that's all part of this...*whirlwind*...ye are," he said, struggling for the right words. "Maybe... maybe it's really all the rest that comes *after*, if ye *did* believe it. Maybe that's the part ye canna face."

He looked at me then, and I know he saw my confusion—the way I leaned in, trying to follow but not quite grasping what he meant. And something in him dimmed. The light behind his eyes faltered, his shoulders dropped just slightly, and he looked...crestfallen.

Like he was about to speak a truth he wished he didn't have to. Like if I hadn't realized what was coming, then maybe he shouldn't be the one to say it.

And still, I knew—whatever it was, it mattered.

"I canna give ye a normal life, Mira," he said, the words slow and heavy, as if each one cost him. "We won't have children of our own...and I ken that alone would be a good enough reason for ye to walk away."

His voice didn't waver, but there was grief in his eyes. I saw it there, plain as day: the image of a life he'd imagined, perhaps only briefly, but deeply. A version of us where we had a family, where laughter echoed through stone walls and small feet pounded across old wooden floors.

And knowing it was a dream that could never be—it gutted him. That truth lived behind his eyes like a bruise, dark and quiet, and it hit me with sudden clarity: he hadn't just accepted this loss. He had mourned it. Before I even realized it might be mine to mourn too.

"This life—it's not easy," he said, his voice low, roughened by the weight of what he was trying to make me comprehend. "Ye stayed with me a week, and I know ye saw glimpses of it. But living it, day after day...that's different. That's heavier."

He didn't look away, didn't flinch, even as the pain behind his eyes deepened.

"And then there's the truth that ye'll grow old, and I won't—unless ye choose to become what I am." He paused, jaw tightening, as if just saying it aloud cost him. "But I wouldn't want that for ye. Not truly. And it would take me a long time to even accept the thought of it."

With every word, I realized just how much he had thought of this—of *us*. He had walked this path in his mind, weighed every angle, every impossibility, every sacrifice. And he was laying it all at my feet now, not to sway me, not to guilt me, but because I *deserved* to see the full truth.

"But if ye ever want to come back," he said, his voice a whisper edged with something that trembled, "know we could make a life together. Here, or on the island, or elsewhere. It dinnae matter where to me—as long as ye are by my side."

The truth of these words weighed heavily on him—no bravado, no shield, just quiet, aching hope. He wasn't asking me to promise anything. He wasn't trying to sway my choice.

"There are a hundred good reasons not to be with me, but it canna be because ye doubt how I feel. I do love ye, Mira. I love ye so much it hurts. So much it frightens me. So much that if letting ye go means sparing ye pain, I'll do it. But not because I dinnae love ye. Never that."

We went to the bedroom then, the silence between us full of tenderness and gravity, the kind that settles in when both people know a chapter is ending. Baird helped me pack, folding my clothes with that same quiet care he brought to everything—methodical, gentle, never rushing. Neither of us spoke much. There was nothing left to say that hadn't already been said with eyes, with hands, with hearts too full to bear.

When the suitcase was zipped shut and there was nothing left to do but face the goodbye waiting on the horizon, we crawled into bed together for one last time.

When we made love that night, it wasn't frantic or wild—it was solemn. I pulled my hair aside and bared my neck to him, offering it not just as permission, but as trust. As a parting gift.

But he shook his head. "Nae, Mira—I want the man in me to remember this. Only the man," he said, his voice hushed and aching as he cupped my face and kissed me deeply.

And so, like the previous night, it was Baird Campbell *the man* who made love to me. Who claimed me not with hunger, but with devotion. With every touch, he memorized me. With every kiss, he marked the moment as something no time, no immortality, could take from us. And he made sure I knew that, so when I left in the morning, some part of him would be with me forever.

# Chapter Fifty-Eight

## MIRA

He'd loaded my bags into the rental and closed the hatch. The sound echoed like the chime mechanism of a grandfather clock, that solemn pause just before the hour strikes—time advancing, inevitable, no matter how desperately I wished it would stop, just for a moment. He came to me where I stood on the curb and placed his hands gently on either side of my face. His palms were cool, steady against my trembling cheeks, grounding me, willing me to look at him—to really *see* him.

My eyes were blurred with tears, clinging to my lashes before spilling down, and I looked up at him through the blur, seeing him clearly in every way that mattered.

"Say something..." I choked, my voice cracking beneath the weight of everything, wanting his voice to fill the void.

He shook his head slowly, a white flag waving that said he would fight no more. "There's nothin' left for me to tell ye," he said, his voice low, thick with the ache he would no longer hide from me. "I've pled my case. I love ye. But it's more than just love, lass—it's fate. I was meant to love ye, Mira Garvie. From the moment I saw ye, I knew."

He leaned closer, his forehead touching mine. "And I think—deep down—ye were meant to love me too."

I wrapped my arms around his neck and pressed into him as hard as I could, needing to feel the solid weight of him, the quiet strength of his arms closing around me. It was the only place I'd ever truly felt at peace—held tightly against his chest, the world falling silent around us.

I needed that one last time.

Just enough peace to carry me through the leaving.

In the end, it was Baird who let go. He eased me back, his hands gentle but firm, guiding me away from the haven I couldn't seem to pull myself from. He gave me the distance I needed, even when I couldn't find the strength to take it myself.

I took a deep breath, steeling myself to ask one last question. "Will you go back to the island?"

"Aye," he said. "That's my home. Bunny tolerates it here in the city, but not for long. I'll close up the house and head back tomorrow."

He opened my door and waited as I slid into the seat and buckled my seatbelt. "Will ye text me when ye get back home?" he asked, voice low. "Just so I know ye made it safely?"

I nodded, unable to trust my voice. If I tried to speak, it would come out in tears.

He closed the door gently, then stepped back to the curb. He lifted a hand in a small wave—almost shy—and then turned away without looking back.

As I pulled into traffic, I glanced once in the rearview mirror and saw him, the street and the city shrinking behind me.

And I wondered how long it would be before he found the box I'd left on his bedside table.

The one with Agnes's portrait.Back at last where it belonged.

After returning the rental car, I took the tram to the terminal. I sleep-walked through security, barely registering the motions—shoes off, conveyor belt, body scan. It all passed in a blur, like I was watching someone else move through the steps of travel, detached from my own body. I found the nearest café and ordered a coffee, just for the comfort of something warm to hold.

When I finally boarded the plane, I curled into my seat, drawing the blanket tighter around me like a barrier against the world, tears still falling down my cheeks. The flight attendant approached, gentle-voiced, offering tissues, a drink—kindness I couldn't bring myself to accept. I waved her off with a small shake of my head. I think she was worried, but she didn't press. I'm sure I wasn't the first wreck she'd seen on this route—someone quietly unraveling at thirty thousand feet, leaving behind a city, a job, a person...trying to stitch together a plan for what came next, even when every piece still felt scattered and raw. As my tears fell, I realized they weren't just for Baird—they were for my parents too. For everything I'd lost, then and now, twisting around and back upon itself. I felt hollow, like a husk—nothing but a bleak cavern inside me, dark and echoing with absence.

I didn't sleep. Couldn't. The idea of closing my eyes and slipping into dreams terrified me more than being awake in this limbo. I knew it wouldn't be Bastien waiting there in the shadows—his haunting had passed. No, the real fear came from what my mind might show me instead: a future without Baird. The silence where his voice should be.

The absence of that steady, fierce presence that had wrapped around me like armor. The thought of waking from that dream, alone, was more than I could bear.

# Chapter Fifty-Nine

## Mira

> (Mira) *I made it.*

I t was all I could bring myself to say. The moment the plane landed and I took my phone off airplane mode, I tried. I stared at the screen, fingers hovering, typing and deleting, retyping. Something heartfelt. Something witty. Something that might carry the weight of what I felt.

Nothing was right.

Nothing could capture the hollowness that had already settled in me, the aching loneliness that had taken root before I even reached the gate.

I'd been lonely before I went to Scotland—lonely in the way of someone who hadn't yet known real connection. But this...this was different.

This was the silence that followed something precious being torn away. This was the ache of a bond severed. And I was the one who'd severed it.

Almost instantly, my phone pinged with a response.

It was the picture—the one he'd taken on the boat.

To anyone else, we looked happy. Two people smiling, windblown, sunstruck, clinging to each other, chemistry electric and apparent. But I saw what was really there, in his eyes and in mine.

*Don't forget this.*

That's what the look said. A silent plea. A promise.

And I wouldn't.

So, naturally, I did the most heartbreakingly teenaged thing imaginable—I saved it as my phone's wallpaper.

Because I needed to see it.Because part of me still wasn't ready to let go.

I waited, hoping for more, something else, more words from Baird. Teasing, something. But there was nothing. Just silence that stretched as the minutes turned into an hour. Maybe it was his own way of closing the chapter.

# Chapter Sixty

## Mira

When the Uber dropped me off at my house, I rolled my bag inside and dropped my tote onto the floor. The post office could wait until tomorrow—two weeks' worth of mail wasn't going anywhere. Tonight, I didn't even want to *think* about my to-do list.

I sent a quick text to Anne and Dillon to let them know I was back. I told them to give me a couple of days and then we could plan something. I'd pretend I was a person again.

I unzipped my roller bag and dumped everything into the laundry pile, pausing only when I came across a few pieces I'd washed at Baird's.

His detergent. His cedar-lined closet. They still smelled like him. I held one shirt to my face and inhaled, sharp and deep, and instantly I was back in his arms, his scent wrapped around me like memory. I set those clothes aside, not ready to wash the last traces of him away.

Just a breath of it made my heart ache—and brought a flush to my skin, the kind of involuntary reaction that reminded me with aching clarity of the way he'd touched me.

Of how he'd made me feel like my body was no longer mine, but something he understood better than I ever had.

One sniff, and the ghosts of orgasms past came swirling through me like smoke.

I stared at my tote bag sitting on the floor. It held my tools, my heavy canvas apron, which Baird had used to wrap around and cushion the box with the necklace, my travel pillow, and my Kindle. I pulled out my Kindle and shoved the bag with all its contents into the hall closet. I just couldn't go through all that. I'd deal with that later, when my mind started to clear, and distance made it easier to recall the sweet memories without unleashing a deluge of tears.

The next few weeks stretched out before me, long and heavy. I kept waiting for the sadness to lift, for the ache to ease with time. But it didn't. It lingered like mist that clung to everything, changing the taste of my mornings, the texture of my thoughts.

It wasn't like the grief I'd felt when my parents died—that had been sharp and consuming, but pure. This was something that was becoming murkier.

Grief tied up in anger.

Anger at myself, for being so unwilling to believe. For needing so much proof, as though this proof could be found in a textbook or some mathematical formula, instead of just felt. For holding part of myself back, the part that could feel, until it was too late.

And anger at Baird too. Since that photo, he hadn't sent a single word.

No *hope you're well.*

No *missing you.*

Nothing.

I wondered if he could still feel me—that bond he'd spoken of, the one that began to form when he drank from me. But maybe that wasn't real. Maybe it was just what he'd said about me wearing my heart too plainly on my face, too easy to read.

Because if he *could* feel me—truly feel me—he'd know I was struggling. He'd know how badly I ached for him, how that ache deepened instead of fading, day after day.

And if he knew...and didn't reach out?

Then I was even angrier still.

I knew none of this was rational. It didn't matter. I was unraveling in tiny, quiet ways. And I started to wonder if I'd ever feel like myself again—if there was still a self to return to. Maybe something in me had changed permanently. Maybe I was turning into one of those tragic heroines from a 1940s drama, the kind who never got over the stranger who swept through town and vanished into the night.

But that wasn't fair.

Baird hadn't disappeared.

*I* had.

Regardless, I seemed to find a new way to be mad at Baird almost daily. Fresh angles. New grievances. Little tortures I crafted just for myself—picking at the scab before it could even think about healing.

If it ever could.

One afternoon, I stopped at the liquor store and bought a bottle of Scotch. I didn't even *like* Scotch. But I left it on the kitchen counter, a constant presence.

Each night before bed, I poured myself a glass. A ritual.

It wasn't about the taste.

It was about going back. About conjuring the memory of whisky-tinged kisses from Baird's lips, that sharp bitterness, the taste of peat and smoke, winding itself around his pain and making it my own.

It was my way of calling his ghost into the room.

So I could yell at him.

So I could sob and beg him—silently, shamefully—to let me go.

# Chapter Sixty-One

# Mira

In the weeks since I'd gotten back, I'd been dodging Anne and Dillon. Texts left unanswered, calls returned half a day late. I couldn't bring myself to face them—*not yet*—not with this strange mix of sorrow and self-loathing still sitting so heavy inside me. I knew I needed to pull myself together—at least enough to pass for functional. Because if I didn't, I was one surprise knock away from an impromptu wellness check.

And that wouldn't end well.

Not with me pacing around in a bathrobe, hair unwashed, looking like the ghost of seasonal depression come to life.

So I leaned into a tradition we held dear. '*Friendsgiving*' had been ours for years, and with my parents gone now, it was the only Thanksgiving that still felt like it belonged to me. So this year, I didn't bother trying to get out of it. I told them I'd host.

We'd do it the day after Thanksgiving, like always, and they could both crash at my place afterward. No driving home in the dark, especially not after what I already suspected would be way too much alcohol. It was the right thing to do. Even if I felt like a shell of the person who used to love planning this kind of thing.

I'd spent the week before Thanksgiving cleaning the house, readying the spare bedrooms, and making endless trips to the store. I'd volunteered to handle the turkey, the dressing, and the mashed potatoes. Anne was in charge of baked goods—her rolls and both pumpkin and apple pies. Dillon, true to form, claimed the green bean casserole and a salad no one would touch but everyone would feel better for having on the table.

My wine cooler and liquor cabinet were fully stocked. Still, when I looked at the bottles—mostly in that fifteen-to-twenty-dollar range—I couldn't help but think of Baird. And like some nouveau riche wine snob who'd been spoiled too quickly, I found myself sneering at my once perfectly fine collection. He'd introduced me to *real* wine. And my heart sank again when I thought of all the little ways he'd changed me.

Thanksgiving Day rolled around, and once again, I spent the day in my bathrobe. This time, though, I started the morning with a donut and a glass of Scotch as I settled onto the couch to watch the Macy's parade, followed by the dog show.

It was what I always used to do with my parents—minus the self-loathing and the whisky for breakfast—so I figured I'd keep the tradition alive, in my own warped way. The first Thanksgiving without them, I felt their absence more strongly than ever.

The turkey was already brined, tucked into a five-gallon bucket in my fridge like some morbid science experiment waiting to be roasted. I was so alone on this day, without my parents, there was a hole in me that was getting deeper by the minute.

At one point, I even Googled *"upcoming holidays in Scotland,"* hoping to find some shared, neutral occasion I could use as a casual excuse to text

Baird. The only thing that came up was the day after Christmas—Boxing Day.

What even *was* that?

Didn't matter. It was still a month away. Maybe I'd hold on to it like a conversational life raft until then.

Just as well. I'd stay right where I was—on this couch, in this robe—stewing in a slow boil of resentment. Resentment at myself for finding a hundred reasons not to believe in what I felt. And at him for letting me spiral without even checking to see if I'd landed on my feet. I wondered if there was an expiration date for hating yourself like this. Or if some part of me would always be what I'd seemingly become—a woman half-drunk before noon, angry at a man halfway across the world, and angrier still that I'd loved him and never told him.

Because yes, he was right.

I loved him.

And supposedly, he loved me too. Above all else. But some part of me still refused to believe it—everything he'd told me. That our love was fate. That he loved me so much, it terrified him.

Because if all of that was true...then how could he just *be there*, in his world, silent?

Not even a text to ask if I was okay. Didn't that say everything? Didn't that prove I hadn't meant as much as he claimed?

I continued to nurse the bottle of Scotch and wallow in misery for the rest of Thanksgiving Day, and by the time I fell asleep on the couch, the bottle was empty.

I woke up Friday morning with a hangover and just two short hours until Anne and Dillon arrived. After I put the turkey in the oven, I shuffled through the house, picking up the empty Scotch bottle and the half-eaten box of stale donuts, wiping down counters and tabletops with the mechanical efficiency of someone trying hard not to feel anything.

The bathrobe—stained and sagging with defeat—went straight into the hamper. I stepped into the shower and let the water beat down on me, hoping it could rinse off more than just the sweat and sadness clinging to my skin.

Thankfully, neither of my friends would be dressed up. So I reached for comfort: a threadbare sweatshirt with a hole in the cuff and my oldest pair of leggings. Still, I made an effort. Just enough to pretend. A swipe of lip gloss, a coat of mascara—something to suggest I hadn't entirely disappeared.

But the mirror didn't lie. The dark circles beneath my eyes made me look as hollow as I felt. Even concealer couldn't cover the ache. I slapped my cheeks a few times, willing the blood to rise, some flush of life to reappear. To feel something other than this numb, endless sorrow.

The doorbell rang at noon, and I summoned just enough energy to fake some animation as I pulled it open. Two smiling faces greeted me, arms overflowing with food, bottles, and the kind of warmth I hadn't felt in weeks. I took the pies from Anne, followed them back out to the car for a second haul, and finally shut the door behind us, sealing in the familiar chaos.

To kick things off—and maybe keep myself from unraveling—I opened a bottle of wine, even though my stomach churned with the lingering consequences of finishing off the Scotch the night before.

"Happy Friendsgiving!" I said, forcing a brightness I didn't feel.

We clinked glasses, and for a moment, the kitchen buzzed with the familiar rhythm of tradition.

Dillon went straight to tossing the green salad none of us would eat. Anne commandeered the oven to warm her rolls. And I lifted the foil tent to show off the golden-brown turkey like it was a trophy I didn't remember winning.

We moved through the motions like we always had—like everything was fine. And for a moment, I almost believed it. Over plates piled high with turkey and dressing and glasses of wine that never seemed to stay full for long, we fell into our usual rhythm.

Anne filled us in on the latest antics of her endlessly enthusiastic, painfully earnest Boy Scout of a boss. Dillon, between bites and dramatic eye rolls, recounted the current saga of his love life—which, unsurprisingly, had evolved into yet another love triangle.

I laughed where appropriate, nodded, sipped my wine, and tried to keep the spotlight moving. But despite my best efforts to steer the conversation away—despite my deflections and strategically timed refills—it was only a matter of time.

Eventually, the inevitable came.

Someone said the words.

"So...tell us about your trip."

I took a deep breath and started with something safe—my visit to Jonathan Blackwell's office. I told them he'd seen other portraits by the same artist but couldn't definitively name him. That part was true.

Then I moved on to Kirriemuir. I talked about meeting Evie and Morag, shared what I'd learned about *rumbledethumps*—which I promised I'd make for them sometime, though none of us were exactly craving a potato-cabbage situation after three rounds of stuffing.

And then, carefully, I dipped a toe into deeper water.

I told them about the reading I'd gotten from Morag's mother, Granny Margaret. But only a little. Neither of them knew about the nightmares. Or about Bastien. That darkness wasn't something I was ready to speak in any room, let alone this one.

"So Granny Margaret..." I said, twirling my wine glass by the stem. "She's something of a clairvoyant matchmaker in their village. She told me I needed to be on the lookout for a man with green eyes."

I left it at that. Not the part about him being connected to Agnes. Not the unspoken threads winding through time. Even Granny Margaret hadn't said it outright—just that *'he's the piece ye be lookin' fer'.*

Anne let out a little squeal. "Is that the hot farmer?"

I nodded, a little shyly. "Baird."

Despite the weeks of sorrow that had settled in me like sediment, despite being mad as hell at Baird for doing exactly what I'd asked him to do—*let me go*—I felt a flicker of something I hadn't felt in a while.

A thrill.

Just the smallest spark of joy, speaking his name aloud. Letting it live outside the hollow of my chest. Saying it to the only two people on this planet who shared space in my heart alongside Baird Campbell—Anne and Dillon.

And somehow, that simple act—his name on my lips in their presence—felt like drawing a line across the universe.

A thread. A connection. The Venn diagram of us, overlapping for the first time. So I pressed on—to how I'd wound up on the island and on the green-eyed man's couch.

"So, the appraiser I met with—*Jonathan*—he mentioned a grave on the Isle of Arran," I began, trying to keep my tone light, conversational.

"It's about four hours from Edinburgh, once you factor in the ferry ride. I drove there the day after I'd been up to Kirriemuir."

Anne and Dillon were listening, forks paused midair.

I pressed on. "After I checked into the inn, I went for a walk down the coast road to the gravesite. There was this little cottage up on the hill above the road, just across from the cemetery—cozy, with cheery yellow window trim and a matching door. I noticed it right away."

I paused and took a sip of wine, trying to steady myself.

Here it came.

The moment he would slip into my story like a ghost through a half-closed door. I wanted it to sound offhand, like nothing special. Just part of the tale. Not the moment my life cracked wide open. Not the moment I met someone who wasn't entirely human—*that* detail definitely wasn't getting aired out tonight.

"So," I continued, aiming for breezy, "I touched the head-stone—*Agnes Garvie Campbell*—and passed out. Again. Like when I touched the portrait."

Anne gasped. Dillon looked vaguely impressed.

"When I came to, I was lying on a couch in front of a fire. In the cottage—the one overlooking the grave." I gave a tiny shrug, like none of this was particularly remarkable. "And that's when I met Baird. And Bunny, his giant dog. Both of them were eyeing me suspiciously. He'd seen me collapse at the grave out his kitchen window and carried me back."

I laughed—unconvincingly, probably.

"Did you know right away?" Dillon asked, leaning in, completely absorbed.

"No. But he walked me back to the inn that night," I said. "And when we said our goodbyes, I noticed his eyes were green. I figured it was just a coincidence."

I shrugged like it didn't matter, like it hadn't meant anything.

"But then I saw him again the next day when I was hiking—he was out checking on some cattle he had grazing nearby—and later we had lunch. He was...just *easy* to talk to. I told him about my visions, my parents, everything. It all came spilling out like it had been waiting."

I paused, letting the memory wash over me. "I felt different with him. Like some part of me I didn't even know was locked up had suddenly been let loose."

Anne's eyes lit up. "So how did he end up back in Edinburgh?"

Of course she'd skipped ahead—she already knew that part. Dillon didn't.

"Turns out the hot farmer from the island also had a place in the city," I said, smiling despite myself. "And he made up this ridiculous excuse about needing to be there. Just so we could have dinner."

Anne let out a dreamy sigh. "*OMG, this is so romantic.*"

Dillon rolled his eyes. "Whatever. Let's get to the good stuff. How was the sex?"

Straight to the money shot. And just like that, the breath caught in my throat.

How was the sex?

*Devastating.*

*Transformational.*

The kind of physical connection that rearranges your sense of self—and then leaves you haunted by it.

I hesitated, the tears already threatening, rising hot behind my eyes. "Mind-blowing doesn't even come close," I said, forcing the words out with a shaky laugh. "I mean...I don't even have the vocabulary. I've never *felt* what I felt with him. And you know I'm no innocent—I've had a few to compare to."

I tried to smile again, but I could feel the corners of my mouth faltering. And they saw it.

Of course they did.

Anne and Dillon exchanged a glance—quick, sharp. The kind you don't notice unless you know people deeply.

They knew.

Knew something wasn't adding up.

Knew the woman sitting across from them, still in her old sweatshirt, who'd dodged their messages for weeks, wasn't glowing with post-romantic bliss.

She was grieving.

And no story—no matter how carefully told—could cover that up.

"Oh...babe," Anne murmured, brow furrowed, voice soft with concern. "He dumped you? Even after knowing you'd just lost your parents?"

That's when I lost it. Tears. Hysterical sobbing. Eyes squeezed shut, shoulders shaking, the kind of grief-scream that lives somewhere between heartbreak and humiliation.

I heard their chairs scrape against the floor before I felt them—both of them—coming around the table to wrap me in their arms.

But then I spoke, and it only made it worse. "No," I sobbed. "He didn't dump me. He said he *loved* me."

As if that explained everything. As if that made any of it make sense. I could feel Anne and Dillon coming to the same conclusion without a word: I needed to be on the couch. And we needed more wine.

Dillon grabbed the bottle.

Anne took my arm and guided me to the sofa, settling beside me with one arm wrapped tight around my shoulder. I wiped my tears on the sleeve of my sweatshirt. Dillon returned with a box of tissues and set my glass on the coffee table, then pulled a side chair in close, like we were in a makeshift support group for the romantically wrecked.

Anne leaned in gently, voice low and careful, as if speaking to someone on the edge of a cliff. "And what did you say...when he told you he loved you?"

I drew in a trembling breath. "I told him it was impossible. He still loves his dead wife...and I feel like some fucked-up second-string quarterback," I whispered, the words landing like stones in the silence that followed. There was no way to explain the rest. Not without saying the words *vampire*, *Agnes*, or *Bastien*. So I didn't.

"Um..." Dillon tilted his head. "How long ago did she die?"

I sniffled, buying time.

"A long time," I said carefully.

Maybe without saying so directly, Dillon had made a point. Maybe Baird *was* ready to move on.

But the truth still gnawed at the edge of everything: I hadn't let him.

"He said we were destined to meet. That he was *destined* to love me." I threw my arms out, exasperated. "And the *fucker* hasn't called or texted since I got back!"

As if that explained everything.

As if that somehow made my tears reasonable.

Anne straightened up, eyes narrowing as she tried to piece together the chaotic mosaic of my confession.

"Okay," she said slowly, her voice turning analytical. "Let me see if I've got this straight. A Garvie family psychic tells you to be on the lookout for a green-eyed man, that he's your destiny somehow. You find him. You have *ultra-hot*, mind-blowing sex. He tells you he loves you. Tells you you're meant to be together."

I nodded warily.

"And *you*"—she pointed at me—"tell him he *can't* really love you. That *you're leaving*. Did you...did you even tell him you loved him?"

I blew my nose loudly into a tissue, trying to stall, the shame already creeping in.

Then just shook my head.

Dillon blinked at me, incredulous. "But, like—Mira. You *do* love him. Right?"

"Yes! *Fine.* I admit it." The words came out sharper than I intended, edged with fury.

"Okay." Dillon leaned back, ticking it off like a checklist.

Then Anne continued. "So...he tells you he loves you. You *don't* say it back. You tell yourself he can't love you because you think he still loves his dead wife—those two things not being mutually exclusive, by the way—and then *you* leave. And now you're pissed *he* hasn't reached out?" She looked at me, eyebrows raised. "That about sum it up?"

I looked between them, utterly deflated.

"Well...when you say it like *that*," I muttered with a shrug, "I sound like an absolute lunatic."

Anne handed me another tissue and topped off my wine. "No, babe. You sound like someone who's scared."

I stood up and grabbed my phone from the kitchen counter, pulling up the photo—the one he'd taken on the boat. The one that had wrecked me all over again when it showed up on my screen.

I handed it to Dillon.

He took one look and let out a low wolf-whistle. "*Fuck me*, Mira. This is him? He doesn't look like any farmer I've ever seen."

"Give me that," Anne said, snatching the phone from his hand.

Her eyes widened as she stared at the screen, taking in our windblown hair, the smiles, the truth behind our eyes.

"Woman," she said, looking at my phone, "you are *clearly* in trouble. This man has '*I love Mira Garvie*' written all over his drop-dead gorgeous face," Anne said, handing my phone back with dramatic flair. "What are you going to do?"

I shrugged, helpless. I didn't know.

Dillon cleared his throat theatrically. "So... can I circle back to the sex for a second? You know, purely in the name of science. Was it all just hot and filthy—the kind of partner who's a specialist in one very specific flavor you didn't know you were missing? Or was he more of an...all-arounder?"

I didn't even hesitate. "All-arounder. He's got all the gears—hot, dirty, frantic sex, slow, tender, emotional sex, even some transcendent kind I didn't know existed until I met him. You know, the 'I love you and never want to let you go' kind of stuff. He's no one-trick sex pony."

"I wouldn't have come home—*and I have a boyfriend*," Dillon said under his breath, not willing to let that go. Anne shot him a '*I don't think that's helpful right now*' look and then just sat there looking at me pitifully.

They seemed to sense it—no more questions, no more pushing. Just the gentle, loving silence that comes when your friends know you're barely holding yourself together.

We curled up on the couch for the second phase of Friendsgiving: cheesy movies, another bottle of wine, and the slow drift toward sleep.

It was Anne who made the first suggestion. "Anyone up for that new vampire movie? It's streaming on Prime now."

"*Absolutely not,*" I said, a little too quickly.

The words dropped like a rock, but no one pressed.

Thank God, because if I started picking apart every tired vampire trope, they'd start asking how I suddenly knew so much. And I wasn't quite ready to unravel that thread.

# CHAPTER SIXTY-TWO

# MIRA

The next morning, the three of us ate leftover pie and tackled the mess from the night before. I felt a little silly, but also a little better—just being around Anne and Dillon had helped. I even considered scheduling a session with my therapist. Once they'd gone, though, I realized I needed to sit with some of the things that had surfaced the night before.

I could admit now that expecting Baird to reach out might have been unrealistic. And seeing everything through Anne and Dillon's eyes had shifted something. Maybe the belief that he couldn't love me—not really, not for who I truly was—had been more about my own fear than about him. About being not good enough, not worthy of a love like that. I found myself thinking maybe I should reach out...but I wasn't sure how.

The rest of the day, I kept replaying our last two days together—every conversation, every look, every touch. And yes, shamelessly, the sex. Especially the sex.

That's when I remembered the necklace. It was still in my tote bag, the one I'd shoved in the closet when I got home, too wrecked to deal with it. I hadn't looked at it since I was with Baird.

I went to the hall closet and pulled out my tote bag. Just seeing it there made my chest tighten—a small, ordinary thing suddenly heavy with meaning. Its presence, small and forgotten, exposed the truth of how I'd been since I got back. I hadn't just set it aside; I'd buried it. Just like I'd tried to bury the memories, the emotions, the raw ache behind all my anger and confusion. Out of sight. Out of reach. And for the first time, I saw it for what it was: not just grief.

I'd been hiding.

I thought of Baird then. Of how he'd walled himself off after Agnes, disappearing into the silence and solitude of his life on Arran. I'd judged him for that, hadn't I? But now I saw the reflection. The way pain makes you retreat, makes you put pieces of yourself in the dark, just to survive.

And I was doing the same.

I dug through the bag until my fingers brushed the rough canvas of my apron—the one Baird had used to cushion the necklace box. I pulled it free. The box slipped from its wrappings and tumbled to the floor with a quiet thud. I reached for it.

The moment my fingers touched the leather, it hit me.

A surge of adrenaline, sudden and sharp. My heart thundered in my chest, my pulse racing. I set the box back down, steadying myself. I needed a breath—a beat—before opening it. Something inside me knew this wasn't just a necklace anymore. It was trying to tell me something.

I sat cross-legged on the floor and drew in a slow, grounding breath.

I wasn't afraid.

My Sight—my gift—had already been tested, stretched, confirmed. I still wasn't entirely comfortable with it, and maybe I never would be. I wasn't like my kin in Scotland, not really. But I couldn't deny it anymore.

It was real.

And something was coming.

When I opened the box, the beauty of the piece hit me like a wave. It stole my breath for a moment—and beneath the edge of panic rising in my chest, there was guilt too. Guilt that I'd let something I had poured my heart and soul into sit hidden in a closet for weeks, forgotten, just because I was afraid of the memories it might summon.

But this...this wasn't memory.

The electric current that rippled through me wasn't about the past. It was something else entirely—something alive. And like always, I was powerless to resist the siren's call of touch, that strange will that wasn't quite mine. The connection that brought truth, raw and undeniable. I didn't resist. I never really could.

I reached out and let my fingertip brush the emerald at the center. Its green shimmer pulsed beneath my skin, promising magic I could almost see—if I'd only let it in.

So I did.

I let the darkness rise and take me, not resisting. Wanting—needing—to understand why my own creation felt enchanted.

And then it came. A flood of warmth, a loving embrace that wrapped around me from the inside out. Images followed, flashing like visions on a reel: me, asleep in Baird's bed. Me, head thrown back in ecstasy. Me, eyes wide with fear. Me, sitting at the counter in his kitchen, laughing. Every moment, every frame, seen through his eyes. Baird's voice, my name. *Mira*—over and over.

And woven through them all was something undeniable.

Love.

Not the word, but the feeling—so profound, so anchored and fierce, it left no room for doubt. I felt his arms around me, his mouth against mine, the full force of his longing and devotion. And something deeper still—the universe's quiet approval, urging me to believe.

This pendant...it had been anointed somehow, marked by the intimacy of the moment I'd worn it for him. The way he'd looked at me, the devotion in his eyes. He'd known this might be the only way to reach me. Just as he'd known to guide my hand to Agnes's gown, hidden in the chest in the spare bedroom.

He'd always known.

Bastien had been right. Baird knew me better than I knew myself.

I came to slumped over but still upright, the pendant clutched tightly to my chest. My heart was pounding, but my breath had steadied. My eyes were overflowing with tears of joy, and with trembling hands, I lifted the chain and slipped it over my head, needing to feel close to Baird—needing the connection this amulet carried, the one we had created separately but together.

I knew from experience that once I'd touched something, once I'd been shown what I was meant to see, the intensity never returned with the same force. I wouldn't pass out just wearing it. And sure enough, the moment the necklace settled against my skin, what I felt was quieter, gentler.

No visions. No images flashing through my mind.

Just warmth.

A steady hum, like a heating element pressed to my chest—but instead of heat, it radiated a soft, unwavering current of love. Baird's love. Not memory, not projection, not fantasy. It was *real*. So real I could feel it pulsing through me, grounding me, steadying me. Proof I couldn't ignore, not anymore.

I wouldn't deny it again. Not to myself. Not to anyone.

I needed to make this right. Baird needed to know—*deserved to know*—what I'd seen, what I felt, what I finally understood. But this wasn't something I could say in a text or fumble through on a phone call. This needed more than words. I had to go back. I booked my flight for the day after tomorrow.

When I told Anne and Dillon, they didn't even pretend to be surprised. If anything, they seemed relieved—happy, even. Like they'd been waiting for me to come to this decision on my own.

That night, before slipping into bed, I set the necklace on my bedside table. I wasn't ready to wear it as I slept, but I didn't want it far from me either. Just knowing it was there brought me comfort.

Then I opened my laptop and typed out a quick email to Evie and Morag:

"Tell Granny Margaret I found the green-eyed man "

I smiled as I hit send, then closed the lid and slid beneath the down comforter, pulling it tight against the late November chill. My body softened into the warmth, and for the first time in a while, I let myself drift into sleep with hope in my heart.

*I walk through a mist so thick I can scarcely see my own hands before me. Yet something draws me onward—not an insidious darkness, but something else. Something I do not fear. Step by step, I move forward.*

*I hear the crash of waves and smell the sharp tang of salt in the air. My bare feet press into damp grass as I follow a path leading down toward the point—the very place Baird's cottage overlooks.*

*The mist begins to lift, just enough for the world to take shape again. And there it is: Agnes's headstone. Just as I had seen it in the vision, the one I'd had when Baird found me. The stone is new, the inscription crisp and clear.*

*I sense a presence near me, though I see no one. A ripple of confusion stirs in me, and then—there. Just beyond reach, a figure begins to take form. Not solid, but spectral, vaporous, flickering at the edges softly, like dust in a sunbeam. She is neither fully here nor entirely gone. Agnes—just as she appeared in the portrait. Alive, and yet not.*

*I glance around instinctively, searching for Baird. Somehow, I feel he should be here. But he isn't. We are alone.*

*Agnes shakes her head slowly, gently, as if to say this moment is meant for only us. She steps forward and reaches for my hand. When her fingers brush mine, an impossible warmth floods my body—an emotion flowing from within her and into me.*

*Peace—that is the message.*

*A small smile curves her lips.*

*And then she is gone.*

Sitting at the gate, waiting to board my flight to Glasgow—closer to the island than the long drive from Edinburgh—I heard the familiar ping of a text, then another, and another. I unlocked my phone. A dozen pictures filled the screen: close-ups of jewelry—gold-filled bracelets, a few 14 karat charms, a small tangle of delicate gold chains, and an old sapphire ring set in 18 karat gold. My heart did a strange little lurch.

It was Honey.

> (Honey) *Any of these float yer boat?*

I looked over the photos and asked for prices on the charms, chains, and one of the bracelets. We settled on a price, and then another text came through.

> (Honey) *Give me yer address, and I'll let ye know how much to add for shipping.*

> (Mira) *Hang on to it for now. I may be able to arrange a pickup. I'll let you know in a day or two.*

Happiness flooded my body just thinking about seeing Baird in a few hours.

# Chapter Sixty-Three

## Mira

I pulled off the Ardrossan ferry and onto the island. Late afternoon on the first day of December was cold and gray, with the kind of winter light that made everything feel hushed and expectant. I didn't stop in town, no scenic turnout this trip. I headed straight for Baird's cottage, taking the same winding road I'd followed that very first time, already knowing it would be a forty-minute drive.

I tuned the rental's radio to the same '80s station I'd listened to before, my nerves jangling with anticipation. My heart thudded in my chest, louder with every mile, and by the time I crested the hill overlooking Lochranza harbor, I could barely keep my foot steady on the gas. That's when the radio signal cut out—just for a moment, a burst of static—and then came back in clear.

It was the same song. *Her* song. My mom's favorite.

Just like last time, right in the same spot.

But this time, there was no gut-punch of grief. Just warmth. Awareness. A presence so familiar and comforting it brought tears to my eyes—not from sadness, but from recognition.

It wasn't coincidence. Not then. Not now.

She was sending a message. Both times.

This place, this road—it was leading me exactly where I was meant to go. To the love I was meant to find. A love strong enough to stretch across oceans, lifetimes, and everything in between.

To Baird.

I was done denying the magic that existed all around me. Less than fifteen minutes later, I pulled into the gravel drive of the cottage. My heart was pounding, but when I looked around, my stomach dropped—Baird's Range Rover wasn't there.

I got out anyway, climbed the steps, and knocked on the door.

No answer.

A chill ran through me that had nothing to do with the cold. Anxiety spiked in my chest. Maybe he was just out—maybe on this cold, gray, drizzly afternoon, he and Bunny were tucked away by the fire at Robbie's pub.

Clinging to that hope, I got back in the car and headed south, the drive taking another twenty minutes that felt like a lifetime.

I was starting to spiral. Second-guessing everything—my timing, my decision to come unannounced, the entire plan that had felt so certain just hours ago. By the time I parked and stepped into the pub, my nerves were coiled tight.

It was packed. Bodies crammed shoulder to shoulder, the air thick with warmth and noise. But Baird wasn't there. I scanned the room, heart hammering, until I spotted Robbie behind the bar.

I pushed my way through the crowd, my voice unsteady as I reached him.

"Where is he? Where has he gone?" I asked, breathless, panic leaking into the edges of my words.

Robbie narrowed his eyes at me, less than welcoming, finally relaxing a bit when he saw the pleading look on my face. "Weel hello, Mira. I'm guessin' yer askin' about Baird?" Robbie asked as he mopped up the bar with a towel, never taking his eyes off me. He looked wary but resigned. Like I was some kind of a problem.

I swallowed and nodded nervously.

"I don't think he's off-island—nae, I keep an eye on his herd when he's away, and he would've told me if he was goin'. If he's not at the cottage, I'd wager he's in the upper valley checkin' on 'em, near where he found ye swimmin' in the Blue Pools the last time ye were here."

I relaxed a bit at that, but my fears of how Baird would react when he saw me must have been written on my posture and prompted Robbie to continue.

"I told him not to hold out hope for yer return, but the daft fool kept it anyway—*hope, that is*—and for his sake, I'm glad ye've come back. But listen to me, lass," he said with a warning in his voice. "That boy's had more than his fair share of heartache, and he doesn't deserve another ounce of it. Don't go back to him unless yer sure. Just...don't hurt me boy—*I do think of him that way, ye ken*. He doesn't deserve another broken day, Mira."

I ran around the end of the bar and threw my arms around him, knocking him slightly off-balance. He stiffened at first, clearly startled by being ambushed by a nearly hysterical, lovestruck woman. But after a beat, he relaxed—just a little—and gave me an awkward, robotic pat on the back, like he wasn't quite sure what to do with all the emotion being hurled at him.

I pressed a quick kiss to his cool cheek, laughing through tears as I pulled back, realizing in that moment just how much he'd been like family to Baird all along. I felt the shock ripple through him, like his body hadn't expected kindness to come in this particular form.

"You have my word, Robbie," I said softly, a promise I intended to keep. And with that, I turned and headed back out the door to the car.

A light dusting of snow began to fall as I drove east. The landscape I moved through had now faded to a rich brown—winter leaching the life from the same heather moorland and hills that had shimmered in deep greens when I was here just a month ago. I pulled into the gravel lot just past the campground, met with the same scene as before: a completely empty lot, save for Baird's Range Rover. Mud splattered the tires and streaked the lower panels, another quiet testament to how winter reshaped the island.

I pulled my rental in behind his SUV, blocking its exit—just in case I missed him before he returned. But I didn't think I would. Some invisible thread bound us still, pulling me forward. I hoped he felt it too.

I tugged the knit cap I'd brought low to shield against the cold and wet snowflakes, locked the car, and headed for the trail. I walked quickly and then started to run, urgency rising in my chest. I needed to see him. I needed to see his face. And then just before the bend that led to the wooden footbridge, I saw him.

His tall frame. Broad shoulders. Long legs. A silhouette etched in my memory, walking toward me, Bunny at his side.

My heart thundered. I wasn't sure if it was the run—or the sheer anticipation of seeing him again—that had set it racing.

He stopped in his tracks.

There was no shock on his face. No relief.

Just stillness. A passive, unreadable mask.

Maybe Robbie was wrong. Maybe Baird didn't want me to come back. Maybe he'd changed his mind.

My stomach dropped. I hesitated. Was I too late?

Bunny had no such doubts. She trotted up to me, tail wagging, and bumped my hand with her nose. I stroked her soft head, my eyes never leaving his.

"I'm sorry," I said, my voice catching. "Sorry I doubted you. I believe you now..."

"What do you believe?" he asked evenly. His tone was calm. Too calm. No hint of feeling. I didn't remember him being this hard to read.

"You love me," I whispered, tears stinging my eyes.

His face remained stoic for a dozen heartbeats—until it didn't. I saw it: the glint. That teasing light in his eyes.

He was going to make me pay for not believing him.

"Oh, well, yes—*breaking news*, Mira Garvie," he said. "I'm quite certain I did tell ye this—*more than once*—before ye left. And how exactly do ye know that now? What finally convinced ye?"

I reached into the front of my jacket and pulled out the gold and emerald necklace around my neck, letting it catch the light between us.

"This," I said softly. "I believe it now. Truly. Will you forgive me? I was such a fool." My tears came freely then, hot and unrelenting.

"Is there anything else?" he said, his expression expectant.

And I knew what he was asking, the last truth he needed to hear. "Yes—I love you." I nodded and hoped he heard in my voice just how true that was. I closed the distance between us in a handful of strides. He caught me as I reached him, lifting me effortlessly, and I wrapped my legs around his waist.

His kiss told me everything I needed to know. It was a kiss full of relief, of joy, of passion held back too long. It swept through me like fire and stillness all at once—fierce and tender. And within it, I felt the same warm peace that had flooded my body when Agnes touched my hand. A peace that told me I was where I belonged.

He broke the kiss and searched my face. "How long are ye staying this time?"

His voice wasn't suspicious—just careful. Cautious. I cupped his face in my hands, feeling the rough stubble under my palms.

"How long will you have me?" I asked.

He didn't answer right away. He didn't need to. His expression said it all—how it shifted, softened, lit from within. The last of the weight he carried seemed to fall away in an instant.

And in that moment, he looked like someone reborn. Almost unrecognizable. The lines that had long etched themselves into his brow had softened, as if time itself had been rolled back. His mouth, the one I'd seen so often drawn in restraint or sorrow, now curved with the faint, stunned smile of someone rediscovering the shape of joy.

But it was his eyes that revealed the greatest change. No longer shadowed or guarded, they gleamed—clear and unshielded, brilliant green—lit not only by the supernatural, but also now by something that came from deep inside him—the promise of a new beginning.

# CHAPTER SIXTY-FOUR

## MIRA

We left my rental at the parking lot, vowing to come back for it tomorrow. He pulled his SUV up the drive to the cottage, skidding slightly on the gravel, coming to a stop just a touch too fast. He was out of the vehicle in an instant, opening the door to let Bunny out, and at mine in the span of a single heartbeat.

And I relished it—this version of him no longer hiding from me.

He lifted me into his arms and carried me toward the cottage, kicking the door open, crossing the threshold. The front door swung wide behind us, Bunny left to fend for herself as he strode through the main room and into a bedroom I hadn't seen the night I woke on the couch.

It was spare, like the rest of the cottage, but a king-sized bed sat centered against the far wall, facing another stone hearth. He closed the door behind us, and in that moment, wrapped in thick stone and silence, it felt like we had vanished into a private cave.

We fell onto the bed together, all breath and urgency, hands grasping, reaching, pulling. Both of us desperate to get to the place we needed to be—to *become* what we had been circling for so long.

To join, finally, as one.

No more fear. No more hiding. Just two hearts, wide open.

We tugged at each other's clothes, desperate for skin on skin. Fingers fumbled, buttons and zippers testing our patience. His lips were everywhere—scorching, electric—and I felt the heat of him, the charge I'd missed so achingly.

When we were finally bare, he stilled, hovering over me as I lay breathless beneath him. He bent low, covering my stomach with kisses—soft, lingering, teasing ones that left me trembling. Then, with one strong arm around my back, he lifted me to him, our torsos pressed tightly together. My body collapsed into his, boneless, pliant.

"Stubborn, stubborn..." he murmured, the words trailing off as his mouth moved lower, finding my breasts.

His playful scolding, mixed with the reverence in his touch, caught me off guard—and a laugh burst from me, unguarded and warm. Joyful. I couldn't help it. He was right, of course.

I *had* been stubborn.

Each kiss, each scrape of his stubbled cheek, sent sparks dancing across my skin. My nipples hardened beneath the cool contrast of his body, the tension between us coiling tighter. I arched beneath him, my neck bared, offering everything. Every inch of me was his. And my body knew it—eager, unafraid, utterly his to command. I searched his face, bracing for a reaction—hoping I wouldn't see the disgust or shame I'd seen before.

He gave a small shake of his head, and I knew he saw my disappointment. The smirk—the one that undid me—made an appearance. My breath caught, heat thrummed through me, the wetness between my legs heavy now.

"I dinnae say no," he said, voice low and deliberate. "Just...not yet. I mean to take my time with ye. If I go straight there, it'll be over in five minutes." Then it was his turn to laugh, a low rumble in his chest—a dark, delicious promise of everything still to come tonight.

He palmed my pussy, the friction of his hand moving in slow, rhythmic strokes—back and forth, back and forth—against my slick, swollen flesh, already aching for him.

Then he brought his hand to his mouth, his tongue lapping at my sweetness, eyes fluttering shut for a moment as he savored the taste.

"Oh, good God, I've missed this," he growled. "The way you taste...it's my second favorite part of you to devour."

His gaze locked on mine—wild, hungry. The playful teasing in his voice barely restrained something deeper, darker. The point on my neck pulsed with a heat that matched the one between my legs, the lava flow awakening.

I knew what his favorite was now. It throbbed inside me, calling to him. And he was listening.

I was emboldened then—driven by the need to please him, to offer something in return. So many times, in our lovemaking, he had made me the center of everything—my pleasure always coming before his.

But tonight, something shifted. I *wanted* to serve him. No—*needed* to.

I pushed him back onto the bed. He went willingly, a lazy, satisfied smile curling his lips as he propped himself up on one elbow, watching me with keen interest, letting me take the lead.

I straddled his legs and lowered my mouth to his cock, my ass raised behind me, offering, exposed. He moaned the moment my lips wrapped around him, my spit and his precum making every movement slick, every stroke smooth. He was thick, hard, overwhelming. I gagged, pulled back, caught my breath, then dove in again with hunger.

"We are getting a mirror for that wall," he said, voice gravelly with lust. "So I can watch your pussy and ass the next time ye suck my cock like this."

His words hit me like a shockwave—filthy, raw, and devastatingly intimate. I'd never been brought so close to the edge from *words* alone. But with him, even his voice could unravel me. A moan escaped my lips, my body wanting all of him.

"Stay like that, lass. On yer hands and knees for me," he said. He was beneath me—and then he wasn't.

The world spun, a rush of air and motion, and I gasped, disoriented—until I realized the cause. His mouth was on me. On my pussy. Devouring.

Lips, tongue, even the press of his nose—every part of him was on me, claiming, consuming. He sucked at me with a kind of desperate precision, like he was starving and I was the only thing that could save him. The pleasure was blinding. My body writhed, helpless. Mindless, broken whimpers spilled from my lips, sounds I couldn't have stopped if I tried. I was utterly undone.

Then—two fingers slid inside me, firm and knowing. He stroked exactly where he needed to, the place only he seemed to understand. The perfect pressure, the perfect rhythm—he wasn't guessing. He *knew*.

My body responded instantly. A gush of warmth spilled from me, and he was ready for it—mouth still on me, drinking me in, fingers still working, coaxing more from me, pulling pleasure from the deepest parts of me.

"Don't ye dare make a face," he growled between moans. "I've *craved* this." His voice was thick with his own pleasure, his mouth unrelenting as he swallowed and licked at everything I gave him.

He pulled back, kneeling behind me, his fingers sliding inside me again—then out. Wet fingertips moved between my thighs, up to the cleft of my ass, his thumb tracing slow, deliberate circles over the tight ring of muscle there.

I lifted my head slightly, startled by the unfamiliar sensation, my body tensing instinctively.

"Tell me what's off limits," Baird said, his voice low and hot against my skin. "Or if there's something ye don't like. You won't offend me..."

I trusted the way my body responded to him—instinctive, electric. I didn't want to deny myself any new opportunity for pleasure.

Turning my head, I looked back at him, breathless but sure.

"If I need you to stop, I'll tell you..." I said softly. A groan of pleasure slipped from my lips, unbidden, as anticipation curled through me. My eyes were heavy-lidded, half-open, my body loose, yielding—utterly relaxed and open to him.

His hand slid between my thighs again, gathering my slickness and spreading it slowly, deliberately, ensuring I was ready. When he finally entered me, the sound of my arousal—undeniable, wet and raw—filled the room.

He moved inside me with slow, deliberate strokes, watching my body respond, clenching around his cock as if trying to keep him there, deep within me.

His thumb traced slow circles around my tight bud as before, teasing me, making me wait, then pressing gently, coaxing my body to open to the dual sensations. I pressed back against him harder, pushing his thumb deeper into my ass.

I threw my head back, a guttural cry escaping my lips as I surrendered to the overwhelming feeling—his body filling me, surrounding me, claiming me.

Each thrust, from his hand and his cock, sent me higher, the pressure building, cresting, pleasure so sharp it nearly hurt. I pressed back into him, wanting more, needing all of it—needing *him*.

My body tensed, then shattered, wave after wave surging through me. My cries were wild, unfiltered, utterly unashamed—echoing through the room, rising with the force of my climax.

He bent over me, soft kisses laid across my shoulders and back. "Ugh...woman...the way your body responds to mine is like magic."

He sat back on the bed, legs stretched out in front of him, and pulled me into his lap. I straddled him, my legs wrapping tightly around his back. His strong hands slid beneath the curves of my ass, lifting me effortlessly, guiding me as I began to lower myself onto him.

He moved slowly, rhythmically, his brilliant green eyes locked on mine with such intensity it stole my breath. His pelvis rolled in a deep, deliberate rhythm, pushing into me with a quiet, aching precision.

I reached up and swept my hair aside, baring my neck to him once more—the part of me that belonged to him, that *called* to him. The need for that final, sacred connection still pulsed within me, raw and insistent.

I wanted *everything*.

All of him.

The bond between us, still incomplete, still hungry.

His eyes flashed—and the darkness surged through him. But this time, he didn't resist it. He *welcomed* it.

Power rippled across his body, every nerve thrumming with anticipation. He swelled with it—stronger, harder, every part of him growing, expanding with the force of what he was.

No longer holding back.

No longer afraid.

"Yes, Mira," he hissed—his voice deeper now, shaped by something ancient, a sound forged in a realm where darkness and light had long since entwined. It filled the room, echoing from every corner, yet it also came from within me, vibrating through my bones, threading through my blood.

As if the voice itself *knew* me.

Claimed me.

There was a sting as his teeth pierced my skin—sharp, precise—followed by the scalding pleasure of him taking from me the one thing that bound us, irrevocably. I had just come for him moments before, my clit still achingly sensitive. But with every pull at my neck, my nerves sparked back to life, pushed to new limits.

His deep, unrelenting thrusts drove me higher, again and again, until the pressure inside me broke—an explosion of heat and intensity radiating outward, wave after wave.

Bliss surged through me, echoing to the furthest edges of my body—my toes, my eyelashes, even my fingernails reverberating with it.

I was completely consumed. And I *wanted* to be.

With my body still trembling in the aftermath, he lifted his mouth from my neck. I felt the slow trickle of warmth—twin crimson trails sliding down my skin. He watched them, transfixed. His eyes were black now, consumed by the darkness within him. But I wasn't afraid.

No—*I knew.*

I held more power over that darkness than he did. And he had given it to me freely, trusted me with the part of himself he had once feared. He had surrendered that part of his soul—and it belonged to me now, just as I belonged to him.

He was still moving inside me—long, deep strokes—my slick heat wrapping around him, pulling him in. His pace quickened, his gaze fixed where the blood had reached the swell of my breasts, trickling down the curves, gleaming against my flushed skin.

I lifted one breast to his mouth, an offering. "Take it," I whispered. "Don't waste it."

And he did.

His tongue moved slowly, reverently, lapping at the blood with a kind of worship. He savored it as his thrusts grew more urgent, his grip tightening on my hips, pulling me down, grinding me into him.

Then he cried out—rough, vulnerable—his climax tearing through him. Each aftershock pulsed between us, echoing along the new, shared pathways forged in blood and desire. I felt his pleasure as vividly as my own, the lines between us blurred, dissolved.

Still panting, his breath coming in short, uneven bursts, he leaned back to study the marks on my neck. Gently, tenderly, he pressed his mouth to them, his tongue soft against the tiny wounds. He pulled me to him, arms wrapped around me tenderly, lips in my hair, my face tucked under his chin. He rocked back and forth slowly.

"*Luaidh mo chèile*," he whispered to me.

"What does that mean?" I asked.

"It means you are the love of my life, Mira Garvie—both of them."

325

# Chapter Sixty-Five

## BAIRD

They lay together in the quiet afterglow, Mira tucked against him, right where she belonged. Baird held her close, reluctant to break the moment with questions—especially the ones he'd turned over in his mind so many times, in all the long hours he'd spent hoping she might come back. He'd promised himself he wouldn't push. That if she returned, he'd be content just to love her. That he'd take whatever she was willing to give—no matter how small—so long as it wasn't nothing. But he was surprised when she brought it up first.

"I don't care, you know," she said, breaking the quiet between them.

He turned his head, lifting her hand to his lips and pressing a kiss to her knuckles. "Tell me," he murmured. "What don't ye care about?"

"What you said. The day before I left. About what life would look like—if I could ever believe you truly loved me. About not having something...normal. I don't care about normal."

She shifted, her voice steady. "I'll trade extraordinary for normal. I want *you*, plain and simple. The rest doesn't matter."

He pulled her into him, holding her close, knowing what it must've cost her to speak those words aloud. The future could wait. The complications, the logistics, all of it—they'd figure it out.

Tonight, this was everything.

# Chapter Sixty-Six
## BAIRD

B aird made his way up the stone path that wound behind the cottage to the new studio nestled just above it. Built from the same weathered stone as the original structure, it wore the same slate roof and sat so naturally against the hillside that, unless you knew the island well, you might believe it had always been there.

Light spilled from the studio's windows—three walls of them—casting golden shapes onto the grass outside. The Dutch door stood half-open, its cheerful yellow paint matching the trim on the cottage below. If Mira was inside, the top half of the door was *always* open.

And it was.

He spotted her through the wide glass—hair swept back, face intent, a heavy apron shielding her from the chemicals she worked with. A torch blazed in one hand, flickering and fierce, the hissing blue flame held steady in her grip like something wild she alone could tame.

Music played from somewhere unseen, the soft thrum of it curling out into the warm afternoon air. She moved with it, hips swaying slightly, a rhythm all her own. She was entirely absorbed in her process—focused, precise, utterly alive.

He thought she looked like a creature out of myth: part alchemist, part enchantress. A fire-breathing dragon in her hand, flame and precious metal at her command.

He leaned against the doorframe, content to watch. She hadn't noticed him yet. She never did when she was lost in creation.

That was something he understood about her, perhaps better than most—this need to *make*, to *shape* the world with her hands. It was a refuge for her introverted soul, time and place to regenerate.

So he stayed at the threshold, silent. Waiting for her to notice him.

He still tended the cattle and worked his fields, his own quiet way of shaping the world, he supposed. Different than Mira's—but similar in its devotion. His daily routine hadn't changed much in the year they'd been together.

But his life had. Completely.

# Chapter Sixty-Seven

## Mira

I turned around and saw Baird leaning over the half door, watching me the way he sometimes did—like I was a magical creature only he could see. And maybe, in some small way, I was.

I shut off the gas to the torch and carefully hung it on its bracket. These breaks, once interruptions, had become moments I craved—needing to see him, to hear his voice, to feel the familiar grounding of his touch.

I crossed the studio and met him at the door, standing on my toes to kiss his lips, soft and cool against mine, my eyes pulled to the view just past where he stood.

The front of the studio looked out toward the point where Agnes was buried and to the sea beyond. I'd wanted it built this way, positioned this way, so I'd never forget.

For a time, I'd believed she stood between us. But I'd been wrong.

Agnes wasn't a wall—she was a thread. A tether. One of many that had drawn me here: her, the painting, Bastien's dark pull, the strange mercy of his final request, even the echo of another woman I'd never met—Clémence.

Cogs in some unseen wheel of time, all moving in concert, bringing me to this place. To *him*.

To a love I hadn't believed I'd ever find.

Big love. Fierce love. Love that rewrote wrongs, granted closure, offered peace.

Love that spanned lifetimes.

And it was the very thing I once believed was a curse—this strange Sight, this pull toward the impossible—that, when reframed, revealed itself as a blessing.

The thing that made all of this possible.

# Chapter Sixty-Eight
## EPILOGUE

A box arrived from Honey. He'd been sourcing pieces for me here and there, and about once a quarter, he'd package everything up—the items I'd already paid for—and ship them to wherever I was staying. Sometimes, when I was in Edinburgh, I'd meet up with him in person. But lately, we'd been spending more time at the cottage on Arran, so when the mail truck pulled into the drive and the postman brought a box to the door, I had a good feeling it was from Honey.

This time, he'd found something exceptional—a loose ruby, unmounted, discovered at an estate sale. The seller's daughter said it had been in their family for generations, but no one had ever set it into jewelry. I was eager to see it in person. The pictures looked promising, but with stones, nothing mattered but how they looked in natural light.

The cut appeared clean, and while the accompanying paperwork was dated—a questionable forty-year-old appraisal from an independent jeweler—it suggested the stone had been valuable even then. I'd gotten it for a steal. I suspected it might have been heat-treated, but for the price I paid, I didn't mind. I planned to send it out for a proper appraisal before setting it anyway.

I grabbed a kitchen knife and sliced through the tape, then peeled back layers of bubble wrap tucked inside a rigid plastic case. A few 14 karat charms and some scrap chains were nestled on top—items I'd likely melt down—but I was only interested in the ruby. Honey had packed the stone in its own plastic case, and even through the clear lid, I could tell.

It was stunning.

The color was intense—what gem dealers call *pigeon's blood*—a deep, vivid red with the faintest hint of blue. That slight bluish undertone, rare and unmistakable, only occurred when the stone's chemical makeup contained chromium. It glowed even in the dim light of the kitchen, like it was lit from within.

But the panic hit me before I even lifted the lid. It was immediate—visceral. A crushing sensation, like being smothered under something vast and unseen. The feeling radiated from the box in waves: something *sinister*, dark and ancient, pulsing beneath layers of time. But threaded through that dread was something else—something equally overwhelming.

*Love.* Fierce, consuming love.

It twisted through the darkness, the emotions coiling around each other in an endless, looping figure eight—one born where the other faded, bound together in something both eternal and impossible to escape. I could nearly *see* them: evil—bleak, black and cold as night, and love—radiant and red, burning like an ember in the dark. Two forces, equally fierce, equally real.

I had never felt anything like it before. Every instinct screamed at me to run. But as always, my gift offered no such choice. My clairvoyance wasn't something I could switch off. It didn't ask permission. I didn't wield it.

It wielded me.

My breath stuttered. My hands shook. Still, I forced myself to lift the lid. Inside, the ruby gleamed like a living thing. And I knew—*knew*—this was the most powerful object I had ever touched.

I reached out to touch it.

Bracing myself against the counter with one hand, I pressed the pad of my finger to the crown of the stone with the other.

And held on for dear life.

Keep reading for a preview from Book Two in the Sanguis Amantium series

# MEMORY OF THE BLOOD MOON

# PROLOGUE

## May 11, 1370 – Biertan, Romania

The blood moon hung low in the night sky, an ominous orb glowing crimson—a portent of birth and death, of the eternal struggle between light and darkness. Tonight, the veil between the physical and the spiritual world was perilously thin.

In the small cottage at the edge of the village, the air was thick with heat and the tang of iron. The gray-haired midwife, Zora, worked with fevered hands as the young woman fought to bring new life into the world. But this was no ordinary villager to her—this was her only daughter, Anca. The labor had started normally enough, but as the hours dragged on, her unease grew. Something was wrong. Anca's brow glistened with sweat, her face twisted in anguish. It had been nearly a full day since her waters broke, and the child refused to come.

"The babe's breech," the old woman muttered under her breath. Her gnarled hands pressed and prodded the swollen belly, whispering prayers—some in Latin, others in the old Romani tongue—until, at last, she felt the baby turn.

"On your hands and knees now, girl," she ordered sharply. "With the next pain, you push—hard. Childbirth is no work for the weak. Do it now, or the babe won't last much longer."

Her daughter clung to the bedpost, knuckles white, a strangled grunt escaping as the contraction tore through her. Her face flushed deep red, the veins on her forehead standing out like dark rivers beneath the skin.

"There—yes! The babe is crowning," the old woman cried, sliding her hands into position. "Don't falter now—one more push!"

Anca's scream split the air as she bore down with the strength of the desperate, and the child slipped free into her grandmother's waiting hands.

"I have a granddaughter," the old woman whispered, tears springing to her eyes. "A beautiful, healthy girl... she looks so much like you did, the day you came into this world. A head full of hair she has, as black as a raven's wing."

She wiped the child clean and placed her gently to the young mother's breast.

"Magdalena," Anca whispered, her voice raw and fragile from hours of torment. "I want to call her...Magdalena."

At last, her body began to relax, the tension melting from her bones in a long, blissful exhale. She gazed down at the tiny face nestled against her breast, wonder softening the exhaustion in her eyes.

But the joy was fleeting. The bleeding didn't stop. Zora worked frantically, packing herbs into a poultice, murmuring incantations, but the color drained from her daughter's face.

As dawn threatened the horizon, Anca pressed a trembling kiss to the baby's forehead. "Take care of her, Mama," she whispered, her eyelids fluttering shut.

By the time the first light spilled over the hills, the young mother was gone.

Magdalena was not the only child born in the village that night, nor the only one to lose a mother to the cruelty of childbirth. Under the same blood moon that cast its crimson glow over the poorest cottage, death crept silently into the highest chamber of the walled castle at the village's heart.

There, within stone walls warmed by roaring fires and draped in silks, the boyar's wife labored through the night. Drago Bourean, the district's military leader and master of the castle, paced like a caged beast as his wife's screams echoed down the corridors. But all the wealth and privilege of his house could not shield her from the same grim fate. By dawn, she too lay pale and still, her life bled out upon fine linen sheets.

Her son—who would be named Caius, was strong and healthy. A perfect heir. He was as different from Magdalena as two babes could be. His hair shone like burnished gold in the torchlight, and his eyes—an impossibly vivid blue—would not dim nor change with age as most infants' did.

Though born less than a mile apart, they had come into two entirely different worlds. She, the granddaughter of a Romani midwife in a drafty, dirt-floored cottage; he, the son of a nobleman destined to command armies and inherit vast lands.

Yet the blood moon, a cruel and watchful sentinel in the sky, had bound their fates together, in ways no one in the village—not peasant nor boyar—could yet imagine.

# MIRA

When I finally opened my eyes, Baird was kneeling beside me, his face a mask of worry as I slumped against the cabinets under the kitchen sink. I could only imagine what he had seen—how the ruby, still clutched in my trembling hand, had dragged me under, pulling me into its relentless vortex of darkness and light. I wasn't even sure I could explain it to him. It wasn't like the other objects I'd touched before—simple conduits that revealed emotional imprints of the people who once held them. No, this was different. This was alive, humming with a malevolence that felt ancient and knowing.

My abilities—this uneasy "gift" I'd only recently begun to accept—had overwhelmed me from time to time, but this was different. The power contained by the ruby had consumed me the moment I'd touched it. It had come to me through a picker named Honey, a colorful character who found vintage pieces and gemstones for me from time to time. The color was what gem dealers referred to as pigeon's blood—a deep, rich red with a tinge of blue, glowing from within. When I'd opened the package he had shipped me, I hadn't noticed anything unusual, that was until I lifted the top on the plastic case the stone had been shipped in. Its surface seemed to pulse faintly, as though a heart beat within it, and when I had touched it, it thrummed with an electrical current that stung the tip of my finger and spread like ink through my veins.

At first, the sensation was intoxicating. Unlike anything I had felt before. With other objects, what I saw made me an invisible bystander at best—or at worst, hurled violently into someone else's reality. I had fought those visions, resisted the emotions they forced upon me. But with the ruby, it was different. Its power coiled through me, heady and electric, and for a moment I felt unbound—no longer flesh and bone but something else entirely. Something vast. I was earth. I was sky. I was no longer human. I wondered if this was how Baird felt.

The air around me thickened, vibrating with energy, every shadow in the room stretching and quivering as if alive. A low whisper rose in my ears, soft yet insistent, threading through my mind in a language I did not know but somehow understood.

*We see you… we know you.*

And I felt it too—the ruby seeing me. Not my face or form, but the marrow of my soul. It gazed into my very being, and in return, it offered me a glimpse of something limitless. But then everything changed, and what came next was terrifying.

My chest constricted. My breath came shallow and the air around me froze, as though the ruby was drawing not just my warmth, but my very life. And then came the visions. Jagged flashes of other lives and other deaths. An old man with brilliant blue eyes on his death bed. A woman with dark hair screaming, dragged away from a young child with the same dark hair and eyes. A village in flames, the smell of burning wood and flesh assaulted my senses. A handsome man young man, a soldier perhaps, lay dying in battle. Desperate voices echoed in my ears. The metallic taste of fear, sharp and bitter, flooded my mouth. But amid the chaos and violence the ruby dragged me through, another, more crushing knowing bled into my mind.

The woman I saw was connected to all of them. The old man who was dying, the young man who fell in battle. And the little girl—no more than five or six—was her daughter. I just knew it. I felt the love that coursed through her veins for all of them, but it was not gentle, not soft or nurturing like sunlight. No, this was a desperate, all-consuming love, shot through with a violence I couldn't begin to understand. It wrapped around me like barbed wire, sharp and piercing all at once.

Then the visions shifted—jerking me into a room choked with the metallic scent of blood. The woman stood amid a circle of men, her dark hair matted, her clothing soaked crimson. Their eyes bulged with terror as they cowered from her, weapons trembling uselessly in their hands. She moved among them with terrifying speed, a predator unleashed. The blade in her fist flashed like lightning, slicing through flesh as she carved her way from man to man. Blood gushed, warm and steaming, and she didn't hesitate—her mouth found their throats, and she drank deeply, draining the very life from their bodies.

There was no mercy left in her. Only vengeance, and a hunger so immense it seemed to devour the room itself. With every life she took, she grew stronger, claiming the power she'd never known in her human life.

She was a vampire now. And as I watched her slaughter them with that terrible, inhuman grace, a single, unrelenting truth anchored me: She had once been human. And somehow, I was witness to her transformation—feeling her rage, her freedom, her terrifying ascension.

As my vision slowly bled back into the kitchen—the worn oak table, the kettle cooling on the stove, the faint scent of peat smoke—I felt my chest rising and falling in shallow, ragged breaths. But the ruby...the ruby was still in my hand.

I tried to drop it, to shake it free, but my fingers wouldn't obey. They remained curled tight around the stone, as if it had fused itself to my palm. Its sinister, electric thrum still vibrated against my skin, pulsing in perfect synchrony with my own heartbeat.

"Take it... please," I gasped, holding out my trembling hand to Baird, my eyes wide, desperate. "Take it away from me."

Baird pried the ruby from my fingers, but even as it left my grasp, a cold thread seemed to tether it to me, like part of me was still caught in its pull. I wasn't sure the connection had truly severed.

"Shh, dinnae fash." His voice was low and steady, a balm against the chaos that still churned in my mind. He pulled me into his arms, holding me close until I could feel the solid weight of him anchoring me, his strength defending me against the icy chill that lingered in my veins.

"Tell me what you saw, love," he murmured into my ear, his lips brushing the sensitive edge of it.

"Magic," I whispered, pressing a trembling finger to my chest as if to ground myself. "The stone holds some kind of dark magic. It spoke to me, Baird—the ruby spoke to me." My voice cracked, but I kept going. "It said, *'We see you... we know you,'* in a language I've never heard. But somehow... I understood it. It spoke to me before it let me see."

"Mira..." Baird's voice was low, thick with worry. His strong hands cradled my face, thumbs brushing my damp cheeks. "Ye look like a ghost, lass." His gaze searched mine, like he was trying to pull sense from the madness I was spilling.

I clutched his wrists, needing the contact to stay anchored. "There was a woman. Her village was in flames, men destroying everything in their path. They took her—ripped her away from her little girl. But then I saw her later... killing those same men. She was a vampire, Baird. At some point, she was turned—and she used her power to get revenge."

A chill rippled through me at the memory. "When I first touched the ruby, my senses... shifted. I could see beyond the shadows; the darkness itself was alive. Is that what it's like for you, when you see in the dark?"

His jaw tightened, but he said nothing.

"And yet," I went on, my voice shaking, "the ruby's power feels older than her. Older than what it let me see. I felt a continuous cycle of death and rebirth from it. As if what I saw was only the most recent chapter in the story of the stone. They're separate—yet somehow tied together. But when it spoke to me, it wasn't about her at all. I can feel it. Whatever that voice was... I don't know what it means. But it knows me."

# DEDICATION

To my husband:

My life may have begun on the day I was born, but my *real* life—the one that finally made me feel whole—began the day I met you for coffee.

Even when I've struggled to trust myself or believe in my own abilities, you've never doubted me. Not once. Not the wildest idea, hairbrained scheme, or fragile dream have you ever deemed me incapable of achieving.

You are the rock I lean on, and the wind beneath the wings you helped me see were always there. You told me to trust them. To trust *myself*.

I love you with every fiber of my being. This book could not exist without your love and unwavering faith in me.

You are my everything.

# Acknowledgements

To A.W., When I smarted off in a text that day this spring and said, *"I think I could write a book..."*, your reply came without hesitation: *"Do it. Start now—right this very minute."* Those words galvanized me. They lit the fire. I went and wrote for three days straight before I told another soul.

To Nancy Smay at Evident Ink, when the universe told me to write this book, I didn't flinch—and as a reward, it sent me a fairy book-mother to guide me. You told me I could every time I said I couldn't. When I veered off course, you gently, patiently steered me back. Not only did you help me take a chaotic 40,000-word draft and coax it into the book that became *A Memory Not Mine*, but you also mentored me through every step of the self-publishing journey. When you said, *"You should write books for a living,"* I tucked those words away as one of the most memorable and meaningful things anyone has ever said to me. If I said *"thank you"* a thousand times, it still wouldn't be enough.

# ABOUT THE AUTHOR

Rebecca Byron lives in Grapevine, Texas. When she's not writing or planning her next travel adventure, she's reading—voraciously, obsessively, and with complete disregard for whatever might be on TV.

As a teen she read hand-me-down paperbacks from romance icons like Janet Dailey, LaVyrle Spencer, and Kathleen Woodiwiss. But after she read *Salem's Lot*, vampires took up permanent residence in her heart. These days, she fangirls hard for Diana Gabaldon (she once wrote her a gushy fan letter in the early 2000s and has no regrets), Christopher Buehlman (because if horror could write poetry, it'd be him), and Mary Roach (science, but make it weird and funny). In addition to all things vampiric, Rebecca has a deep love for ghost stories, witch-lore, and all forms of clairvoyance—which she may or may not secretly possess.

Rebecca was born in Southern California, where she grew up riding horses, hanging out at the beach, and serving as president of her high school FFA chapter—because honestly, if you've never learned how to castrate a lamb or aren't fluent discussing chimeras in citrus crops, are you truly *living*? She even spent a year working on a horse ranch in Southern Italy—mainly for the pasta.

Her hobbies include eating, baking (not really cooking, just baking—let's not confuse the two), drinking cocktails, swearing a lot, barely exercising, parking with chaotic energy, and hiding her disaster of a closet from her ultra-organized husband.

If you'd like to stay up to date on Rebecca's latest books, or sign-up for her newsletter, visit her website at:

https://rebeccabyron.com/

Or follow her on Instagram (@rebeccabyronbooks)